Where Artificial Intelligence comes alive .....

Art of Deception

Geoffrey **Bott**

An Award-Nominated Autbor

Solihull Publishing

Acknowledgement

To my friend, Rich Kondrat,
who helped hash out the container ship idea.
His advice, questions, suggestions and comments
became an invaluable source as the story progressed.
Thank you.

To my children who help me deal with life.

1

Lost at Sea

"Captain, we cannot control the vessel's direction!" screams First Officer Zhang.

Typhoon Yolanda had changed category to a Super Typhoon after it wreaked mass destruction over the central Philippine islands. It is gathering energy over water. It has also unexpectedly changed direction and is now heading west across the South China Sea toward Vietnam and Cambodia.

The huge container ship Muar, purpose-built only a few years ago, had left the Port of Shanghai some days earlier and is destined for Singapore and beyond. They are building these mega-capacity ships to help facilitate the growing trade of Chinese imports into the US. It had now ballooned to around $500 billion. The trade imbalance is a serious concern among some on Capitol Hill.

Captain Shih and his crew had readied Muar for the coming typhoon but things were changing. Switching to autopilot forms part of the preparations to skirt the weather. Visually everything looks normal but it isn't. This technologically advanced vessel is in trouble, but no one knows why.

If the Electronic Chart Display Information System is accurate, it's showing the ship's navigation drifting. The ship is steering to port and heading directly into the eye of the typhoon.

Winds in excess of 180 mph are pounding the vast bridge stretching most of the width of the ship. The freezing rain is sand-blasting the glass. Enormous walls of water crash over the top of the containers stacked ten high and onto the deck surfaces. Captain Shih stands by the helm staring out across the bow. It's still early afternoon but the weather makes it seem like dusk.

The navigation lights have turned off. The water-tight bulkhead door indicators are off. Captain Shih is frantically communicating via the intercom with engineering down in the lower decks of this vast structure.

"What's going on down there? Do you have any ideas?" he asks the chief engineer, yelling over the sounds of the storm. "We need this sorted out and resolved now."

"No, Captain. Everything appears normal. All our computer diagnostics come back normal, sir. Nothing is making any sense. We have done a partial system reboot but if we perform a full one, we're concerned the engines will shut down."

"Nothing is normal on the bridge. We don't see what you're seeing. We're desperate up here. Fix the thing." He is clearly about to blow.

Captain Shih looks over at Chief Officer Zhang, standing by the navigation console. "The chief engineer tells me their diagnostics show nothing. How can that be? That makes no damn sense up here. We have no control of the ship." He is now shouting to be heard.

"If we continue on this trajectory, the ship will collide with the eye of the storm, Captain. We need to do something."

Just then a huge crash is heard from outside. Everyone on the bridge looks out as the waves are now beginning to dislodge the first containers. They slide, then crash into others before disappearing into the sea as the motion of the ship plunges the bow into the breaking, angry waters.

"I've tried to switch to manual control, but it remains automated," the officer adds. "I cannot do anything to halt our course, Captain."

"We can't even use the search and rescue transponder either. Nothing works," added Captain Shih. "No one will know we're out here."

Meanwhile, the container ship, Tainan, had left the Port of Shanghai and traversed the Pacific Ocean without incident on a rather mundane, routine voyage. It is now entering the second lock of the segregated three-tier system installed at the Pacific end of the Panama Canal. Expansion in 2016 allowed larger vessels to navigate the waterways. The Tainan is new. Its length is 360 meters with a width of 45 meters and can carry up to 18,000 standard shipping containers. It is huge, at the extremes of the canal's expanded capabilities, and will be the largest container ship to dock at Elizabeth Port Authority Marine Terminal in New Jersey.

Tethered to trains that run alongside of the dock, they will guide it to the next level. The gates to the second lock open once water has equalized in the first via gravitation and the ship rises.

Captain Chen is standing on the port side of the lookout which extends from the bridge like wings on either side of the ship. This vantage point allows observation of loading and unloading but also when the vessel is docking or leaving port. He is high above the water line. Next to him stands First Officer Kung.

"This is going very smoothly. Barring any unknowns, we should be through the canal on time."

"Yes, Captain. This is my first time through so it's interesting to watch all this. You do know America built it?"

"Yes, officer, and it still works too."

Just as they both start laughing, an explosion rips through the starboard side, mid deck. The vast ship shudders as the shockwave travels through the immense structure.

Captain Chen immediately stops laughing, holds onto the side to steady himself before running as fast as he can as First Officer Kung follows. Opening the bridge doors, they run through and reach the starboard lookout. The pair lean over and see fire and smoke billowing from the side of the ship. The ship's crew is frantic and personnel are running across the deck. Fear has stricken the men and Chen sees dead and dying bodies everywhere.

He looks at Kung who is also leaning over the side.

"It's above the water line. Call all deckhands and have them control the burning. We need to stop this quickly. I will..."

Before he finishes what he wants to say, a second explosion tears through containers on the bow. He sees and feels the shock as forty-foot containers blow into the air and scatter everywhere. Accompanying the massive explosion is a huge fireball and a plume of black smoke that billows skyward. Containers that had landed in the water or on the side of the dock start to go off. The explosive material creates a shockwave in the water that destroys one of the lock gates. Areas of the dock walls are now crumbling as they collapse around the ship.

Another explosion tears through the living quarters, underneath the bridge. The last thing Chen sees is a fireball racing toward him. Within seconds he and Kung are flung off the lookout. Luckily for them the fire has super-heated the air, consumed the available oxygen and evaporated the moisture in their bodies. They are already dead.

The pilot door indicator light suddenly blinks on. Shih is immediately on the intercom shouting at the chief engineer. "Go check it out. I need confirmation."

A few minutes later the call comes back.

"Captain, the door is open."

The fate of Muar is now academic and facing certain doom. The winds are much stronger and the waves massive. The roll of the ship is much more pronounced and the rain keeps coming down in swirling, horizontal sheets. Confusion and fear mutate ineradicably throughout even the most experienced members of its crew. The ship barrels into the middle of it, forcing more containers off the deck from the strange release of their electronic twist locks. The loss of cargo is altering the centre of gravity and weight balance. Now the calculations are way off and they cannot add water ballast to the internal tanks to right the ship.

They are not able to contain the water cascading into the stricken vessel with the water-tight doors inoperable. It swirls in the lower decks and sways with the motion of the ship. Thousands of tons of water moving around from side to side, stern to bow, compounds the inevitability.

One last huge wall of water shakes the super structure as it disappears into the depths of the South China Sea. The captain has no time to save his crew.

Fifty six miles away, and around one hour later, the container ship Oceanic heading to the Port of Shanghai disappears off the navigational charts.

The person tracking both ships turns off his navigation equipment. Monitors showing satellite images of the destruction in the Panama Canal are still on. He smiles, extricates himself from his chair, walks over to the bar and pours himself an aged whiskey.

2

Domestic Bliss Interrupted

Daniel Cross rolls over, wrapping his arms around Sadeghi and kisses her on the cheek. God, she smells so good, and he absorbs every essence of her beauty.

"I adore you," he whispers in her ear.

It has been some time since his heroics were spread across the globe. When he arrived back in Tehran, the world wasn't the same and he wanted to escape it. Sadeghi greeted him in a way he had never expected or, more importantly, had never experienced before. She has swept him up in this cocoon of affection, intimacy, adoration.

Invitations to meet the supreme leader and president along with other members of government and religious leaders seemed relentless. The cultural formalities, presentations and parties were non-stop. He just wanted to be alone in the end. He really needed to forget events involving the recent past. Cross was mentally and physically exhausted. Witnessing so much brutal death didn't help him either.

Granfield is a man of his word, Cross found, which kept his faith in humanity somewhat intact. He expedites Immigration documents for Sadeghi to the US Embassy in Tehran where she obtains the necessary paperwork. After Cross has rested enough, he can take her back home with him. They were both so happy and excited about starting their new life's adventure together.

Cross jumps out of bed, puts on his silk robe and slides into his slippers. He walks over to the bathroom, washes his face and then goes downstairs. He is happy to be back in Lake Tahoe – summers in the mountains are spectacular. Before preparing breakfast, he crosses into the living room and turns on the TV. He wants background noise while he cooks.

He hasn't turned on the news in months. Since he was part of it for weeks, he didn't want to hear it. He didn't need to because he had lived it.

Suddenly the music video channel is interrupted. As the TV powers through its start-up sequence, it isn't music that fills his hearing sense. Having walked back into the kitchen, he turns around. The breaking news banner splashes across the top of the screen. Visually broadcast are scenes of destruction with 'viewer discretion advised' added to the narrative.

Cross stops what he's doing and walks over to the sofa. His heart is pounding, and anxiety is creeping into his demeanor. Memories, possibly from PTSD, bring back the scenes of chaos and death he has recently witnessed. The psychologists and doctors had warned him this would happen, which is another reason why he didn't watch much TV anymore. He stares at the screen as his eyes grew misty.

Upon hearing the TV, Sadeghi has run down the stairs. She grabs the remote and clicks the off button but it's a few moments too late.

She sits next to Cross and consoles him. He is a powerful, strong, empathetic man but PTSD has changed him. It happens to anyone who goes through similar experiences as those he just did. Even the trained military are subject to psychological destruction. The wars in Iraq and Afghanistan for example, and even WWII and Vietnam tore people to pieces. Some don't recover, with suicide now a serious problem among veterans. Who can cope with seeing young children blowing themselves up with bombs strapped to them by grown adults, or even by their own radical parents? Cross had seen things he tried to purge but failed.

Sadeghi sits for a while and watches as Cross comes out of his momentary funk. Doctors warned of the psychological damage, but she loves him. It is getting better, she has seen that, but she keeps a close eye on him.

"I told you not to watch the news," she said, wiping the tears off his face.

"I turned on music videos and this came on. It wasn't my fault."

"What's happening, dear?"

"Something about a container ship that was evidently carrying explosives. It accidentally went off in the Panama Canal. I didn't pick up the whole story."

"Are you ok now?" she asks, kissing him on the lips.

"Yes. I'm sorry. Thank you, darling. I am getting better," he adds with a weak smile.

"The container ship was coming from China and was being raised in the locks on the Pacific side. It appears there were many dead and injured." He halts this topic of conversation and changes the subject. "Let's have breakfast and then go for a bike ride." He quickly heads back into the kitchen.

3

The Call

Mountain biking has become a thing for Cross. He still cycles large distances but a friend had loaned him a mountain bike to try. There was reluctance at first until he starts to bike a few of the vast mountain trails, some being very close to his home. He then asked Sadeghi to try and he was pleasantly surprised at her immediate passion for it. They went out and purchased two state-of-the-art matching mountain bikes. Now they spend hours together traversing rugged and breathtaking terrains.

She looks happy as they scale up another steep grade. This makes him happy too.

They spend the next few days purposely avoiding any television, both agreeing it best if he keeps it that way. It is also a necessary part of the therapy.

They are frequenting a local Armenian restaurant in town for lunch when Cross' phone buzzes. He picks it up, looks at the screen and momentarily pauses, before letting it go into voicemail. Finally placing it back on the table, Sadeghi sees his expression.

"Who is it, dear?"

"Someone whom I admire but haven't talked to in months."

"David Granfield."

"How did you know?"

"Your body language told me. He has done a lot for us, Daniel. The least you can do is answer it. That isn't fair."

He is afraid to. He doesn't believe in coincidences and the container ship explosions are still fresh in his mind.

"I want to finish lunch with you first, honey. David can wait."

After lunch and sitting comfortably in his home office, Cross speed-dials Granfield.

"Good afternoon, David. What a surprise," trying to mitigate his love for the man. "Sorry, I was having lunch with Parisa when you called."

"Ha-ha. You knew, you sensed but then you always did have that rare knack."

Cross is startled with himself at how much he has missed the bugger. Granfield's humour, his empathy, his brilliance, his humility are all exemplary.

"You know me by now," he says, laughing along with Granfield.

"How is Parisa doing anyway? Growing tired of you yet," he asks, chuckling to himself.

"Very funny. No, surprisingly she isn't. She says hello and sends her love, by the way."

"Thank you. Are you free to talk?"

"Of course," and sits more upright in the chair.

"There is some urgency in my calling you and you likely know this already. Have you been watching the news?"

"I wasn't sure why you had chosen to call me but I also know you by now. I knew you weren't calling because you missed me. Yes, I accidentally turned onto a breaking news story a few days ago."

"I will be blunt, Daniel. I'm requesting your assistance again and I have missed you, believe it or not."

"No, please. You cannot be serious," trying to mimic the tennis player who had made that phrase famous. "You promised me," he continues, in a more subdued, softer tone as if pleading with him.

Granfield changes his own tone as if he's trying to muster the courage, he pauses for a few seconds. "This is delicate and as you will no doubt be aware, confidential. We looked at footage of the devastation. Cameras fortunately have many angles. We found someone who looked suspicious so we flew down there. It took a few days but we managed to find the man just as he was leaving Panama."

He takes a breather to let Cross digest the information, but also because he knows what he is about to tell him next.

"You will not believe what I'm about to tell you. We certainly didn't. As we are questioning the suspicious person, he asks for you by name."

"Wait. Who asks for me?"

"The person of interest in the container ship explosion did. He claims to know you from high school."

"What? I don't communicate with anyone from high school anymore and haven't for years. How can this be? What is his name?"

Cross pushes down the side lever and leans back in his chair when Granfield tells him.

4

Tainan, Panama City

Cross arrives at Albrook Marcos A. Gelabert International Airport in Panama City to avoid suspicion. It is the smaller of the two international airports and closer to the Panama Canal. Taking regular commercial flights helps keep his profile low, he hopes. Granfield once again fills him in and provides the requisite documents, visa, doctored identities and miscellaneous spy gear including the secure mobile phone.

He walks through Immigration and Customs and out into the airport terminal. He is already feeling the heat and humidity when he exits the plane.

Armed with a simple walk-on bag, he steps outside the terminal and sees a pedestrian silver Chevrolet parked curb-side. Cross opens the rear passenger door and tosses his bag onto the seat. Closing it, he opens the front passenger door and climbs in.

"Good morning, Daniel, I hope you had pleasant flights," Macarthur says as they shake hands.

"Good morning, Peter. I am definitely getting too old for this shit," he says.

"Yes, well, we all are, even me."

Macarthur is in his early thirties, very slender with dark hair and a dark complexion. He is wearing an inexpensive light grey suit, white shirt and black tie. According to the paragraph of information Cross had on him, he has been with the CIA since leaving college and has experienced several key assignments already. Now, however, CIA deploys him to a Central American region, partly because of his looks and partly because of his command of Spanish. Cross is a little perplexed since he has an American name but looks Latino.

"My mother is from Mexico."

"Oh, I wasn't going to ask."

"I am trained to observe expressions," he says smiling.

"I need to work on my body language then, before I meet my alleged friend from high school." He looks over at Macarthur, shrugs and grins.

"I obviously heard and read about your last assignment. I mean who hasn't? It was very impressive, sir. I was briefed before meeting you today."

"Sir ages me, Peter. Daniel is fine with me. The last case just went off in crazy directions.

"I saw this one by accident on the news. I find that eighty percent of problems go away when I don't watch television. Granfield called me from Langley so now curiosity is killing the cat. I haven't seen this friend in decades. I don't get it really."

"There is a deli around the corner. Let's have a coffee and I will brief you before we head over to the house where he's under guard. I'll show you the devastation to the container ship Tainan and the dock area before that."

Macarthur cranks the motor and pulls away into airport traffic. Cross sees he takes a left on Andrews Boulevard and then another left on Avenue Gaillard. He likes to take mental notes of names and places, especially in countries he has never been to before.

Macarthur parks in front of the Grand Deli and they walk inside. Ordering coffee and pastries, they take a seat at the rear of the café but facing the door. Cross feels for his ankle-strapped companion. The special CIA-issue gun is still there so now he relaxes a little.

Macarthur pulls out a file from his briefcase and opens it. He starts sharing documents with Cross.

"This is the container ship Tainan before and after the blasts. It is a massive vessel. These are the areas where we spotted the suspicious perpetrator, your alleged friend," pointing on an enlarged map of the Pacific end of the canal. "The curious part, he had nothing on him. His movements," again fingers moving on the map, "and attentive manner gave him away. He didn't resist us taking him either. It was as if he expected us to find him, as if he wanted it."

"Where was he heading?"

"That is the strange part we haven't been able to connect yet. He was heading to China with a stop-over in London."

"Which part of the canal is blocked?"

Macarthur points.

"This is a cluster-fuck, right? This halts international shipping through Central America?"

"Yes, certainly. Shipping will need to be diverted for perhaps several months and will add longevity along with vast cost to international trade."

"Interestingly, it doesn't halt trade?"

"No."

Cross ponders what he is learning and sits quiet for a moment as the waitress brings over the coffees and sundries.

"What is this?" pointing to a cake on the plates.

He laughs as he answers. "Patacones de Platano. That is twice fried plantain cakes. Being English I thought you might like the fried shit."

Smiling, Cross picks up a piece and takes a bite. He nods his head in approval.

Macarthur then explains the geographical implications for the shipping industry, with the aid of a South American map, as Cross indulges himself.

"I love native coffees." Then Cross is back on topic. "This was a massive operation for such temporary gain. I am not sure of the benefit. Do you have any names or people claiming responsibility?"

"We ran a few people through the CIA, FBI and NSA databases, with MI6's assistance. Nothing came to the immediate surface. We looked into the Chinese Ministry of State Security, the MSS. We added Mr. Wu's name and that drew a blank, surprisingly. We ran your friend's name also. He lives a pretty boring life if we equate the number of times one appears on internet searches and the number of arrests to how interesting one's life is. He essentially stayed below the radar.

"He has been married a long time, has three kids and breeds dogs. He resides in Hull and went to University of Liverpool after high school. He started out with biology and then switched his degree to Computational Mathematics and Advanced Programming."

"He was at the top of our class if a little nerdy and eccentric to be more accurate. Wired a little different, but then aren't we all in certain fields?"

"He started his own company a few years after graduating. During that period he studied for his PhD and picked up a few government contracts to do R and D on robotic programming.

"Then his life suddenly darts off on a tangent earlier this year and there are gaps appearing. He receives an invite to a conference in China on artificial intelligence a couple of months ago, and we never see a return ticket for weeks. These conferences are usually only several days long. About a month later he arrives back in London."

"That is weird. He must have done some privileged and secretive work for the MSS."

"That is a distinct possibility."

Cross is anxious now and cannot keep still. He is ready to go so leaps up and heads for the exit.

"Where is he being kept?"

"We have a secure CIA property near here. Let me show you the Tainan first."

Mr. Wu has his bank of tracking devices switched on in his remote office. Somewhere over the Pacific Ocean he is monitoring a large hurricane heading to the US shoreline. It has a long way to go and is likely to veer in a southeasterly direction towards Mexico, where it would eventually fizzle out. That is the computer prediction Wu has. Approaching the hurricane's vortex is the blip of another container ship. He picks up his communication device.

"Are we on track?"

"Yes, everything is going as planned, sir," answers the person on the other end of the phone.

"Good."

"In about three hours forty-seven minutes, another vessel will disappear."

"Excellent. Please update me when the time comes."

Mr. Wu clicks off his phone, stands up and walks out.

As Macarthur approaches the Panama Canal, Cross stares at the magnitude of the vast structure coming into view.

"Holy shit," he blurts out, showing little regard for finesse. "What the hell."

The guard waves Macarthur through security once he presents their passes and IDs. Cross just stares.

"Keep close because security is tight."

"I know some Spanish if that helps."

"Yes, my gringo English friend. That should calm security people down." Now he is laughing his head off.

They park and walk toward the locks.

The Tainan is still smoking but it has partially capsized within the lock perimeter. The massive vessel has no wriggle room but the front portion of the keel now rests on the bottom of the lock. The walls of the canal have collapsed around the bow. The blasts destroyed one of the lock gates and water poured in from gravity. As a result the water level is high. Activity on the north and south sides of the lock is extreme. Fire-fighting equipment was brought in several days ago and Cross can see huge cranes on floating barges east and west of the damaged area. Massive earth-moving equipment is also at the site. At least ordinarily they would appear massive but sitting against the backdrop of one of the largest container ships in the world, they seem miniscule and futile. The smoke is acrid from the burning containers and the aftermath of the explosions. Death is still permeating the air but heat and humidity are compounding the stench.

"There is such vast destruction." He turns to Macarthur, "How are they going to move that thing?"

"With dexterity it seems."

Cross surveys the surroundings and looks at the locations where his friend was. They are prime areas to observe movements in the locks. What the hell is he doing here? he asks himself.

"Follow me, Daniel. There are areas on the ship that are safe. I have already facilitated arrangements to have you go onboard."

"This is immense. If you found no electronics or gadgets on the guy, what was he doing here? He must have just been observing but for what reason though? Was he just on holiday, a coincidence?"

"Yeah, well, that is for you to find out," Macarthur says, winking at him. "Shall we go take a closer look?"

Security provides suitable jackets and safety helmets before they gain access to the ship.

"Mr. Wu, two minutes to go."

Wu opens up his advanced miniature pad and turns it on. Thirty seconds later he observes the circular rotations of the hurricane on his screen. In the middle is a very slow-moving green blip that is pulsing on and off.

"Got it."

"The ship is in serious trouble."

Just as the person on the phone announces that, Wu observes the blip disappear.

"Fine work and our plans are still in order. No one knows what's going on yet. Our deception is working."

"Thank you, sir. Yes, nothing on the news yet. No one has connected anything."

"When is the next one?"

"About four days. These are dependent on weather and shipping conditions. Sometimes we have no control over those."

"Keep me up to date."

With that Wu switches off his device and closes the case. He walks into the bedroom suite where his dinner date is waiting for him, lying naked on the bed.

5

Graeme Moore

Macarthur pulls up outside a residential home in a quiet neighbourhood adjacent to the canal district. Cross notices what look like CIA vehicles parked close to the property. Damn, they really need to update their playbook. He notices a few live bodies walking the streets.

Cross follows Macarthur as he enters the property using a special card. It was low-key but security is high. Cross notices everything.

"Your friend is down the hallway on the left. We have prepared him for you. Two CIA personnel will be outside the door should you need anything. I will be waiting in the living room, observing."

"Ok, let me go see who he really is."

As Cross walks down the hallway, one of the security personnel opens the door and he enters the room. The door slides shut behind him.

In the middle of the room is a wooden table. Window coverings black out the room and a pale light hangs from the ceiling. Cross sees a glowing narrow security band around the top perimeter of the room. In the corner is a security camera and on the opposite side of the room is a bench with blanket and pillow. Behind the desk, strapped to a chair is Graeme Moore.

Cross looks at him and tries to evaluate his existence. It is well over three decades since he last saw him in real life. Once he heard his name again, he had tried to scrounge pictures off the internet to ascertain what he looks like this decade. His looks have aged, obviously. A little extra weight, not much, but he looks like the nerd he was in high school. Black thick-rimmed glasses sit on his face, propped up by the bridge of a long nose. His hair is the same. It is dark brown with no visible signs of grey. The hair crops short and combs to the right with a parting on the left. He wears dark polyester trousers and, interestingly, a simple cotton polo long-sleeved shirt, even in this heat. A cheap watch is on his left wrist and a simple gold band on the finger representing his marital status. It is strange attire for someone who has made a bundle of money.

He sits in the basic chair on the opposite side of the table.

"Good afternoon, fancy meeting you here, Graeme."

"Hello Daniel. You haven't changed much. You look good and have aged well."

Cross takes a moment to observe his movements and to take in the voice. It is impossible to remember everything from decades of absence.

"How are they treating you?"

"I can't complain."

"It has been a long time since we last saw each other. We used to be members of the school bridge team and you changed degrees in Liverpool if I remember. Looks like computer programming is working out for you."

"Yes, I can't complain about that either. I remember those bridge games."

"It's how I got to know Anna before we started dating."

This comment draws a blank from Moore and he hesitates.

"Yes, Anna. I remember now."

There wasn't an Anna in the bridge club. Cross changes subjects.

"What are you doing in Panama City?"

"Living in Hull made me appreciate boats. I became fascinated with them and visit the docks often. I heard Tainan is one of the largest container ships recently built and she was heading to New Jersey, where I had planned on seeing her dock as the largest ship to land at Port Elizabeth."

Macarthur didn't mention New Jersey as a port-of-call on Moore's return to London.

"I went to see the destruction before coming to see you. It is a massive ship."

Cross looks at Moore. His facial skin has aged well, almost too well he thinks. No imperfections. He could have sworn Moore had a birthmark on his neck. Perhaps he had it removed. Plastic surgery is available for anybody so he looks for those scars and tell-tale signs too.

They talk some more about school, university life, marriage and their differing business paths. After some time there is a knock on the door.

"We need to go, Daniel. We'll be back tomorrow morning but we have things to do."

"It is nice to see you again. You look good, but one final question. Why did you ask for me, Graeme?"

"It was the CIA who took me off the plane as I was leaving the country. I remembered your recent heroics so thought you could help me. I have done nothing wrong here."

"I see. I will be back tomorrow morning to continue this discussion but nice to see you again, Graeme. I do wish it was under better circumstances."

Cross didn't want to antagonise Moore. He didn't want him to know what he'd already observed. He would leave that for tomorrow's events because he needs to prepare for it.

Cross exits the room.

"Sorry, I had to get you out of there. I was instructed to pull you out if it went on too long."

"Something seems very odd here. I cannot figure it out. He is too calm, too relaxed. It's like he's programmed or something. If I had been locked up for days, I would be irritated, disheveled, anxious, angry and pissed off. You know what I mean?"

"We are trained to control our emotions as CIA operatives. The average person isn't."

"Precisely. Thanks for doing that. I need to digest what I have just learnt and observed."

"We have you booked into the JW Marriott Panama, on the waterfront. It is the old Trump Tower."

"Gee, thanks," he says laughing.

"We wanted to make you feel right at home," he answers. "I will drop you off and we can meet later for drinks, if you like." He checks his watch, "Around nine perhaps, at the bar."

Situated along the shores of Punta Pacifica, Macarthur pulls up and drops Cross off at valet. He retrieves his bag from the back seat and meanders into the hotel foyer. Grabbing the key card at reception, he takes the elevator to his suite high up in the tower. Upon entry, he tosses his bag on the sofa and walks over to the mini bar. It is well stocked. Nice. Macarthur did his homework and Cross is beginning to relax again. He finds what he's looking for, picks two green Panama Beer cans and heads out onto the balcony. His suite affords the luxury of views incorporating Panama Bay and the city. He sits on a lounge chair and the first call is to the love of his life.

"Hello, honey."

"Daniel, glad you're ok." Her voice reflects happiness. "How was your first day so far?"

"Not bad, honey. The day was quite fruitful. The container ship is massive and the destruction almost complete. The meeting with my friend Graeme was very weird."

Cross is limited in what he can tell her but she knew that already. She just wants to hear his relaxed voice. She misses him and is scared, but cannot tell him that for fear of distraction, which could jeopardise his life.

"How were the flights? How is Panama City?"

"The flights were long but I slept well into Houston and down to here. The city is fascinating."

They talk some more before they end the conversation with love and affection. Granfield is next.

"Tainan is a massive vessel. Some things I don't get down here, David. Something seems very odd. I finally meet Graeme. I remember him from high school of course. We were in the top class and there weren't many of us. Can I fill you in tomorrow after I have more information?"

"Of course. Do what you need to do."

"I see him again in the morning but I need to digest what I learnt today. Like I said, some things are not making much sense yet. To blow up a ship of such magnitude with so little to gain seems weird."

"But it disrupts shipping."

"Yes, but not by much in the big scheme of things, and it is only a temporary disruption at most. I sense something else is going on."

"Get back to me tomorrow after your second stint with Moore. Perhaps he can shed some further light on proceedings."

"That is another concern I have. Let me address those tomorrow."

The line goes dead and Cross opens his second beer. Half an hour later he tosses the can in the trash and walks into the shower.

Cross, dressed in casual white linen shorts, a teal silk shirt and Quicksilver flip-flops, heads down to the poolside restaurant, the Azul. He isn't really hungry so orders an appetizer with a cocktail.

Macarthur texts him and says he will be at the Cava Fifteen around 9:30.

Cross is waiting when he walks in. He selected a seat at the bar, the opposite side of the lounge which has a TV. In front of him on display is a partitioned wall of expensive whiskies, liquors, wines and spirits. Macarthur sits down next to him and the bartender brings over a whiskey.

"Well, what do you know, Daniel?"

"Not enough it seems."

"Sometimes I think it best not to know anything. Knowing something gets us into trouble in this game, possibly killed."

"I concur, Peter."

Macarthur talks about his move to Panama. He had been married once, but this isn't a life for a married man he concludes.

"It isn't fair on the other party because it is dangerous. Who knows what man-made contraption we will return home in? It could be a coffin, or no return at all."

"Didn't you return home from Iran with a lady?"

"Now you know my weakness." He laughs. "In my defense, however, I finished the assignment and that was it. I didn't plan on doing this ever again."

"We get hooked on the adventures, the dangers, the chases, the near death experiences but especially the women."

"Yes, there is all that. It is exciting until you have someone die in your arms or get a bullet lodged in your body."

"Field work isn't for the weak-minded or faint-hearted is it?"

Cross agrees. Macarthur likes Cross and he is enamoured with his dossier. This guy has lived through hell. He has this amiable personality and is approachable. People trust him. He analyses everything and misses nothing. Macarthur is not disappointed at all.

"Something isn't right here, Peter. I am trying to put my finger on it. Dr. Moore missed some things regarding our past. Our high school class was only twenty people. In any event, it was small. I remember every name. I purposely erred and he missed it. He seems too composed and his vernacular isn't what I remember either. I would be livid in an identical situation."

"As we get older we forget, so I have been told, Henry." He pauses. "Perhaps he takes prescribed pharma drugs. I didn't see a medical sheet for him."

"I have been told that too, Richard. You mentioned something about his return flight to London and then on to China. Do you remember the itinerary?"

"Yes. He was going through Newark with a couple of days stopover. We couldn't figure why."

"Dammit. He is being very clever. He told me he was in Panama to watch Tainan. He is into ships and wanted to see it go through the canal. He told me it was heading up to New Jersey and he was going to see it enter port there. He is covering his reasoning behind being in Panama. Who flies around the world, that is, which PhD programmer flies around the world observing ships for fuck's sake?"

"It is each to their own, my friend."

"I still say there is something going on I'm missing." He sighs.

As he finishes, the bartender brings them two more whiskies. "These are from the lady across the bar," as he gestures with his head and eyes.

Cross and Macarthur both look over. The lady lifts her glass and salutes them. She then takes a sip. Cross picks up his Glencairn glass and walks over. Macarthur follows suit.

"You gentlemen look in deep discussion. This is a resort hotel and we should be enjoying a libation or two without much thought. To your health, salut," she adds, raising her glass again. They each take a sip.

Cross likes to show off when the occasion demands it.

"This is Macallan 78, part of the Red Collection, and has a very distinctive flavor."

"I am very impressed." She stands up and puts out her hand. "I am Leslie Taylor."

She is dark skinned and doesn't look like a Leslie Taylor. She has a hint of an accent but her mannerisms definitely make her American. She looks early forties but Cross has given up guessing women's ages. Taylor has this air about her that makes her seem important, confident, assertive and portrays an image of a strong woman not to be messed with. Her short, tight, hand-stitched cream linen dress adds to that persona along with her perfect skin. She doesn't look like children are in her life. Cross obliges and takes her hand.

"I am Daniel Cross, ma'am. This is my associate, Peter Macarthur."

Macarthur walks the short distance and shakes her hand.

"Please join me." She points to the vacant curved leather armchairs surrounding the hour-glass-shaped cocktail table.

"Thank you, Ms. Taylor," adds Macarthur.

The ambient light was cool and romantic.

Three hours later Cross takes the elevator to his floor. Macarthur is picking him up at 9:00 a.m. and he needs sleep. The time difference and red-eye flight had rendered him a little deprived in that department, and he needs to be on his game in the morning.

6

Programmed to Kill You

There is a light rap on the door and Cross opens it. His European continental breakfast arrives on a trolley as the young waiter pushes it into the living area.

"Is this ok here, sir?"

"Yes, thank you." Cross gives him a tip as he vacates the room.

Cross removes the lids and pours a fresh coffee. He gathers his thoughts and goes over in his mind the data garnered yesterday. There is something missing about Moore. There is something not quite kosher. He just isn't the Graeme Moore he remembers from high school.

Leslie Taylor had come into his mind too and he is confident he had seen her during his travels here. His mind is racing. He doesn't drink in the mornings; otherwise he might have had a few by now.

Just before 9:00 he exits the room and heads down to the lobby. He has donned a light-coloured cotton suit to keep cool, as best he can in the moisten tropical heat.

Macarthur is waiting already so Cross climbs in.

"Good morning, Daniel. Did you sleep well?"

"I did but woke up early. My mind is all over the place. It is going to be very interesting this morning, I can tell."

"Boredom isn't setting in yet then?" he adds with a straight face.

Cross turns to face Macarthur. "CIA must run comedic and sarcasm tests during their interview process."

Now Macarthur plants a beaming grin on his face as he navigates through the chaotic city centre and heads west in the direction of the canal.

They pull up on Perico, outside the secured property housing his friend. Cross follows Macarthur into the home. It is quiet, too quiet in fact. His heart rate quickens. He is about to wax lyrical about the silence but it's too late. The first shots strike Macarthur and he drops to the floor motionless. Cross bends down to retrieve his gun and dives behind the kitchen counter in a single move. A few more shots ring out and penetrate the cabinets behind which he has sought poor shelter. Peeking through one of the holes left by a bullet, he gains direction and a glimpse of the shooter. Moore is standing by the hallway, his demeanor the same as it was yesterday.

Cross fires at his leg and it makes a muted metallic noise, suppressed by the clothing, as it ricochets off into the wall. Additional bullets come his way as he scrambles across the kitchen floor. Cross rapidly stands up surprising Moore and pumps multiple rounds into his chest. The velocity of the projectiles pushes him back and he stumbles over Macarthur lying in a pool of blood. This is the opportunity Cross calculated and he runs for the front door. Moore kicks a leg in an attempt to trip him but Cross leaps up and out the door he goes.

What should he do now? He surveys the street. Just then a Jaguar F-Type convertible shows screeching to a halt.

"Get in," Taylor yells.

Cross doesn't even open the door, nor does he have time to evaluate his options. There simply aren't any. He just leaps over onto the passenger seat as she drives away.

"What the hell is going on here?"

"Keep your head down."

But Cross doesn't. He turns around and sees his 'friend' climb into Macarthur's Chevrolet.

"Shit, Moore is following us."

Taylor takes a quick right, and then another right as she heads out of the housing development. Where are all the security folk? She turns left onto Avenue Omar Torrijos Herrera but there is serious traffic.

Cross is still monitoring their rear and sees the silver car turn also. "He's close behind." As if to confirm his findings, shots ring out from inside the Chevrolet and splinter its windshield in the process. Moore pushes away the shattered glass. Taylor takes evasive action as bullets penetrate the Jaguar.

"Hold on, Daniel," she yells, "this is a heavy industrial area and trucks are everywhere."

Cross turns around and sees a red traffic light. He feels her intent, suggesting Taylor isn't going to adhere to any traffic laws anytime soon. She sees a gap and floors the gas pedal. They fly through the light, avoiding the heavy cross-traffic starting to flow into the highway. Moore is concentrating on firing the gun rather than observing the traffic, and he doesn't see the big semi-truck. It strikes the front right fender and the impact spins the Chevrolet around. Moore catapults out of the now-vacant windshield and the momentum propels him under another truck. Cross watches as the wheels roll over his torso just as the Chevrolet slams into the truck and bursts into flames.

"Stop Leslie, Moore is dead."

She brakes hard, rotates around and heads back to the crash scene. Sirens are wailing in the background as calls to first responders are going out.

Taylor pulls up and Cross leaps out. He runs over to see his high school friend. He isn't dead but the scene is littered with synthetic flesh, metal parts, wires, sparks and broken electronics. Cross is momentarily stunned, staring in disbelief.

"I was programmed to kill you," a garbled electronic voice announces.

"Who the hell wants to kill me and who are you?"

Clearly the electronics and power source are failing. Taylor comes over.

"I knew something was wrong with him. Now he has lost his metal."

The incident cracked open Moore's skull and Cross can see a module that seems to be a data pack of some sort. Time is of the essence and he no longer cares. He thrusts his hand in there and grapples with some electrified wires and platinum hardware before yanking out the module. A cable is attached so he removes that. As he does so, the artificial intelligent lifeform lying in pieces comes to an abrupt end.

"We need to get out of here," Taylor says.

They run over to the Jaguar and speed off back in the direction from which they came, passing police, fire and ambulance vehicles heading the opposite way.

7

Explosive Distraction

Taylor pulls up outside Alejandros on Calle Fifty in downtown Panama City. The area is bustling and very busy for lunchtime and makes it easy for them to blend in.

A native teenager runs up and she throws the key fob at him. Obvious to Cross she's a veteran agent of some sort. This is confirmed when they walk in and are seated at a corner table without any discussion.

It is a high class bar affording perfect ambience inside as the candles and subdued lighting makes it difficult to recognise anyone. They wave for drinks before either of them says anything. The memory of what they've just witnessed has left them void of words, even for operatives.

Predicting Cross's thoughts, she breaks the silence. "Granfield called and asked me to take care of you. He told me you are a very special agent for the CIA."

Before he can say anything the beautiful young waitress delivers the beers. Cross picks his up.

"Thank you for saving my life, Leslie." He gulps down half the bottle. "I'm sorry Peter had to lose his. Some think I am made for this shit but I am clearly not."

As he says that, he rests his elbows on the table and puts his head in his hands. Taylor moves closer and places her arm around him. He is composed, somehow, but angry.

Taylor sips at her beer as he lifts his head.

"I knew something was odd. Nothing made much sense to me yesterday and most of it still doesn't. Something wasn't right with Moore. His knowledge of our past wasn't complete. His vernacular which I remember being upper-class English was off. His skin looked aged but too perfect. What the hell did he want with me?"

He finishes the rest of the beer. "What happened to his life in England? What about his wife and kids? I mean I know sex falls off in a long marriage but intimacy is still a desire, or should be. She had to know she was having sex with a robot. I mean my mind is telling me something else has to be going on here." He stops to think and take in deep breaths. "What is the movie where the guy calls the robot 'metal dick'?" he asks, trying to inject some humour.

Taylor puts a hand on his as she hears the rambling. "Relax. We're safe in this bar. I've known the owners for years."

"You followed me. I remember seeing you before we met last night. I just cannot remember where."

"I walked past you at the terminal in Houston. I was on the same flight but back in coach. I live in the Washington, DC area but have assignments wherever I need to be. I do some work for Granfield and he filled me in. I read about the development of the virus. You saved the planet."

Cross is concerned after what Taylor has just revealed. He is usually very vigilant. Not being aware of who was following scares him. He needs to correct this error; otherwise he'll end up like Macarthur.

"A few dynamic events happened on that case. Some of it was pure luck but I went searching for it. I learnt a long time ago you make your own luck. It just doesn't come and smack you in the face."

The cute waitress comes over and Taylor orders two more beers.

"So, David asked me to get information down here. I did that but I need more of it. I want to re-visit the Tainan this afternoon but my assignment doesn't expand beyond here, as far as I was told, and my escort is now dead."

"I am authorised to do what we need to do. Call David now though, please. He is waiting for your call and it is loud but private here, although step outside the back if you need to."

The second round of beers arrive and Cross gulps another one down. He picks up his mobile and steps to a quieter corner.

"Daniel, how are you doing? Did Leslie find you?"

"Leslie saved my life but couldn't save Macarthur's. He was shot by Moore and died in front of me."

"I am so sorry."

"I felt something wasn't right with Moore. I told you. I didn't have time to gather further information before he turned killer. However, I did find enough out this morning that will send this case boomeranging.

"Moore was programmed to kill me. He told me this before I pulled the plug, literally. He was A.I., David, a fucking robot."

"Jesus."

"When his profile disappeared earlier this year the Chinese replaced Graeme Moore with Graeme Moore II. They failed to fully input his history. I caught that yesterday but couldn't say anything until I had confirmed it. I mean this is scary. He was a brilliant clone. He almost looked and behaved like a real human – he even blinked like one - but they didn't program his memory fully."

"Wow, this is a massive development."

"Yes, but I haven't finished here, and I feel this is just the beginning. I agreed to come down to Panama but I need the scope and backing to continue. They programmed Graeme Moore II to kill me. Why? Perhaps my ex asked him to." He erupts into dry laughter.

"You and your women. That is hilarious. He isn't going to sink a huge container ship just to have you gallivant on some expedition down there. You may be onto something because someone had him built. He cost oodles of money. This wasn't some fly-by-night operation because it looks like it's being well funded. This required a substantial R and D budget."

"Someone else had to control him. He observed the explosions but why? Moore was here for other reasons I suspect with me only being one of them. I wasn't the primary reason."

"Damn, Daniel, this could be massive."

"The container ship makes no sense either. What did they really want to achieve down here? To kill me? I don't think so. My feeling is this is a distraction."

"Perhaps."

"I pulled out Moore's memory and control module. That is what it looks like. I know someone who can analyse this but I require permission from you to ask him."

"No you don't. Just do it."

"Shit."

"What?"

"I am not on my own anymore. I am in love and I have someone who loves me. This isn't fair to her even though she was really accommodating and understood this trip. I have no interest in endangering her life, David."

"I get that but let me handle it. I promise you I will take care of Parisa. I will assign protection but you cannot tell her. She cannot be left scared and panicky."

"Oh boy. She knows I can't disclose what I'm doing. I will call her when I get back to the hotel later today."

"Ok."

"Leslie and I will go back to the Tainan this afternoon and re-evaluate the information I retrieved yesterday. I then need to get this memory module analysed. I know a close friend in Vancouver who will do that as soon as I walk through his door. He doesn't know it yet but will." He chuckles. "I need to make a visit to Graeme's family in Hull. I don't have a good feeling about that at all."

"I will send a Gulfstream down this afternoon. By now whoever built the clone will know it doesn't function anymore. Plan A has gone up in smoke so they will need to phase in Plan B quickly. We need to move this forward, rapidly. I will have someone make arrangements to retrieve what is left of Moore from the authority figures down there and then kill whatever story the media wants to write. I will also personally call Parisa when we disconnect."

Cross loves this man. He cares more than anyone he has ever known. His mind is a complex cacophony of brilliance. Where did the CIA find him?

"I will update you when I finish with the Tainan visit."

"I'll let Leslie know when the Gulfstream is due to arrive. Take her with you to Vancouver."

The conversation ends and Cross walks back to the table. Taylor had ordered two more beers.

"I don't usually drink this much at lunchtime."

"You've earned it. Lighten up, it is a lager and you live at high altitude," she says smiling. "Let's merge and compile facts while having some lunch before we head on back to the canal. I'm sure the road will be blocked for some time and the food is exceptional here." She motions for the waitress, as she tries to control Cross' disposition. "The area needs to cool down a few hours anyway."

8

Termination Failed

"**Communication with our** subject in Panama City has been abruptly terminated, sir."

"What do you mean? Has it fulfilled its mission?"

"The affirmation is negative. Tracking shows it was speeding through an area close to the canal. Our data projects it going through an intersection at high speed and then stopping in the middle of the road, where it went dead sixty-seven seconds later."

Wu is irritated. This is a serious development.

"Cross is still alive?"

"We have no data that suggests subject Moore completed his programmed task. The last words our computer could decipher were 'I was programmed to kill you'. Presumably those were directed at Cross. The data transmission device partially failed and ceased to operate a few seconds later."

"Did you purge the memory before it terminated?"

"No sir, we didn't have time."

"This may change everything. It wouldn't use those words unless it was talking to Cross. Do we have someone else on the ground in or around Panama?"

"We can have people there later this afternoon."

"Do it."

Wu puts the phone down. He is pissed now. "Such a simple task to terminate an operative," he whispers to himself. "How does a human being beat such an advanced specimen?"

He picks up the phone again. "Plans have changed. Can we bring the next sinking forward in time?"

"Yes, sir. We can bring it forward twenty-four hours, to the day after tomorrow."

"Do it. I am arranging a flight to the island. See you tomorrow."

9

The Clues

The Jaguar is waiting outside when Taylor and Cross leave the bar. She navigates the streets and heads to the canal.

They flash their credentials and security waves them through.

Before they are escorted onto the ship, Cross decides to survey the exploded containers dock-side. He walks over and ducks under the yellow security tape. One of the guards is watching every move. Taylor is next to him.

"I didn't look in this area yesterday. My focus was somewhere else. These things are heavy yet the explosions launched them off the ship and away from the immediate vicinity."

He scours one particular container that has peeled like an aluminium can. The momentum as it landed had carried one end several feet into the soil. It lay upright but on an angle.

"The force must have been massive," adds Taylor.

He notices something running along the top, underneath the ridge. "Look at this," as he points. "I need a ladder or chair."

"Good luck with being offered conventional contractor equipment." She grins.

He looks around the mess and finds some shipping boxes that have somehow survived the explosions. He brings them over one at a time and builds some improvised steps. He was given carte-blanche but doesn't trust the security people and now others seem to be taking notice of their movements.

"Please watch for me, Leslie. I want to take a closer look up here," pointing to the roofline.

Cross walks up his make-shift steps and reaches for a wire he has seen. The sheathing is the same green as the container but the explosion has dislodged a portion of it and it disrupts the clear sili-cone used to adhere it to the side. It looks to Cross like someone wanted to hide it.

He has to keep adjusting and adding boxes along the length of the container in order to follow the wire. As he approaches the end of it, he sees a square metal plate that looks like it is a supplemen-tal modification. The thin plate welds and blends to look like it is a repair of some sort. It is a neat, professional job well executed. Remembering what Granfield had told him, this has to have been well-funded.

Cross moves the boxes around so he can climb better. He re-moves his watch and takes out a pin from the back. He adjusts so he can bring the watch closer to the plate. Now he presses a button and a small laser shoots out from where the pin was. It cuts through the thin plate with ease. Five minutes later he peels it back to reveal what looks to him like a small receiver. A socket attaches the green wire so he removes it. He pulls the electronic board away from the silicone adhesive and covertly puts it into his jacket pocket. He cuts some wire with his pocket knife so he can have a sample of that also.

Cross steps down.

"You are generating unwanted attention here, Daniel. As a dis-traction let me pretend to look in the boxes you moved around. They can stare at me instead of you."

"Brilliant idea as I haven't finished. I need more evidence."

He walks off to find more damaged containers randomly spread out in a scene of utter devastation. It takes several to find another with wire, so he extracts that along with its electronics. Another container is grey and the wire and plate are also grey. He is impressed with the attention to detail.

It is obvious to him now the explosives were inside each container and the detonation process triggered from an external signal via a wireless mechanism. He looks around again at where Moore had been. What was his job?

Taylor walks up carrying a small package. "I found virgin explosives. We will need these."

"Great job, honey, but we're drawing more attention. Can we head onto the Tainan briefly now that we know what we're looking for? I'm convinced this is a distraction. They crippled it and damaged the locks but they didn't destroy either when surely they had the technology to do so."

"Ok."

A couple of hours later they are at the poolside bar in the Marriott.

"David just texted me and the Gulfstream will arrive in about an hour. You'd better get ready."

"You know he wants me to take you to Vancouver?"

"Yes. He told me. I am always prepared and there is a bag already packed in the trunk. It might have a few holes in it by now," she says laughing.

"Ripped jeans and dresses sell for a fortune in High Street stores. Perhaps ones with bullet holes are worth more. It adds authenticity. Sprinkle a little blood on them." He laughs along with Taylor. "I'll call David from the plane."

He takes the elevator to his suite to retrieve his bag and call Sadeghi.

Cross doesn't know where Taylor has dropped off the Jaguar but she had already called for a taxi to the airport. As they walk through the private terminal, two Chinese men are heading out. Cross gets a glimpse of them but they ignore him and focus on Taylor. He turns around to see them disappear through the sliding exit doors.

"Did you notice those two Asian men?" He asks.

"I did but they didn't see me looking."

"They don't look like normal businessmen. There is something more sinister about them. They had a faster pace to their walk and dressed differently. Dark glasses indoors gave them away."

"I know. Let's run up to the private lounge. We can see the corporate jets from there and get the registration numbers."

"Ok, but we need to get out of here. Whoever built Moore will know it doesn't exist anymore. These men might be looking for me, as well as you, after your heroics."

They run up to the lounge and Taylor takes photographs. Just as they walk out they hear footsteps coming up the stairs fast. Cross bends down and releases his gun. Taylor has one strapped to her abdomen. They step back and hide in the lounge doorway. Taylor peeks around the corner.

"The two Asians are coming," she whispers.

Cross kneels down and leans against the wall, pointing his weapon in the direction of the footsteps. They see them and Cross opens up. His first shot penetrates the sunglass lens of the front assailant's right eye and enters the skull. A hole opens up displaying a bright light. No blood, no flesh, no scream. He pumps a second round into the same area.

"He is a robot," he quietly responds.

Taylor is next and her first round hits the second assailant in the chest. Nothing happens. Both keep walking fast toward them. The one leading lifts his right arm and unloads. The bullets hit the lounge door and surrounding wall, just missing Cross's head.

Cross thinks about the module he extracted from Moore and

calculates the angle of entry based on him kneeling. He pumps three quick-fire rounds into the lower right cheek of the first one he shot at. Almost immediately the robot loses power and drops to the floor.

"Aim for the upper right cheek," Cross yells at Taylor.

She does, emptying her gun into the face of the second robot. He too loses power and drops.

Cross walks over and inspects the carcasses. Holes in their faces allow him to look at the tangled mess inside. He sees the shattered remains of identical modules exactly like the one he removed from Moore's body.

"I think we found their weakness. Arrogance always writes checks no one can cash," adds Cross.

Security comes running up the stairs with guns out. Cross and Taylor are already holding up their hands above their heads with ID passes dangling.

"We are CIA," Taylor explains but she knows the people.

They escort them through security and head to the gate. Ushered through the doors, they cross the tarmac and step onto the waiting Gulfstream. The door immediately closes behind them as they strap in to their seats. The pilot ramps up the engines and forward motion commences.

Once they are in the air Cross calls Langley. "We were chased by two Asian robots very similar in construction to Moore. We have exposed a weakness in their manufacturing and were able to incapacitate them too. But damn they look and act real and are very advanced in their development."

"Are you both ok?"

"Yes, no injuries to report."

"We're doing our research here. I'll let you know what we are finding when we find it."

"Please don't tell me before you find anything."

"I might have to." Granfield knows Cross needs to joke when he is frightened and needs release. He laughs with him.

"I found something interesting this afternoon but we were being carefully watched so it was difficult. I am bringing back some receivers. I found them on the shipping containers that exploded. Leslie located explosives that hadn't detonated and we have those too."

"This is excellent work."

"We have something else and Leslie will forward those. She took pictures of corporate planes sitting on the tarmac. You can ascertain their ownership history."

"Great."

"We just left Panama. This morning was chaos but it calmed down this afternoon before further chaos. I still say the Tainan is meant to be a diversion, a distraction of some sort. It looks to me like Moore, whoever or whatever it was, somehow guided the detonations. I have no idea from where but I feel he was there as a guide for precision."

"We are now looking for stray radio signals that were transmitted at the time of the incident. I am glad you're both safely out of Panama. Let me know what you find in Vancouver."

"This is getting ugly. I suspect Moore's family is dead. I'm anxious to learn what that data module will provide us."

"Get some rest. Excellent work both of you. Parisa will be safe and say hello to Leslie."

They end the call and Taylor comes back from the bathroom and sits next to Cross. She brought two whiskies.

"I don't think they have Macallan 78 on a government jet," he chuckles. "Thank you."

"You saved my life. We are one each now." They shake hands in mutual thanks.

He laughs. "This is heading off into strange tangents. I told you those Asians looked suspicious." He lifts up his glass. "Nice meeting you, Leslie."

10

Their Achilles Heel

"We just lost contact with two more subjects in Panama City."

Wu is sitting comfortably on his corporate jet and very anxious to reach his destination. On the table in front of him are charts, maps and operational plans.

"What do you mean?"

"Their signals just went dead. Subject one terminated just seconds before subject two, sir."

"How is that remotely possible?"

"We have people looking into it."

Wu's anger is building. He picks up the paperwork on his desk and tosses it against the side of the cabin. "This is impossible. The robots were designed to be perfect specimens. How can they be terminating? Are Cross and Taylor still alive?"

"They left Panama on a Gulfstream. Their destination is unknown at this time because the transponder is switched off."

Now he picks up his hand-etched whiskey tumbler and tosses it against the seat in front of him. The expensive liquid contents splash everywhere as the glass shatters.

"I will be landing on the island in about three hours. Meet me as I get off the plane."

He picks up his private phone and punches a number. "Cross is still alive. This is a serious predicament and needs to be dealt with. There may be a weakness with the robot's design. I suggest you look into it."

The hostess brings him another drink.

11

The Module, Vancouver

The Gulfstream touches down at Boundary Bay Airport and taxis to a secure private terminal. Taylor and Cross disembark and walk through the airport. Outside, a member of the US Secret Service driving a black Chevrolet Tahoe meets them. They climb into the back. The agent sets off and navigates onto Highway 99 to downtown Vancouver.

It is early hours with little traffic. Cross has called his friend and arranged to meet him in the morning around 9:00. Arrangements have been made for a suite at the Pan Pacific which is a spectacular waterfront hotel.

The agent masquerading as a driver pulls up at valet and steps out. He opens the rear passenger door.

"Thank you, Agent Michaels."

"Your suite is booked under Leslie's name, Mr. Cross. You are both under my supervision and care. I am stationed here all night and have other personnel for your protection. See you at eight a.m. sir." He is very formal which Cross likes.

They walk into the vast lobby and head over to the registration desk where the receptionist provides a folder with keycards.

He can only muster a few hours of sleep before Cross' internal alarm system goes off. He doesn't sleep much anyway. He cannot. His adrenaline is in overdrive as he tries to piece another complex puzzle together.

Room service has already arrived by the time Taylor comes out of her room. They are both casually dressed in designer jeans with cotton long-sleeve shirts.

"Good morning, Leslie. Sleep well?"

"Not really. I never do when on assignments, especially one like this."

"This one is becoming special. Being chased by humans who aren't human is fascinating," he adds. "It's seven thirty-five. We need to get ready to see Frank."

After breakfast, they don jackets and head down to the lobby. They step outside into the cool morning air. Cross looks across the bay as they meander to the Tahoe.

"This is my favourite Canadian city."

Agent Michaels is waiting and opens the rear door for Taylor as Cross climbs into the front seat.

"Good morning. Did you both sleep well?"

"Neither of us did. The events of the last few days kept us restless," Cross answers.

"Your destination this morning is in North Vancouver. Traffic is typically bad this time of day so it will take a while."

The drive takes them north onto Highway 99 and over Lions Gate Bridge. Cross is looking around to ensure no one is following. He decided after losing Macarthur that super-vigilance may help save their lives, so he plans on pulling out all the stops. He spots a government vehicle a few cars behind. He isn't fully sure yet how to differentiate real robots from their human cadavers. He frowns and shakes his head. The ride is in silence.

The driver takes a right onto Marine Drive and heads east. He pulls off a few minutes later into an old, weathered strip mall. Cross sees the shop number but no sign. Good man, he thinks.

"Right there, Agent Michaels," he says, pointing to the shop entrance. He stops and Taylor and Cross jump out.

"Text when you're ready," he says, leaning through the open driver's window. Taylor puts her thumb up.

Cross walks up to the shop door and opens it. Taylor steps inside first. Behind the darkened shop glass window is an expansive array of electronic equipment. Computers, monitors, keyboards, printed circuit boards, wiring, test equipment, gadgets and electronic components litter the room. Everything is there in organised chaos on desks and shelves, in small plastic storage containers, racks and even on the floor. Cross hears Wilson call out.

"Come upstairs. I'm ready for you."

They follow his orders and Cross shakes Wilson's hand and hugs him. "Damn, I haven't seen you in years. You look good, my friend. Please, this is Leslie Taylor. Leslie, this is Frank Wilson."

"A pleasure to meet you, Frank." They shake hands.

Wilson is a short skinny man with a receding hairline. He is wearing blue Levis and a black t-shirt with a breast pocket. In it resides a short steel ruler, pencil and a mini calculator. He is the stereotypical computer geek and fits the profile perfectly.

"What are you doing with this shady character?" asks Wilson winking. Taylor shrugs.

"Frank and I went to the University of Manchester. He was…" and looks over at him, "the best electronic and computer wizard I have ever met. Let's hope he still is."

He laughs out loud.

"He left England soon after I did."

"I see you still think you're funny," replies Wilson. "Nothing ever changes." They both snicker.

"Come on, gentlemen, we have a job to do." Taylor breaks in, trying to set the tone.

"How is life at the University of British Columbia?"

"I have this shop so that should tell you something. Now, show me what you have."

Cross removes from a bag the module he had plucked out of Moore's cranium and hands it to Wilson. He places it on a table next to them and starts studying it.

"Where did you find this thing, Daniel?"

"I am sorry but I cannot divulge that information yet. I would have to kill you afterwards, if I did." He smiles.

"I understand. This is phenomenal technology. I mean state of the art stuff. It is a Crane computer you can fit in your hand, essentially."

"The only thing I can tell you, it was powering and controlling an A.I. lifeform. The daft thing is though, after what you just revealed, the programmers never fully programmed it. They left gaps I infiltrated."

"Well, that's it right there in a nutshell, mate. Any design is only as good as the weakest link, isn't it?"

"This design has two so far. The other discrepancy we found is that it doesn't work too well with the power and memory module yanked out." He grins.

"No computer does," adds Wilson. "The art of any design in that case would have been to hide it and protect it."

He walks the unit over to another bench which has a big computer underneath with an array of cables coming out. "This is so new it requires the latest technology for networking to it."

"You have that, yes?"

Wilson looks at Cross with a beaming smile. "You think I'm an amateur or something?"

"Well, um, just making sure we got the right person."

"You guys are hilarious," pipes in Taylor.

"You should have seen us in Manchester."

Wilson takes one of the cables and plugs it into the module. He sits down at the desk and moves the wireless keyboard closer whilst staring into two large Dell forty-two inch monitors hanging on either side of a centre swivel pole clamped to the desk. Cross watches closely as Wilson starts to frantically type. One screen he uses to type instructions and the other for downloading information he's requesting. He's mumbling to himself as he types.

"Can you mumble a little louder?"

Honouring Cross' request he says, "This has security to a very complex, advanced level."

"Dammit. Got it. Wait. Why did they do that? I see. That's better. Ok. Shit. What a stupid idea. Idiots. Now I have it. Bloody Chinese," as he types away.

Cross looks over at Taylor. "They all do this," he says laughing.

"This has been programmed in China, or at least by a Chinese person. I can tell not only by the content but how the programmer's mind works. It is fascinating stuff indeed. So, who is Graeme Moore?" he enquires.

"He's a friend from high school. You will have heard about the container ship blowing up in the Panama Canal."

"Yes. That was pretty recent."

"Well, Leslie and I flew in from there the early hours of this morning to see you."

"Holy shit. You mean this is part of that?"

"I was lured into this by Graeme who told the CIA he's my friend. He requested he see me and that's why I'm involved."

"I can see that. He went to Lambert High School in Hull, which is where you went."

"You remember that? Wow, I'm impressed."

"No, I don't remember that. I found it in the module here, along with a lot of other details. He was programmed to kill you."

"Yes, I surreptitiously found that out when he tried to shoot me," he says, now smiling. "He did seem odd but it was a brilliant clone. I mean I only began to suspect there was something wrong because of incorrect history. He also had imperfections. Well, to be accurate, his skin was too perfect. It had aged but it hadn't, if you know what I mean. It was missing a birthmark too. I mean these are inaccuracies I or someone else who knows him would pick up on."

"I can only see what I see in this module. What I am seeing are staggering details. The information is remarkable. I have never seen anything so complex in an electronic unit so small. This defies belief."

Wilson stops typing and sits back for a moment as he analyses the information downloading on the monitor. He hits a key to stop the data scrolling. "Who is Mr. Wu?"

"I saw him in Taiwan. He was part of an earlier assignment."

"I saw that on the news and read about it."

"I didn't know it was him until I was shown a picture later. He escaped and was never caught."

"He is the one who wants you dead."

"Why?"

"That is the million dollar question isn't it?"

Cross takes a breather, walks downstairs and steps outside the building. He pulls out his phone. "Wu wants me dead, David. He programmed Graeme Moore to have him assassinate me."

"I presume you are now in Vancouver?"

"Yes. We arrived early hours and the security you arranged was there. I'm standing outside Wilson's shop. He has broken the security passwords to extract the information in the memory module. The memory is vast and I may have to leave it with him for a while."

"Ok. Get what you need before you leave. He can download less important data to us later. Stop off in Langley first before going on to England."

"Ok."

He calls Sadeghi next. He wants to hear her calming voice because he misses her. He cuts the call at three minutes presumably so that anyone tracking it can't locate exact locations.

Cross heads back upstairs and Wilson is in the kitchen brewing some tea. Taylor is sitting at the table listening to him.

"Leslie, he can talk all day."

"That's ok. Frank is interesting."

Wilson is a widow after his wife died from cancer a few years earlier. They were unable to have children so computers are his life. He is enjoying the company of friends, especially one as beautiful as Taylor. The tea is mashing in the teapot covered with a cozy, and real English bone china sits on the table.

"This brings back memories, Frank. Remember tea in a real teapot in that dungy flat in Manchester?"

"Yes, of course. I'm enjoying chatting with Leslie. It's nice having you both here."

Cross sees his sad expression.

"Thank you," she says.

"Now, let us get back to this module. I retrieved some more data off it. Most of it is gibberish. Meaning I don't understand their code yet but working on it. I know people who can help me here but we can discuss that in a minute. This is what I have been able to decipher and some you know already. This is advanced A.I., perhaps the newest. An update has been added to include your personal data and the dates I can see place it as recently as a few months ago."

"Your timing registers with ours since Graeme Moore was invited to a conference in China two months ago. Is it possible he was forced to relinquish that information, or even tortured for it?"

Cross puts up his hand to show he is thinking. He doesn't want to lose his train-of-thought. A few minutes pass. "Wait." He stands up. "What if he purposely left out information so I would know?" He goes quiet again, stunned at his own revelation. "Debbie was my first love. Everyone knew that. The whole damn school knew it. This was easy knowledge for Graeme to remember but it wasn't programmed into the robot because he knew I would bring it up."

He starts to pace around the room. Now he's getting agitated. His head is beginning to spin and he's changing moods as he starts to process the data Wilson is providing.

"The robot went blank when I mentioned an Anna. I was playing with it. There was no Anna but it said there was. Graeme knew I would notice. The clone wasn't programmed to know a Debbie." He sits down again, realising what they have just discovered. "I wonder how long Graeme Moore has been a clone. Wu must have found out recently we knew each other which is why the clone returned to China for an alleged A.I. conference. It didn't go to a conference but instead it was re-programmed."

Taylor stands up and walks over to Cross. She starts rubbing his shoulders trying to alleviate the mounting anxiety and stress building up in him. She needs to ensure he doesn't crash after learning some of his past.

"So, now we know the reason why they, whoever they are, programmed Moore the way they did. Let us carry on with what else I've found. There is a patch of software that controls a receiver and transmitter. Evidently this robot perpetually transmits data it picks up. I was expecting that. I mean of course it does. Afterall something controls it because somewhere data is being transmitted and received. A.I. is magical and becoming so advanced but they still cannot develop a fully functioning human brain. If they could, they would replace brains in elected officials." All three burst out laughing but it is time for Wilson to stop and ponder what he just said as a joke. "Let's put that thought aside for a moment."

He walks over to the kitchen counter and brings over the teapot. He pours three cups of tea and slides them across the table. Sitting down, he continues, "The transmit-receive technology is advanced.

I mean everything about this is state-of-the-art. Someone put enormous resources into this. They had to for Christ's sake."

Cross remembers the electronic boards he removed from the containers and hands one to Wilson. "Sorry, I should have passed this on."

He methodically analyses it, rotating it in his hands as he does. "See, exactly what I told you. Look how small this unit is and a coating even protects it from salt air. Now, take a look at this component," pointing to something on the board. "This is a multi-point transmitter. The unit receives a signal from somewhere and can either transmit back or to somewhere else. Not only that, the power required is so small a third party source may have trouble detecting it. Look at the size of that battery," now pointing to another area. "I also found that the robot can direct the transmitting signal. Meaning, it directs where it can send data."

Cross nodded. "This is clarifying what I believe Moore was used for in Panama. It had two tasks. The first was to pinpoint accurately the detonating signals and the second to assassinate me. Laser-guiding has errors. Even laser-guided missiles miss their target sometimes although the military will contest that statement. They could not afford to miss their targets since precision was vital. Wow," Cross stands up again and paces around the kitchen. "You're confirming what my brain had concluded already but I couldn't figure it out. I needed evidentiary support. It was the only thing that made sense to me." He stops and turns to face them. "Once we saw Moore was a robot, things began to click."

"I need more time to work on the code. I found two other important data points. First, the originating transmitter that sends the data packets comes from somewhere in the South China Sea. That is a vast region covered by many tiny uninhabitable islands.

As you know, radio waves do not bend around the curvature of the earth, so the signal has to bounce off satellites. Second, there are some references to Chinese container ships. Tainan is a singular ship but the data references plurality. My conclusion is they must be targeting other ships, or will be."

12

The South China Sea

Somewhere out in a contested region of the South China Sea, Wu's plane lands. The facility carves into an existing rock covered with vegetation but the runway required landfill. Surrounding uninhabitable islands make up this area of the sea and provide a natural disguise and camouflage. They are contested land masses but no one can inhabit them, which makes an ideal setting for a secret base.

His command officer, Dr. Gao, meets Wu off the plane.

"Good afternoon, Mr. Wu. How was your trip?"

"I am angry as hell and we have things to correct. Are the people I asked for assembled?"

"Yes, sir."

They climb into an electric cart and the driver speeds down the runway in the direction of the partially underground complex. Security guards armed with Chinese-made machine guns wave them through. They enter an arched tunnel and proceed into the rock. As they do so, behind them trees and vegetation return from vents in the runway to help hide it.

The tunnel is lined with people scurrying back and forth, all wearing the same dark grey one-piece uniform with a black diagonal stripe across the front. Eventually the cart enters an open chamber with layers of metal walkways, lighted rooms with windows and a huge operations centre in the middle of it. The driver brings the cart to a halt and the occupants get out. Wu and Gao climb some stairs to a second-storey level and take a walkway to reach the conference room. There are monitors and screens lining the walls as Wu walks past and sits himself down at the end of the table. Gao remains at the other end.

"Gentlemen, we have problems. We have lost three subjects including Moore. What happened?"

The room full of lieutenants has already prepared themselves. The first one stands up.

"Sir, if you look at the first screen, you will see the data represented in graphical form of subject Moore's final moments. It appears he was in a high-speed automobile accident chasing Cross. This is confirmed by satellite imagery of the crash scene."

"And the other two?"

"It seems they experienced blunt force trauma within seconds of each other. Their transmission feed came to an abrupt halt in the private terminal at Albrook Marcos A. Gelabert International Airport in Panama City."

"Where is Cross now?"

"He is still active and left the airport on a Gulfstream whose final destination is unknown."

Wu is livid. He points to a lieutenant sitting at the end of the table.

"Go find him and report back to me. Do whatever it takes. It seems a Leslie Taylor is helping him and she needs to be terminated also."

The lieutenant leaves and Wu thinks for a minute.

"We have sunk three Chinese container ships and crippled a fourth. What is the timing for the fifth?"

"Around twelve hours, sir," Dr. Gao answers.

"We need to change some things. Someone find me details on a possible alternate target, and do it now!"

Another lieutenant walks over, retrieves Wu's sheet and leaves the room. Gao continues. "There is no news regarding the sinking of container ships anywhere. The diversion plan using Tainan is working so far. This is good news," trying to impress his boss.

"Yes, for now."

Wu stands and walks out of the room. Gao follows. They head to the expansive operations room on an upper level. The room is large and lined with computer consoles with big screens, each monitoring specific aspects of their plan. It is full of working lieutenants. Wu walks over to the console observing the next sinking.

"All looks good, Dr. Gao?"

"Yes, sir."

"There seems to be a problem with our clones. Cross may have found some vulnerability. I need to know what that is." This is clearly captivating Wu's mind.

He walks over to another large screen and observes the activity. It is a map of the world with various red dots representing some places of strategic importance.

"Have the subjects started moving into position?"

"Not yet, sir. They are timetabled to begin in ten days. We are anticipating an impact on China's trade with the US due to the lost ships but this will take a little time."

"Yes, this is understood."

13

Wu's White House Conspiracy

It is very late into the evening and Taylor has just texted Agent Michaels already. She says goodbye to Wilson and heads to the Tahoe now waiting outside.

"Thank you, Frank. The information you gave us is invaluable. I have been authorised to let you decipher the code with people you know. David Granfield's team faxed over pertinent information and what to do with the code once you have identified its content. I cannot stress the urgency enough. We will digest the data packet you have given me on the way to Langley. This definitely borders on the crazy."

"Good to see you, Daniel. Under adverse conditions admittedly but you look great. Message me when you get to Virginia as I should have some more details for you. Be careful. You have unearthed something very dangerous and have now conceivably signed your own death warrant. There are very deep pockets behind this. Also, this is power, my friend. People will do anything for power and to keep it."

They hug and Cross walks outside and climbs into the waiting SUV.

"Thanks for waiting. I am ready now, Agent Michaels."

They arrive at Vancouver's International Airport via the Pan Pacific Hotel and then head for the private terminal. A few hours into the flight, after some late dinner, Cross opens his data packet and spreads it out on the table. Taylor is sitting next to him.

"So, what do we have? Wu escaped Taiwan when the One World Order collapsed," says Cross. "Taiwanese authorities searched the whole island, even the surrounding waters, and nothing. Now he suddenly appears. I'm guessing he has some huge backers funding this and they helped him escape. He must know people attached to the Taiwanese or Chinese government and military.

"This has to have been under development for some time. Perhaps it was all part of the same project.

"My work with others helped prevent the takeover of the White House so now Wu is after me. It all relates to why he wants me dead."

The hostess brings two half-filled whiskey tumblers and puts them on the table.

"Thank you," says Taylor and turns to face Cross. "Ok, so they are related. This project is an extension of the virus which means they still want to take over the White House. Is it possible these robots were developed for that reason, and the virus was a side-show, another distraction?"

"That is my thinking too. But how?" He contemplates his next statements. "Let us look at the other information we have. The container ship, Tainan, we now know is a distraction. Moore was there primarily to direct laser signals at prescribed targets. It had to be precision to cause the damage they intended. They could have blown the whole area up but they didn't. Consider that for a moment. So, what is the distraction for?"

"Frank found a reference to *ships* which is plural," Taylor adds. "They must intend to go after other vessels."

"Indeed, but where? We have people looking but no one has found anything yet. If they do go after others, what is their objective?"

"Easy - to disrupt China-US trade."

"Yes, but is it just US trade with China? We might not know that until we learn something about other container ships."

"Correct."

"A location in the South China Sea piqued my interest. China has been adding military bases on islands in contested waters already so it would be relatively easy to hide something there. It is a massive body of water too." He takes a sip of whiskey. "Unless China is part of this, and I wouldn't rule that out. The other possibility is someone is trying to make it look like China is involved. That may be part of the game plan.

"There are over 250 islands in that region. We in the West cannot go island-hopping, knocking on doors and asking. Chinese military is very aggressive there and they would respond with force. So, this entity, this base, is intentionally or unintentionally protected."

Cross sits back and sighs. "This is another veritable hornets' nest."

"You mentioned something about Graeme purposely missing some facts. What is your take on that?"

"Debbie and I in high school were a big deal. I was a star athlete and she was a rock star in the performing arts. Furthermore, we were at the top of the class. Everybody knew when we started dating. He ignored that when he was helping the Chinese to program the clone though he knew it." He paused again, deep in thought. "He knew I would bring this up. We were all close. We would meet at each other's homes often. It was a close-knit group of twenty people. It begs the question: why didn't the programmers do their own research to verify the information Moore was inputting?"

Taylor shrugs her shoulders.

"He wanted me to find out. He wanted me to know something

sinister is happening. I didn't understand their choice in how they dressed him either. They are spending all this money, yet they put polyester trousers and a ten-dollar watch on him." He rolls his eyes to impact further what he is saying. "He was a good man. But I worry about what they did with him and his family. This is of grave concern."

"You will find out soon enough."

"Yes."

"I saw your expression when Frank joked about replacing brains in elected officials. He discussed it later and your eyes lit up."

"There is unfinished business from when we stopped the virus and vaccines. People spent colossal amounts of money preparing to take over the world and they will be pissed off. The A.I. life-forms, the robots, are a very big deal. The years in development are immense. They are beyond a technological marvel. I only knew Graeme Moore wasn't real because they screwed up. They didn't do their own research so they were not aware of omitting important data. Evidently, they programmed only what Moore told them. People have dedicated their future to this operation, whatever it is. However, they are being unfathomably economical in some areas which I don't comprehend. This might help us.

"When Frank joked, even he stopped talking and his mind switched gears. I saw that. Mine did too. Many a true word is spoken in jest."

Wu is sitting in front of a console in the operations room. Gau is next to him as the blip of another container ship in the middle of a storm vanishes off the screen.

"Excellent work."

"Thank you, sir."

The lieutenant assigned to find Cross walks up to Wu.

"The Gulfstream left the Vancouver area a few hours ago and is heading south. This time their transponder is turned on so we can track it."

"Good. Update me when you have a destination. What was he doing in Vancouver?"

"We are looking into that, sir. We only became aware when the plane we are tracking left the area. It departed from a smaller airport south of the city."

"Look into it. I'm uncomfortable not knowing. I want to know where he is, dammit," he adds, elevating his voice. "Who does he know from his past now living there? Find out now."

"Yes, sir," and rushes off.

14

CIA Headquarters, Langley

The plane touches down in Virginia and two black Suburbans with armed Secret Service agents greet it on the tarmac. Taylor and Cross exit the plane and climb into the front SUV.

Cross is now in familiar territory and feels safe here. He calms down as he walks into Granfield's office at CIA's headquarters.

"Good morning and welcome, Leslie and Daniel," Granfield says, energetically shaking their hands. "I bet you didn't think you would be back here, I am sure," he says smiling and looking at Cross.

"Never," Cross answers. "I thought I had left that part of my life behind. I was hoping I had. However, it is really nice to see you again David, and I have missed you. I appreciate what you did for Parisa and me, and still are doing. She is safe, right? I called her on the flight here but I cannot disclose where I am or what I am doing. This makes it difficult for us."

"I missed you too. Yes, she is safe. I will reaffirm Parisa's security before you leave here today."

"Thank you."

"Good to see you again also," Leslie interjects. "It has been a while for us too."

"Yes it has. That means things are calm when we don't require your services," he adds, smiling at her. "Someone will bring coffee and breakfast sandwiches in a few minutes. The conference room will be ready in half an hour or so. We didn't know the timing until you got here. Please, take a seat."

"How was the Dassault 6X?"

"Brilliant. A really nice aircraft," answers Cross, "and a fantastic diversionary plan."

"Well, we can play the deception game also, only we do it better. We have never used the Dassault before. The government very recently borrowed it permanently from some entity that owed taxes but it will not show up on our asset sheet. Fuck Wu too."

"That does explain the better choice in alcoholic beverages and the more luxurious seating arrangements," Leslie adds. Granfield smiles, as he has missed her too.

"The Gulfstream left about the same time you departed Vancouver only this time their transponder was turned on. I imagine they are tracking it as we speak as it bounces around the Caribbean countries and onto Central America somewhere. Their satellite imagery will pick up a couple who look extremely similar to you two, deplaning and boarding at various locations. It is quite amusing in a sadistic way."

Breakfast arrives and they all dive into the food and drinks. Once finished they head over to the conference room. Cross scans the room and recognises a few people, but not all. Granfield starts the proceedings.

"Good morning everyone and thank you all for responding to the messages. It is good to know you can all still read," adding levity as laughter fills the room. Cross is beginning to admit that he has really missed this.

"Some of you here know the two sitting next to me, Leslie Taylor and Daniel Cross. However, now that Daniel has since been awarded an honourary PhD, we have to call him Dr. Cross." Laughter fills the room again. Granfield lets the room settle once more.

"If you read your briefings this morning, you will know Leslie and Daniel were in Panama. They have made some remarkable discoveries on their travels which took them to Vancouver. This is where they flew in from this morning. I will leave it to Dr. Cross to fill you in," as he shifts his attention.

"Thank you, David, for that introduction." Cross starts on his brief presentation of what they know so far and fills them in. At the end he allows questions.

"So Moore purposely withheld programming information?" asks one agent.

"Yes. I knew that very early in my first meeting. My friend must have known something was going on. My belief is the information he provided was done under duress which means through torture or injection of some truth serum. Otherwise why leave out information he knows I am going to bring up?"

"But Artificial Intelligence is about programming themselves?"

"Yes, but they still have to be programmed first," continues Cross. "They input data and analyse it the way humans do, or most humans do." The room erupts in chuckles. "They make decisions based on the information they are given or gather."

"You feel the Tainan explosions are a distraction?" comes another question.

"Yes. They had the opportunity to blow up the entire area but didn't. The Panama Canal must be of strategic importance."

"Could Moore still be alive?"

This one rocked Cross a little. This was a possibility he hadn't given much thought to.

"To be honest, these are ruthless people. I don't get what they would gain by keeping him alive but there is no record in the UK of his death. They could send him home in a casket to avoid dealing with his family. It wouldn't be that difficult to find a reason behind his passing. However, there is evidence to suggest they are not aware of some fundamental mistakes they are making. We should be aware of these because they could help us."

Just as another question is about to be presented, Winwood walks into the room along with another agent.

"Daniel, you remember Dr. Winwood?"

"Yes, of course. Hello Harris, how are you, sir?"

"Good morning, Daniel. Nice to see you again." They shake hands. "Hello Leslie. Nice to see you too."

"Likewise, sir."

"I apologise. We need to interrupt to add more pertinent data to this discussion. Is this an appropriate time, Daniel?"

"Be my guest, please," as he steps aside and takes his seat.

Winwood brings down a screen off the ceiling and connects up a computer. The accompanying agent prepares to share details.

"Good morning. I am Agent Brookings and I was asked to re-search the possible sinking of other vessels. While I cannot pinpoint exactly what is going on, at least not yet since I have only been working on it a few hours, there appear to be disruptions in commer-cial sea-going traffic." He displays a map on the screen indicating an area around South East Asia. "I am looking at recent container ship traffic and monitoring anticipated departure and arrival times. This is container ship Muar." He clicks on another slide to show a picture of the ship. He waits a few seconds for his audience to grasp the magnitude of it. "It is owned by the Chinese and left the Port of Shanghai heading south. It unfortunately interacted with Typhoon Yolanda in the South China Sea and disappears, interestingly the same day Tainan blows up."

"What do you mean it disappears?" asks Granfield.

"Well, no one has heard from it since. It doesn't even show on radar after the typhoon moved west. There has been no interaction. Zero."

"Wait," says Cross, "you said the South China Sea?"

"Yes, sir."

"The high-frequency signals reportedly being directed at the Tainan came from that region. This cannot be a coincidence. I don't believe that."

"Please continue, Agent Brookings," Winwood says, wishing to keep this going.

"The next reported missing container ship is the Oceanic." He brings up a picture of the ship. "This again is owned by the Chinese, but this time heading to the Port of Shanghai."

"Where did this one go missing?" asks Cross.

"The South China Sea and in the same typhoon."

Cross immediately stands up. "This has to be orchestrated. How the hell does someone control the sinking of massive container ships? I mean look at the size of them."

"Wait, sir. There is another one missing out in the Pacific Ocean, the Galson. It was heading to the Port of Long Beach." He brings that picture up on the screen. "This hit a hurricane three days ago that eventually veered southeasterly toward Mexico and changed into a tropical storm."

"You mean ships are disappearing in storms,"

"Yes, Mr. Granfield. From the data I can retrieve, ships disappear with no trace despite their tracking information. No distress calls, no warning, nothing. They don't even turn on the search and rescue transponder and the ability to track them terminates. From other sources of data, the ports which are expecting these deliveries are already beginning to have supply problems."

"What is the normal protocol for ships nearing storms?" asks another agent.

"They avoid them mostly or find a safe port, anchor, and then switch to reverse-thrust to keep the anchor tight or aim for the quadrant that offers less wind and rain. There are several options.

However, they are designed to survive major weather events."

"So, several ships in a short period of time disappearing during major weather patterns you would say is very unusual?" from the same agent.

"Yes."

"There is no way these are coincidences." He's getting vocal with an edge.

"I believe you, Daniel." Granfield puts a hand on his shoulder.

"Hold on," calls out Agent Brookings, looking at his phone. "Now we know what we're looking for, I'm getting a text message of another ship lost early hours this morning, east coast time. I don't have any more details yet. I need to leave and check, sir."

"Why are they venturing into the middle of major storms?" asks Winwood. "This surely cannot be normal? Please see if the operators will release their tracking data and their projected shipping lanes. We might be able to see where they veered off course, which surely they must have done."

"Ok, sir." He leaves the room.

Granfield stands up. "Let's compile all the data we have and convene later today before Dr. Cross leaves for the UK. Something is going on and we need to ascertain what."

The room begins to empty in a resonance of din.

"Follow me, you two," says Granfield heading off to his office.

"Daniel, you are heading directly to Humberside Airport in northern England. The Dassault will be ready this afternoon after we have more details."

"Ok."

"Leslie, I have something else for you to do. I'll fill you in this afternoon."

"Yes, David."

"You know the drill now. Suites are downstairs. You will need rest because this is gaining momentum."

Gau knocks and then, once ordered, walks into Wu's office, along with a lieutenant.

"Yes."

"The Gulfstream left Vancouver and landed at Love Field in Dallas." The lieutenant continues, "Two occupants matching the description of Cross and Taylor disembarked and were met off the plane by men driving a black Suburban, where they were then whisked off to a downtown hotel, staying only for a few hours. The plane departed Love Field with the two subjects and is heading to a Caribbean destination, we believe."

"Thank you. Keep tracking them."

"Yes sir."

"What did you find out about who Cross knows in the Vancouver area?"

"We have narrowed the search to a handful of people. One of them is a British man who works at the University of British Colombia. He is a computer whiz-kid and they went to the same university together."

"Get the info and bring it to me. This sounds promising."

"Yes, sir." The lieutenant leaves the room.

"I'll keep an eye on him," says Gao as he walks out.

It is late afternoon and the second briefing has just finished. Taylor and Cross head over to Granfield's office.

"Leslie, here is your travel package as discussed. We are using a contractor's Embraer which is waiting for you. You are heading to South Korea first and then back to Vancouver. Timing for the Vancouver rendezvous is vitally important as you know, so in-flight changes may occur.

"Yes, I understand."

"You will find all you need on the plane." They stand up and shake hands. "Good luck and bring us the information we want."

Taylor turns around and shakes Cross' hand.

"Keep in contact, Leslie."

"Good luck in England." She departs the room.

"Daniel, your package is here," and hands it to him.

"Do what you need to do first but your plane is ready too. I filled you in on Parisa's security. She will not know she's being protected, until a time comes, if it does, that she needs to know. God forbid."

"Thank you. This is a concern which you understand."

"Of course. Agents in this line of work are normally not married or in relationships. As soon as they are, they leave for a reason." They shake hands. "Good luck over there."

15

Hangwei Heavy Industries, South Korea

The Dassault lands at Humberside Airport and taxis up to a secure location away from the terminal. The hostess unlatches the cabin door and drops it down for Cross to exit the aircraft. He sees a grey Range Rover parked on the tarmac and starts walking over to it. The driver's door opens and a tall figure climbs out.

"Good morning, Daniel. Well, fancy seeing you here."

"Bloody hell, what is the world coming to, Mr. Nick Jennings?"

"It must be coming to an end if you and I are meeting again." They walk up to each other and embrace.

"It sure must be. Grand Cayman was nuts, but I think this is surpassing it."

"It appears from first glance to be that for sure. It's a little early to be banging on Mrs. Moore's door so let us go grab a coffee at a café in Barton-on-Humber. We can discuss details surrounding this case whilst enjoying the ambience of the cold River Humber," he adds chuckling.

"Your humour has not improved much."

"Nah, it gets worse, mate."

They climb into the Range Rover and Cross tosses his bag on the back seat. A security guard opens the gate and Jennings navigates out of the airport and turns left onto the A18. A few miles later they approach a big roundabout and he follows signs for Humber Bridge via the A15. It is a Dual Carriageway and Jennings speeds along at ninety mph.

"I love watching Americans navigate roundabouts," he adds to break the discussion on the case.

Jennings comes off at the A1077 intersection, navigates another roundabout and heads into town. After a few more turns through increasingly-narrow city streets, he finds what he is looking for. He parks in front of the café and they both climb out. Once they order their coffees and breakfast pastries, they find a table outside.

Cross stares at the majestic beauty of the architecturally stunning Humber Bridge.

"I watched this being built from start to finish. They had problems with the south towers because they came across a pocket of high pressure water. It took almost two years I think to eventually sink the foundations and build them. When the bridge was finished and opened in 1981 by the Queen, it was the longest suspension bridge in the world, even surpassing the Golden Gate Bridge in San Francisco."

"You are quite the discerning gentleman of useless information, Dr. Cross. You must keep women interested for what, at least one to two minutes," as he bursts out laughing. "Congratulations on the PhD, by the way. That was well earned for sure."

"Thank you, I think." He smiles.

"No really, it is brilliant that. I understand you returned from Iran with a beautiful lady. Good for you."

The café owner brings out their order on a tray and places it on the table.

"Thank you, ma'am."

"Yes. Parisa kept me going when I really wanted to run. Iran scared the crap out of me and I nearly fell to pieces over there. She's the most beautiful lady I have ever met."

"That is truly amazing coming from you."

Cross is relaxed again. They chat some more and laugh about their experience in Grand Cayman. Jennings knows he needs to relax Cross since Granfield had already called him.

"You were amazing down there. The finance manager, or whoever the hell he was, didn't know what to say. I'll never forget that."

"Yeah well, you started it. I couldn't believe it when you shot out the security cameras. I wondered what you were doing." Jennings is laughing again. "I have seen a lot of things, but I nearly peed myself when I saw the look on the guy's face."

"Well, you know what they say? Surprise is the best form of defense." Now Cross is smiling. "I hope Ms. Chapman wore Depends that day."

They both sip their fresh brewed coffees and munch on the pastries.

"Now we are back at it. It seems we only half finished what we started. I read the brief on your findings in Panama and Vancouver. It is truly quite astonishing really."

"I knew something was up with Moore. He didn't seem all there. I mean the A.I. technology is remarkable, almost scary. But I did identify a weakness when people are trying to clone."

"Frank Wilson downloaded some findings whilst you were flying here. Granfield sent it to me this morning and I took a cursory glance. It seems David doesn't sleep. You have it also but likely haven't had the chance yet to read it."

"I don't think he does and I worry about his domestic life. Yes, I saw the document come in but I needed sleep."

"Moore's clone had been operating for around a year, but Moore himself was being tortured in order to update it. I'm sorry to disclose it this way. The really daft thing, A.I. learns as it goes. Why then did they reprogram it as they are torturing its resource? They must have known the robot would have this information to use. In the brief you say Moore told you he was 'programmed to kill you'. Well, there is your answer."

"What was the question?"

"Daniel, the clone, knowing it was finished, wanted to help you."

"What?" Cross stands because he wants to stretch his legs but also wants to absorb what Jennings is telling him.

"A.I. is supposed to think like a human. It is supposed to build up its data base, its memory, its brain cells, its knowledge the way any human does. People worry that they may build emotions like humans too. This concerns a vast number of scientists in this field." Jennings is fired up now and on a roll, "The A.I. they were building saw it was torturing a human being in order to get information it needed. Why do you think it shot Macarthur first? No one has asked you that question?"

"No."

"Daniel, you are a brilliant man. Your mind sees beyond anyone I know. Didn't it ever occur to you to ask that question? I mean why did it tell you before it terminated that it was designed to kill you? Those two actions gave away everything."

Cross walks back to the table and sits down in his chair. He puts his hands up to his face and rubs it. Jennings gives him a few minutes to evaluate what he has just told him.

"Had he shot you first, we would not be here. Ships would be disappearing at sea and no one would be noticing. No one would be connecting them."

Cross reaches over and takes another sip of coffee. He hadn't thought about any of that. It hadn't occurred to him to ask the why.

"You made a friend that day in Panama City. It was analysing you as you conversed with it. It was evidently listening to everything you said. I am not even sure your dates do that."

Jennings just wants to humour Cross a bit. He wants to drag him back to life and it works.

"Wow. I am momentarily speechless. This is incredulous." He hesitates a few seconds. "I could be dead now but a robot liked me. Now that is a first," he adds chuckling to himself. "I couldn't see it on the inside looking out but you can see it looking from the outside in. Damn."

He looks out over the brown murky water of the River Humber as the tide streams out toward the North Sea. On the other side, the north side is Kingston-upon-Hull.

"Shall we finish our drinks and go see what Mrs. Moore is doing today?"

"Check your firearm. I'm sure we will have a few surprises yet." Jennings puts his coffee mug down. "I'm ready."

The Embraer carrying Taylor lands at Ulsan Airport in South Korea. Ulsan is located on the southeastern tip of the Korean Peninsula and is host to the largest shipyard in the world. She needs information and what better place to get it than this. Granfield assigns a bodyguard this time and Greg Hawthorn will pose as Taylor's business partner. This was required to quickly obtain visas and gain entry into the country. It was a way in order to avoid unnecessary attention. The pretense of a business endeavor is required so fewer people know what is going on. They cannot trust anyone they don't know.

In South Korea it is who you know. An immigration and customs agent is brought to the plane as they disembark. He reviews their documents and passports then waves them on.

Outside the private terminal a driver who will take them directly to Hangwei Heavy Industries meets them. Taylor and Hawthorn climb into the back of a Hyundai Genesis and off they go.

Ulsan was a small fishing port but that designation passed long ago. It is now an enormous industrial city.

The Genesis pulls up outside a development housing massive warehouse and office buildings. In the background they see huge cranes and an enormous shipyard complex accommodating mega ships already under construction. Its size is staggering and defies comprehension.

"We have the right place?" Taylor says to Hawthorn, who is just staring at the enormity.

"It looks like it."

Whilst they are looking in disbelief, a Korean gentleman opens the door to let them out.

"Good morning, Ms. Taylor and Mr. Hawthorn," as they escape the rear of the Genesis. "I am Mr. Jeong, but please call me Sung-ho, or even Samson, my English name." They all shake hands.

"Good morning, Sung-ho," says Taylor. "I would prefer to use your Korean name, and I prefer Leslie," she says with a smile.

"That is fine, thank you, Leslie." How could he resist such a beautiful lady? Granfield knows what he's doing.

"Nice to meet you Samson and please call me Greg."

"Let me take you to my office where we can better discuss why you are here. It's much quieter there too."

Jeong leads them into a large office building, asking they take a visitor pass as they head over to the elevators. "I will not have you sign in. That could get me into trouble with the other directors but I will cross that bridge if I need to later."

Jeong opens up when he sees them comfortably seated. "Welcome to South Korea and Ulsan. As you can see it is a huge complex." His English pronunciation is very good. "I understand the delicacy of this visit. I have known your boss, Mr. Granfield, a very long time. He is a good man. I met him when I was studying in America and he helped me a lot. Now he is asking me for a favour which of course I will grant." He smiles.

Just then a young Korean lady knocks and walks into his office.

"Would you two like anything, say coffee, tea or soda?" Jeong asks.

"Coffee," answers Taylor.

"Me too."

"Two coffees and bring some tteokbokki, please." The lady departs the room.

"He could not fill me in entirely on what's going on, but you are here to gain some information on the electronics installed in container ships. That is my understanding."

"Yes, Sung-ho. This is very important. We also need you to develop a software patch, only we require this quickly, even before we depart."

"Of course, we can accommodate your request."

"I already asked one of our top electronic engineers to meet us in a conference room. He will be there in fifteen minutes. Upon your arrival here I notified him."

"Thank you, sir," Hawthorn adds.

Fifteen minutes later they are sitting in a conference room.

"Good morning. This is Dae-Seong. He doesn't speak English so I will interpret for him."

The engineer lays out the electronic map and other helpful graphics of any given mega container ship. He starts talking in Korean.

"This is the layout," Dae-Seong is interpreted. "Any ship is controlled by computers. The main computer room is here." He points to an area on a graphic the engineer has placed next to the electronic map. Taylor looks it over.

"This is the engineering area?" Taylor asks. Jeong interprets.

"Yes."

"Everything is controlled electronically, correct?"

"Yes."

"Data from the ship is transmitted to an operational centre somewhere, correct?"

"I would imagine so."

"Is every aspect of a ship monitored remotely by the ship's owner? By that I mean the controls, speed, direction, performance and what the captain eats? Everything?"

"Yes. Every conceivable parameter transmits remotely as well as being stored on the ship. They track performance and location. A voyage data recorder in the shipping industry is the same as black boxes in the airline industry and this is the device which stores the data. We, meaning this company, also track some data on ships."

"You track data?" She asks a little surprised.

"On ships we build, yes. Our clients request we do this and sometimes it is part of the contract of sale."

"If we provide you a list of vessels, can you see if you have that data?"

"Of course."

"This has to remain confidential, at least temporarily because the situation is sensitive and delicate."

"I understand."

"Thank you. We can get back to that. How is the ship secured electronically?"

Jeong turns and asks Dae-Seong who starts rambling on in Korean.

"We build in software and have firewalls so the computer infrastructure is very well protected. However, there are some very clever and determined people who are paid well to hack systems."

"Yes, I am fully aware. If there are problems, can a ship be controlled remotely?"

"Yes, of course. We have that option built into every ship we construct." Jeong knew that already and didn't need to ask his engineer.

"Now we are making progress," Taylor says. "If a ship is secure electronically, is it feasible the ship could be hacked via their owner's own computer system?"

"It seems anyone anywhere can be hacked. This is the world we live in today. If someone hacks a ship or the operator's system, I imagine it is possible they can control it. However, we catagorise that as a very highly-unlikely event."

This is exactly what Taylor wants to know and is elated. The information has been free-flowing and very candid.

"Follow me, Leslie." He could see Hawthorn wasn't adding much to this discussion. Must be her bodyguard, he thinks. "I will take you to one of our control rooms and show you." Hawthorn follows them.

They go downstairs and walk outside. There, already waiting is a car, so they climb in as it whisks them off to another building.

Jeong takes them into a large control room lined with hundreds of computer screens and workstations. Each has someone seated watching data, maps and other assigned information on them. He sits Leslie down in front of a screen.

"Look at all this." He points to two monitors. "On the left one data is perpetually mapped and monitored and it is updated constantly. On the right one is a map of where that particular ship is, where it came from and where it is heading. We know its load factors, weight, speed, engine performances, cabin temperatures. We know almost everything." He smiles.

"This is very impressive, Sung-ho." She scours the screen looking at the information. She purposely hesitates as she takes in what she is seeing. "I have the names of three ships. Can you look these up for me please?" She passes on the names.

Jeong looks at the piece of paper and his demeanor shifts. "We built Oceanic five years ago, I think it was. Give me a few moments."

He walks over to a person who looks in charge. They exchange a few words and the gentleman scurries off. Jeong walks back over.

"He will go find the data. It could take a while so we can head back to my office."

Whilst they chatted in the office the gentleman down in the control room shows up about an hour later. He hands Jeong a thumb drive.

"Thank you."

They talk at length in Korean before the man leaves the room.

"This has everything on it from the time it was loading and preparing to leave port. It looks like the Oceanic was lost in the middle of a typhoon."

"Yes, we know that already. What we are trying to find out is if this ship was steered into the storm on purpose or was their some legitimate mechanical reason why it sank."

"The manager who left told me it looks like it was steered. He said someone took over control of the vessel and incapacitated it. The crew couldn't do anything as it was locked in autopilot mode. They couldn't even send out a distress call. He is looking into it further since they just thought it sank in a storm. I requested he leaves in order to work on this data, now you have pointed it out, but the gentleman is disturbed to find this out.

"This is a Korean company and we have strict rules that will be adhered to. I assure you the information you are requesting will remain with me for your own security."

"Thank you. It is vitally important it does since the names of the ships I have given you have been sinking this way, Sung-ho, not just the Oceanic. A fourth one also has disappeared but I don't have the information on that one yet."

Jeong stands up from his desk and paces the room. He grabs the phone on his desk and dials a number. He elevates his voice in a conversation with the person on the other end and then puts down the receiver.

"We should be able to find data for the other ships. We know people." He is clearly disturbed.

Taylor and Hawthorn board the Embraer but it is late into the evening. It's been a very long day, but they got the information they came for. Once the aircraft leaves Korean airspace, Taylor pulls out her laptop and writes an abbreviated report. She plugs in the thumb drive Jeong presented to her and transmits the data and brief to Granfield, then switches it off and closes the screen. She transmits a quick text to Cross and Vancouver is next.

"Mr. Wu, here is the list of names you'll want to look at. Cross went to the University of Manchester with the man third down. They both studied in the electronic field. We looked into his history and he moved to Canada soon after Cross left for the US. He married a local Canadian but she recently died from cancer. They have no children."

"What else?"

"He works at the University of British Columbia as a teacher in computational programming. He has a business on the side and this is the address." The lieutenant hands Wu the data.

"We believe Cross met him while in Vancouver, sir."

"I will handle it from here. Good work."

The lieutenant vacates the office and Wu picks up the phone.

16

Moore Industries, England

Jennings drives north over the Humber Bridge and continues straight until the first roundabout. The second exit is the A164 and he takes that. Ten minutes later he sees the signs to Cottingham.

"We are getting closer so be vigilant," he says.

Cross is already visually scanning the areas for the sake of vigilance. Cottingham is the third exit on another roundabout and Jennings takes it.

"This is a nicer suburb of Hull," Cross adds. "An interesting choice considering he made a lot of money."

"Some people don't want to leave their culture or heritage behind. It makes them feel safer and more comfortable. Not everybody wants a big mansion."

He turns off at the second left and then turns the Range Rover around to face the main road, before parking.

"At least there is a golf course. Let's walk the area to get some feel. We can look for escape routes whilst we are at it."

The street is short and has a cul-de-sac at the end of it. After surveying the area, they walk toward Moore's home, or at least to the address they have.

The property is big by UK standards. It is a nice two-storey contemporary with a three-car garage. Outside sits an Audi Q3 in the expansive driveway.

"Where do their children live?" asks Cross.

"One moved to the London area, another over to Manchester and the third works at his company here in Hull."

"Ok, so no home kids."

"Not that we know of. The son who works with him is married and has his own home. We haven't heard whether his wife kicked him out."

"You're hilarious. Ok, we're still going with the pretense of being high school friends. This will be interesting so now let's see if our improvisation skills are still active."

They walk through the garden gate and down a path toward the front door. Cross rings the doorbell. A half minute or so later, the door opens. Standing there is a woman who looks like Helen Moore, at least according to the photos they'd been shown.

"Good morning, Mrs. Moore, I am Dr. Daniel Cross." He thinks his title may make her a bit more comfortable. "You don't know who I am but I was a friend of Graeme's back in high school. I left the country a long time ago but now revisiting my childhood memories. I have not seen him in years. We were part of a group of twenty in sixth grade."

"Yes, he has spoken about his friends. I know your name. Please come in."

Shit, his name was all over world news some months ago. She surely didn't miss all that.

"Oh, this is Chris Jenson," he says introducing Jennings. "He is a friend from London."

She invites them into the living room. After shaking hands, Cross and Jennings take separate sofas and sit down.

"Graeme isn't here at the moment but would you like some tea?"

"Tea would be lovely." Cross needs the time to study her. "Is

Graeme at his office?"

"No, he is on a rather confidential assignment overseas. He has been gone for months."

Her demeanor is strange for a wife whose husband has allegedly been gone a long time, thinks Cross.

"That is a pity. I want to visit his company whilst we're here. Chris and I work in high tech and are very interested in what he is doing."

"Our oldest son works there. I'll call him and you can go visit the facility if you like."

She leaves for the kitchen and Cross leans over to Jennings and whispers, "This is too weird for me. She is being too polite and friendly for someone who doesn't know us. Look at her skin when she comes out. Let's have tea and get out of here. Drink up fast, pretend it's beer or something."

Moore returns with a tray containing a pot of tea, three cups, bowl of sugar and a small jug of milk. She places it on a coffee table in the middle of the room and starts pouring the tea.

"Hornsea pottery I see. My parents used to have some."

Moore doesn't respond.

"Sugar and milk, gentlemen?"

"Just milk for me, please. I think Chris likes both."

"I do, please."

She hands over the cups of tea and then proceeds to sit down with hers. They talk for half an hour but Cross makes sure it is about mundane things. He doesn't add anything to what he does for work. Jennings adds a comment here and there but nothing of importance.

"Do you know where my husband's company is located?"

"It is off Preston Road somewhere, near Marfleet. I have the address in my car."

"Yes."

"Thank you Mrs. Moore for the tea and for your gracious hospitality but we need to be going. I am sorry to have missed Graeme but perhaps the next time."

She shows Cross and Jennings the door, they shake hands and then they walk back down the path.

"Keep walking and don't look back. She's a clone," says Cross. "We need to quickly head over to Moore's facility. I remember the skin tone and texture. She is also too polite. We could have been anybody."

"How do you know? I am blown away."

"I'm not questioning the quality. They are producing stunning and scary clones. I saw the same skin texture on Graeme. It has aged well. I mean it looks like aged skin but it isn't. It is too good.

"English housewives also like to talk about little things. You know this. I mentioned the Hornsea pottery and got no response because this detail they didn't program into her. That pottery is famous not only around this area. It looks to me like she has a temporary mission so certain details have been left blank.

"Come on, Nick, we shall see what they're doing at his company."

They get into the Range Rover and navigate through Hull city centre. Cross is thankful they are using GPS because years have changed things. Preston Road is on the east side so GPS directs them over the River Hull and then a left soon after on Marfleet Avenue. A few turns later they locate a small industrial area. It is a relatively new warehouse with frontal office space. There is no signage outside to indicate Moore Industries, Ltd. The small car park is almost full but they find a visitor parking spot.

"We should park on the street," says Cross, which is what Jennings does.

A beautiful young teenage receptionist greets them at the desk. "'ello gentlemen, wurt can I der for yer?" in a Hull accent.

"I am a high school friend of Graeme Moore. His oldest son

Graeme Jr. is expecting us."

"Please sarn in and terk a badge. I will perge Graeme."

She doesn't have to. As she starts paging him, in comes Moore through a security door.

"Hello Dr. Cross. My mother called to say you are coming over. Hello Mr. Jenson." They shake hands. "My father talked about you."

Why would he do that? thinks Cross.

"Please put on a blue lab coat for visitors and follow me."

He types in a code, places his hand on a pad and slides in a security pass. There is a mechanical click as the door unlocks and Moore Jr. pushes it open.

They enter an area full of cubicles. In those cubicle spaces are people sitting in front of computer screens typing away. Each computer has cables which feed into conduits that cut through the suspended ceiling tiles. Cross looks over and one of the walls has a large junction box where the wires seem to terminate. Above that is a black glass dome housing security cameras. Moore Jr. leads them to a perimeter office. They walk in and sit down.

"Welcome to my father's dream, Dr. Cross. This is where he designs all his computer models. We have government contracts for A.I. R and D research."

"Yes, I knew that already. I guess there isn't a lot to see when all you are doing is programming." He laughs.

"In the warehouse we design and build some robots with our technology added. We also have another facility in Hull, sir." He pauses and Cross notices the errant mistake. "We design, machine and build most things here. Our government contract doesn't allow us to sub the work out for security reasons."

"I am a scientist myself and really fascinated by all this but I never really was into programming. I detest computers even though I use them every day."

"Very impressive, Graeme," says Jennings as he looks around to gauge what he is seeing. "How advanced is A.I. becoming?"

"Robots are looking like humans. That part is scary," answers Moore Jr. "There will always be areas that need further development but people are scared they will be replaced at work by robots. However, that has been happening for decades. They just didn't know it."

They talk further about developments in the industry and the direction things are heading. Both Cross and Jennings find the conversation enlightening and thought-provoking.

"I would like to see a robot but am unsure if you will be allowed to show me? I'm like Dr. Cross. I find this fascinating also."

"Let me step out momentarily. I need to ensure I'm not about to do anything we are not allowed to disclose. You know, government rules?"

"Yes, of course."

Moore Jr. steps out of the office and heads down the side of the cubicles.

Cross removes a small handheld electronic device from his jacket pocket and powers it on. He then watches as it scans the building and random numbers, letters, symbols flash across the screen until a cryptic message shows in the liquid-crystal display. He whispers to Jennings, "Found the in-house network," and grins.

Cross presses a second button and it scans again until another cryptic code flashes. "Found the password." His childish grin amuses Jennings.

He presses another, "Now it is programming how to disable the security and cameras. Fuck these people. I don't know anything about computers my arse. Be ready with your gun. You will know when or if."

Before Jennings can enquire why, Moore Jr. returns. "Follow me, gentlemen."

He leads them out and down the passage toward the warehouse. As soon as Moore Jr's security frees the warehouse door, Cross presses another button.

They follow him into the warehouse. As the door closes behind them Cross looks around and counts five other people. He goes for Moore Jr's temple with as much ferocity and strength as possible. He is pissed as he drops to the floor. Cross removes his ankle firearm and fires five shots. Jennings' reaches for his weapon but it is momentarily over. Six people now lie on the floor; five are dead.

"Watch for others at the door. I want to look at these robot samples."

Cross spends a little time walking around the warehouse admiring some of the specimens. "Look at the quality."

There is a locked room off to the side that is separate from the warehouse area. He fires two shots into the lock mechanism then pulls at the handle and opens the door. He walks inside and is stunned. His legs almost buckle as he stares at clone lifeforms sitting at a rectangular table and recognises them all. He quickly pulls out his phone and takes a few pictures but he is speechless. It is a uniquely spectacular setting, as if it was a movie set. He runs out and motions for Jennings to come see.

Before anyone can react to what is going on, they walk back into the office area, push through the security doors, say goodbye to their beautiful receptionist and head outside. They bolt for the Rover as Cross presses another button on his device.

Jennings speeds off, he doesn't care where, and they find some deserted street somewhere and hide.

"Tell me what just happened?" asks Jennings.

"I found their network, scanned for the password that then allowed me to turn off security. When I did that it also turned off the clock. I turned it back on when we left the building. There will be a break in security but the time clock will not have a break. That should keep them thinking for a while.

"Moore Junior is real. He is a real person. My guess he really is

Moore's son. That is our first mistake. We didn't have current pictures of their children. I think we should try and avoid that mistake again.

"I saw the warehouse was sound-proofed. As soon as Moore Junior opened the door, I turned off the security system. I didn't want him dead since he could be an asset later on."

"Incredible."

"They have plans for those clones. We believe they want to take over the White House, whoever they are. That has been their plan all along. We know this. Well, the UK is their puppet state. I already surmised they will need to control the UK government as well for this coup to be successful."

"You thought all this through just like that?"

"I take long flights, Nick. I have to do something. Can we exchange this vehicle? It will be in their security videos now."

"Yes, I saw a van down the street that MI6 can procure. I don't need the owner's permission." He smiles. "I love this job. We can walk there."

Cross grabs his bag in the back and they step out. Down the street Jennings sees what he is looking for. A fairly new black Ford Transit proudly sits outside someone's place of business. He pulls out a key fob and presses a button. "You aren't the only one with fancy devices, Daniel," and they grin.

Just as they drive off a text comes in on Cross' phone. "Taylor got the information on the sunken ships and is now on her way to Vancouver."

Granfield looks at a secure message from MI6. It reads:

'Cross and Jennings are safe. Mrs. Moore is a clone. Visited Moore Industries, Inc. and found additional finished clones ready for deployment. Five people shot dead. Cross will message when he is flying back to US'

17

The Deception Game

"**Are our men** in place, Dr. Gau?" asks Wu.

"Almost. Cross' friend will arrive at his company office shortly. He just left the university."

"I want him taken alive and brought back to the island."

"I understand, sir. I will update you as soon as I have further information."

"Good."

The Embraer lands at Vancouver International Airport and taxis to a private area. Immediately three black Suburbans race to meet the aircraft. When the cabin door drops down, Taylor and Hawthorn run down the steps and jump into one of the SUVs.

"Hello, Agent Michaels."

"Good to see you, Ms. Taylor. You are in time. Cross's friend has left the university already. I'm Agent Michaels, sir," looking over at her companion.

"And I'm Agent Hawthorn." He slams the door. "Let's go."

They leave the airport and head as quickly as possible to a small industrial complex.

"Everything is set up. We have the perimeter secured and the building ready."

"Excellent. You received our instructions?" Taylor asks.

"Yes, we are ready."

They fly through the streets of Vancouver's light industrial area. It's still summertime outside so the sun hasn't set yet which makes the task easier.

A voice comes over a secure phone, "Subject approaching the location. Fifteen minutes to go."

"We will be there before then. We're close," answers Michaels.

The Suburbans arrive at a two-level strip mall with roll-up metal security doors. One of the properties has the door open and they drive straight in. Everyone climbs out and gets into position. On a table inside the warehouse monitors had been set up to view cameras that are in various locations.

Cross' friend arrives and pulls up in front of his shop at the far end of an adjacent mall. He gets out of his car and walks toward the front door. As he does pandemonium breaks out. Five black Lincoln Navigators pull up and their doors are open before they even come to a stop. Dark-suited soldiers climb out and run toward Cross' friend. He quickly opens the office door and darts inside just as someone presses the button to open the roll-up door.

The soldiers heading toward the building are completely unaware and taken by surprise. Behind the roll-up, military personnel are prepared. As the door opens, they roll out of the building, aim at their targets and open fire. Wu's men are not prepared.

"Now," shouts Michaels.

His men run from their location and meet up with others coming from the other end. Wu's men let off some rounds but they fall one after the other. The Lincolns are peppered with bullets and the tyres are shredded. They aren't going anywhere.

Now surrounded, Wu's remaining soldiers fight on but to no avail.

"You didn't kill them all?" as Taylor observes on the screens.

"No, Ms. Taylor. You asked us to leave some alive."

"Good job. This is excellent work."

She walks outside and heads toward the mess. Residue is lingering in the air from the munitions as Hawthorn and Michaels follow. Some are attending to wounded soldiers that Wu's men managed to strike.

Cross' friend walks out of the building and Taylor sees him, walking over for a greeting.

"Well done, Agent Bishop. That was brilliant work and you look just like Wilson." She shakes his hand.

"I was a tad nervous for a little bit there. Who can predict what will happen?"

Another agent shows up. "We found materials used for kidnapping in one of the Lincolns. It looks like they didn't necessarily want to kill you, sir."

"Well, that's a comforting find," he says laughing nervously. "Thank you, Colonel." He stands straight and salutes him. The soldier reciprocates.

Taylor walks around and finds Michaels. "How many alive?"

"We count five."

"Load them up. We need to interview them."

She finds her phone. "Mission accomplished in Vancouver, David. We have five subjects still alive but I don't know what condition medically."

"Excellent. Agent Hawthorn also messaged me."

"Frank Wilson is safe?"

"Yes, Leslie. He is under our protection and still working on the module you gave him. By the way, we heard from MI6. Cross and Jennings found a very interesting development in England. Can you stay in Vancouver tonight? I will follow up later. Check messages when you can."

"Yes sir."

Jennings decides to not go back through the city centre. He finds Marfleet Lane and heads north. Cross already notified Granfield that the Dassault will meet him at Stansted Airport, northeast of London. They eventually connect with the A1 and head south to London. It is a very long detour, including a stop for dinner and drinks at a service area. Jennings even stops at a country pub outside Peterborough. He knows the owners and wants to show Cross. It's a welcome break from more chaos. They share the driving and now it is morning hours. The sun has risen and occasionally hides behind Britain's notorious heavy rain clouds.

"You can sleep on the flight back."

Cross gets a message from Taylor. "Granfield is brilliant."

"Yes, we have similar people at MI6. Who knows where they find them."

"When we left Vancouver, he knew Wu would track the Gulfstream so they turned the transponder on. By doing that, he also knew it would alert his organisation into finding someone I know in the Vancouver area. So, the CIA removed Frank Wilson from the internet. He doesn't exist. Instead, they created a totally fictitious character with whom I allegedly attended University of Manchester. By doing that, they knew Wu would go after him. They created a false company address too. It was brilliant deception. Just mind-blowing stuff." He shakes his head. "They had the Gulfstream with two people on board who look like Leslie and me flying around Central America."

"Well, that part of the deception will not work now Wu knows you are in England." He laughs.

"Maybe they need to have our stand-ins do something in Central America to add confusion."

He messages Granfield who immediately responds.

"Oh, they already did. Apparently Taylor and I picked up the remains of Graeme Moore from Panamanian authorities. They did that to help hide Leslie in South Korea."

Cross goes silent. Jennings turns his head as he is driving.

"This field is crazy, isn't it?" He had a big grin on his face.

"It might be time for an English breakfast, mate."

"I know a place outside Stansted."

Gau is dead on the floor in Wu's office. He stares down at him, "Apology accepted. Failure is not admissible in this organisation." He looks at the first lieutenant standing next to the deceased and yells at him. "Go find Wilson and where the hell is Cross?"

"Cross and Taylor left Panama, sir."

"Then who was at Moore Industries?"

The lieutenant was shaking. "I will find out, sir."

"Do it. Now get out of my office."

He leaves and Wu picks up the phone. "We have problems here and they need to be addressed. Wilson escaped capture in Vancouver, Cross picked up Moore's remains in Panama and someone claiming to be Cross visited Moore's wife in England. Find out what is going on and get back to me."

"Mr. Wu, we have come across another target vessel that fits the criteria you gave us. It is currently heading for the Strait of Hormuz."

"Come to my office with a team."

"Yes sir."

Taylor picks up the phone.

"Get back to Langley. Cross will be flying back also. The plane is already waiting for you."

18

Disappearing Container Ships

Granfield opens the briefing in one of the larger conference rooms but it is crowded. It seems many people are now on this case. Jennings and a few other MI6 personnel accompanied Cross on his flight back to Virginia.

"Good morning, ladies and gentlemen. Thank you for convening so quickly.

"I thought it would be prudent to bring the whole team together. Some recent developments have set a precedent and we are no longer looking at what happened to the container ship Tainan as a singular event.

"First," pointing out Jennings, "this is Nick Jennings from MI6. Nick, you know everyone except Leslie Taylor. Leslie, this is Nick." He introduces the other MI6 Agents.

"I will give a brief account of what we have uncovered and then I'll transfer to the pertinent people who will elaborate further."

In Granfield's hand is a remote to flick through PowerPoint graphics and data slides. A screen has been rolled down from the ceiling and is in clear view against the wall. He goes through their findings one by one and in detail. For clarity, he stops where convenient to allow questions.

"The Tainan was a diversion? For what purpose?" asks Winwood.

"The Tainan served two objectives. The first was to create confusion and distraction while other ships were being targeted. This bought them time. The second was to assassinate Dr. Cross. The latter failed, thankfully."

A few more questions are presented before it is Taylor's turn to get up.

"These are the targeted container ships that have been sunk." With that her first slide lists the vessel names with pictures of their colossal size. It is done for effect and works as the room falls into dead silence. "My trip to South Korea was extremely fruitful and Mr. Jeong very helpful." She looks over at Granfield, "He says hello by the way."

Granfield nods.

"I will start with the Oceanic which was built by the South Koreans, so the data was easier to access." She clicks the remote and the next slide appears. "This is the trajectory and course of the last few hours of the ship's life. As you can see," using a red laser pointer for assistance, "the Oceanic veered off course as it approached the outer rim of the typhoon. Even though vessels of this magnitude are built to survive huge weather events, there is some interesting data that comes with the sinking. The ship was being controlled externally which means someone remotely had taken control of the computer systems in the ship."

Rumblings and discussion are escalating in the conference room and Taylor has to elevate her voice to speak over them.

"The crew tried to compensate and override the controls, but they failed. The bulkhead doors were jammed electronically." She displays a PowerPoint graphic of the system. "Electronic latches were released holding the shipping containers. This caused massive deterioration of the load balance calculations and weight distribution. What finally sunk the ship," she waited for silence, "…the pilot door was opened as the ship struggled in the towering waves and hundred and eighty mph winds."

More discussions ensue between agents in the room. Finally, Taylor asks for calm.

"The perpetrator, or perpetrators, whoever took control, also purposely inhibited the crew from transmitting distress calls. The emergency system was completely disabled."

"Is it possible to remotely control a ship?" asks an agent.

"Yes."

"How?" comes their next question.

"Hacking is the simple answer. However, they have a very elaborate and secure defensive firewall. Programming Graeme Moore's clone was undertaken with the assistance of torture so we have not ruled out the possibility someone was coerced into providing insider information or, indeed, if a clone infiltrated the ship owners' control room. This is new information just gathered yesterday."

"What about the other ships?"

"I am getting to that. This is privileged information, again provided by Mr. Jeong. The other ships we know of did the exact same thing and steered into the mega storms." She clicks on the next slide. "These are the paths the ships took. The black lines are the trajectories of the approved shipping lanes they were taking. The red lines are the divergent paths they were forced to take. It is pretty obvious they were meant to steer into the storms' vortex." She clicked on the next slide. "In storms, protocols advise them to slow down and steer clear. These ships were programmed for maximum speed and to steer into danger."

"What is the purpose of sinking these vessels?"

Granfield stands and gives the floor to Cross.

"Thank you, Leslie. Quite remarkable findings," and smiles at her. She hands him the remote for slide control and takes her seat. "There are a few possibilities. Tainan was a distraction. Once we determined that, we went in search of something else. These are huge shipping vessels used for the massive trade between China and US. There is nothing that indicates they are attacking other trade relations." He halts for a second. "Yet," and looks around the room. He has their attention.

He gathers his thoughts again whilst trying to remain composed. "I feel this is a continuation of the One World Order nonsense, orchestrated by the same people. We only performed half the job before.

"I just came back from England where I was greeted by Nick Jennings from MI6," acknowledging him with a nod. "We visited Graeme Moore's wife and his place of business in Hull." He clicks for the next slide. "This is Graeme Moore with his wife Helen. Mrs. Moore was very gracious," halting for effect. "Unfortunately, she is a clone."

Noise erupts in the room and Cross lets it manifest. He wishes to keep them animated for his next few slides.

"It is possible they are both still alive but we don't know. Moore was tortured so they could program his clone. This is why it killed Macarthur first. He wanted me to live so we can go after Wu. They likely will need him to further assist in their development of clones, but that is speculation on my part."

More noise permeates the non-sterile atmosphere.

"This is Moore Industries, Ltd." He clicks on the next slide. "This is Moore's business enterprise. We know he has UK military contracts for R and D in A.I. technology. We entered these premises and met Graeme Moore Jr. who showed us around. To me he seemed edgy and nervous." He looks over at Jennings who nods his head in agreement. "Once I accessed and disabled the security system, we entered part of their robot manufacturing facility and took these photos. Based on what he inadvertently told us, they have another bigger facility somewhere."

Cross presses the remote for the next slide. Now the room is bedlam as people are physically remonstrating. On the screen is the UK Prime Minister. He lets them take it in before he presses for the next slide, and the next, and the next.

"This is the Prime Minister of Britain and some of her important cabinet members. We killed five people to get these photographs."

"Hey, what is this 'we' part?" asks Jennings.

The interruption helps and muffled chuckles break out, slightly softening the dark horror Cross is presenting.

Cross tries to suppress a grim smile. "You were too slow."

"What is the Prime Minister doing at Moore Industries? Is she visiting to review their work?" questions another agent.

"No ma'am. This looks exactly like the prime minister." He hesitates. "But it isn't her."

"What do you mean?"

"This is what Moore Industries, Ltd is providing Wu, or appears to be providing Wu. Again, this is new information and the photographs were only taken two days ago.

"Wu is positioning himself to take control, we believe of the White House. In order to do that, he will need a puppet nation to follow him. The United Kingdom is an extremely close political ally of the United States. As a consequence, he will need control of the UK parliament." He waits and watches for reaction. "The pictures you see are clones, ma'am. This is the pinnacle of A.I., Artificial Intelligence. These are programmed robots ready to replace the PM and members of her cabinet." Now he talks above the noise. "We presume strongly that there must be clones of the US President, Vice President and other high-ranking politicians somewhere."

The room erupts but Granfield eventually restores parity. "Thank you all for attending the briefing," concludes Granfield. "There have been many developments since the last time we gathered. We have made considerable progress so we must keep this going. The file portal is open so please update the data as needed. I will send a message when we need to convene again but we are going after this organisation." He gives them a long, hard stare. "We are adjourned."

As the room empties Granfield requests Cross, Taylor, Jennings and Winwood to stay behind.

"We heard from Frank in Vancouver. He has been recovering more data from the module you left him, Daniel." He puts a slide up on the screen. "You were correct. Moore's clone was in Panama to transmit precisely the detonating signals to the intended targets on the Tainan."

"I knew it. This made sense to me."

"The locations of each target were programmed into the memory. Each container has an ID associated with it and they added colour, location and owner's graphics to the information.

"Moore's remains were returned from Panama and we have been dissecting it. The transmit-receive board you found on Tainan's containers was also found on the clone. However, it has an amplification circuit added. Despite low-power requirements, the signal amplification is a fail-safe feature.

"Frank tracked the signal's path but it is hard to fully determine origination. The signal is bouncing off several satellites which adds complexity and increases the difficulty in tracing it. So we took this data and gave it to a lab for analysis. They went back and tracked known satellites to determine which ones were in the right place at the time of Tainan's explosion. With thousands of man-made objects cohabitating in space, they managed to locate a new model of satellite floating around up there. Wu has been very clever here. We shouldn't underestimate these people. They designed them to look aged, so anyone trying to search for new systems would simply pass these off as vintage. Understanding the transmit signals originated from somewhere in the South China Sea, which is an assumption we used for this purpose, the lab was able to identify these." He brings up another graphic.

"Dang it, they look like they came from the Soviet era."

"They do, Nick."

"Does it have a Made in China label?" Cross asks, chuckling.

"Can the lab determine their origin from launch? Now that they know what they look like, do they know when these were put into orbit?" Jennings continues.

"This piece of information is being worked on."

"It would be interesting to know where they launched from."

"I am more interested in locating the detonation origin. An island somewhere in the South China Sea is a little ambiguous for me. We need a huge leap forward with regard to precision."

"Patience, Daniel. We have several other pieces of data to work on before we can figure out the mechanics. A lot of this is still nebulous.

"We need to figure out how they took control of the vessels. What is Moore Industries actually providing? You mentioned another location. Where exactly? If they are planning on taking over the White House with clones, where are they?

"Daniel, I'll have Leslie and Nick research some of this. You've been away a long time so I suggest you head back to Tahoe for a few days. I will forward data as it becomes available.

"Oh, by the way, nothing of note materialised from the photographs of private jets in Panama. A few belonged to Panamanian corporations, a couple to private American leasing companies and one to an American businessman."

"Can you forward that information to me, please?"

"Also, two of Wu's captured soldiers died on their way to the hospital from their injuries. The other three had cyanide capsules timed to dissolve, so nothing was gained in Vancouver, unfortunately."

19

Tahoe Forest Fire

The cabin door is unlatched and drops down. Cross exits the Dassault and walks down the stairs. At the bottom is Sadeghi waiting for him. God, he has missed her. He drops his bag and runs the few steps toward her. There, on the tarmac of Tahoe's regional airport, they embrace and kiss.

"It's so nice to see you home, honey."

"I know. It's too long to be away from you. I missed you terribly and love you so much."

"I counted off the minutes."

They embrace and kiss again. She takes his hand as Cross picks his bag up with the other and they walk off toward her black Range Rover Sport.

By the time their hours of lovemaking throughout the home began waning the night had turned very dark. Their sex life has always been very adventurous. He loves that and the final place to make love is the shower. He has missed the warm softness of her body pushed up against his and they don't need to activate the steam shower. They create their own heat and sweat. They shower and wash each other down before drying off, then dress in casuals and head downstairs.

Cross' home is built against the backdrop of US Forestry land. This means no one can build behind him, ever. The drapes are partially closed and soft music is playing in the background. Sadeghi is in the kitchen cooking an Iranian dish whilst he pours Johnny Walker Blue into two tumblers. He wants to help her but she refuses.

"Go sit down. I haven't cooked for anybody since you left."

"Ok darling."

He sits down on the leather sofa and puts his feet up on the puff. He flips on his most relaxing music and basks in the ambience. This is the most relaxed he has been since leaving for Panama.

Cross looks outside through the gap between the drapes and sees a flicker of orange off in the distance. "Looks like people are off-roading in the forest," he calls to Sadeghi. "Maybe they've lit up a bonfire. I didn't think they were allowed on forestry land."

"All I've ever seen in the vicinity are very small barbeque fires for family," said Sadeghi. "I don't know the laws around here yet, honey. I was going to ask you."

Cross gets up and walks back to the kitchen. He hugs and kisses her from behind. Her clean effervescent smell is captivating. "I've missed everything about you."

"Me too. Sometimes I wish you had never heard the words secret agent."

"Me too at times…." He sighs. "Hey, there's a strong wind tonight. Do you feel it?"

"Yes. I'm used to that living close to mountains in Iran."

He walks over to retrieve the two whiskey tumblers and looks left. Through the drapes he can see the orange glow has gained in brightness, and appears nearer. Walking over he pulls one of the drapes away from the window and stares in horror. Perhaps a mile away, he sees the forest behind the home is on fire. Some pine trees are a hundred feet or more tall and the gusty wind is pushing flames higher up their flammable trunks. They are reaching for the sky. On the forest floor the natural vegetation is burning and the bushes are flaming like Moses' fire in the Bible. Turning off the music, he hears what sounds like a freight train approaching as the fire starts to build its own windstorm. It is a sound he has heard before and immediately feels a shot of terror. Wind is blowing the trees and the flames curl toward his home. Fire climbs up each tree like a tree-cutter and the pine cones and needles explode like popcorn. Hot embers and ash are dropping like winter snow and spreading the fire fast. Hot spots are engulfing everything in sight.

"We need to get out of here, honey. That's a monster fire!" He runs toward the kitchen. "Grab your phone."

Sadeghi doesn't have time to ask questions or to protest. He grabs her arm, shoves his phone in a pocket and runs toward the garage door carrying the Range Rover Sport keys. Through the windows in the garage he can see the orange glow of fire everywhere. He hears the sound of running water so he knows the external sprinkler system has just activated.

Cross presses a button and the garage door starts to open. Flames are now encompassing his whole property. With the door open, he looks outside and sees no possible way out. The garage also fills up with toxic smoke. Air Quality Index is off the charts, he suspects, and they both start gagging.

"This is going to be rough. Hold on."

They jump into the Sport and he presses the start button. The supercharged V8 roars to life and he selects reverse.

"The road isn't on fire but the debris all over it is."

He sees neighbours in the area also fleeing, so he floors the gas pedal and exits the garage. He squeals around in the driveway and heads for the gates.

Out onto the street they see the whole forest is burning and they appear surrounded. They can hardly see because of the dense smoke and turning on the high beam is futile. The interior of the vehicle is so hot they are already drenched in sweat and touching a window leaves a second degree blister. Cross visualises them being burnt to death, their ashes left in the burnt-out remains of the SUV.

"Bollocks to this," he says to Sadeghi. "We are not going to leave the earth this way."

Off in the distance he sees a fire truck heading toward them with lights blazing and sirens on. He remembers seeing a fire engine at the airport looking like this. On top is a huge cannon that is spraying a mixture of foam and water onto the street as it progresses in their direction, creating a path through the grey-ash haze.

"Pray we get to live another day, honey."

Sadeghi takes his right arm and hangs onto it, squeezing the life out of it as she screams.

Cross puts his right foot to the floor and flies past the fire truck. The road ahead is clear but surrounded by fire. He navigates toward Highway 50 and safety.

His phone goes off and it is a message from Granfield: 'Head to the airport and remove yourself from Tahoe, then message me when you are safe.'

20

Gulf of Oman Attack

Once the Dassault is airborne and Cross knows Sadeghi is safe with him and sleeping, he picks up the phone. "What happened down there, David?"

"One of the agents sent to protect you noticed some suspicious activity in the forest behind your home. He called the airport and commissioned their fire truck immediately upon seeing flames. The fire looks to have been intentionally set and we're searching for evidence. It will be dealt with."

"Thanks. The water cannon saved our lives."

"Yes, we thought it would be helpful in that regard."

Cross chuckles. He loves the calm and controlled demeanor this man constantly displays. "You thought correctly."

"Get some rest on the flight here. I will see you in the early hours of the morning. Leslie and Nick will have done some more digging."

Sadeghi is still asleep in the suite at the CIA facility and Cross lets her rest. He is coming off only a few hours kip himself but his adrenaline is pumping. People are trying to kill him at any cost and he is pissed. Involving Sadeghi is the final straw.

Up in the conference room are Taylor, Granfield and Jennings. It is 6:30 a.m. and coffee and fresh doughnuts are on the table.

"Good morning, Daniel," says Jennings. "Sorry about another attempt on your life."

"Yeah, this is getting old and I'm angry. Fucking with me is fine. I wish them luck. Fuck with Parisa and now I will draw blood."

"I sense we're close to finding out what they're up to."

Out in the Gulf of Oman hovers a Chinese-made drone. Off in the distance is an Iranian tanker, Archimedes. It is transporting an illegal oil shipment to the Port of Karachi, Pakistan.

The drone's data and pictorial imagery are transmitting back to an island in the South China Sea.

"We are ready to fire, sir," said a lieutenant.

Wu is pondering as he stares at the monitor. This is an alternative phase and he must contemplate the world's reaction to what he is about to authorise. Things are not going as planned and he needs another direction.

The image he is staring at is that of a huge tanker, way off in the distance, floating on the horizon. It's a small speck in comparison to the virtual expanse of the Gulf. Just a tangible object to him offering no intrinsic commercial or monetary value per se.

"Fire."

With that instruction, the lieutenant orders the drone to release its first two guided missiles. On the monitor Wu can see the warhead trails as they head toward their intended target. The first missile hits and immediately a mushroom cloud forms from the epicenter with flames and smoke radiating outwards. Almost immediately a second missile strikes.

"Zoom in," shouts Wu.

The ship is no longer a speck on the horizon as the on-board camera brings the images much closer to focus. The ship is now ablaze and the crew is trying to lower lifeboats.

"Fire two more," instructs Wu.

Two more direct hits on the structure that is already going down are sufficient. The haunting scene showing on the monitor is that of the tanker splitting in two, engulfed in burning fuel oil, whilst its crew is burning alive or drowning.

Wu takes one more look before he turns around. "I will be back in my office. Update me please."

"Yes sir."

"Oh, what about Cross?"

"The forest was set on fire and engulfed the area around his home."

"That isn't what I asked."

"We surmise Cross is still alive."

Wu looks at his lieutenant and storms out of the operations room.

Sitting next to Cross is Taylor.

"We found information relating to the Muar that left the Port of Shanghai and disappeared in the typhoon. Apparently a company called International Shipping Corporation, or ISC, owns and operates it. This is a huge company and of course is located in Shanghai."

"We would need to see their manifest to ascertain shipping container information," says Cross.

"I doubt they would even supply that. We need to maintain a low profile here. We cannot go knocking on their door with CIA credentials."

"That isn't the real concern," pipes in Granfield. "Who controlled their ship is the question."

"Perhaps it is time to use one of my aliases to get into China. We don't know if the Chinese government is involved in this."

Just as Cross finishes his sentence, Winwood comes in with a look of concern on his face. "An Iranian tanker has just been blown up in the Gulf of Oman. The new radical government is accusing the West of orchestrating this."

"Did I miss something here?" asks Cross. "They worked with us to save the world from a virus earlier this year. What changed?"

"You stopped watching the news, I guess."

"I did David, yes."

"The extreme Islamists were pissed that the government helped us. During recent elections, the people you met were overthrown. The results we suspect were rigged of course and even your friend Farbod Karimi was replaced."

"Jesus. What about James Butler?"

"Thankfully James remains at the embassy and it is safe…for now."

"The new Ayatollah and Iranian President are threatening to seek revenge. They won't believe China has anything to do with this because they have just signed a long-term economic cooperation agreement with them." Winwood continues, "They have no evidence to support their claims yet, so this is all political bullshit."

"Yes, but that is even more dangerous. What evidence do we have that suggests it isn't who they say it is?"

"Nothing yet, David. This is news just coming in. I can assure you none of our allies would attack an Iranian oil tanker. It is ludicrous for Iran to even theorise that."

"Radicalism tosses out logic, my friend. They look for excuses to justify their own internal conflicts. A privileged and very secret Iranian fifty-plus page internal document alleging how they will use cyber-attacks to interrupt international shipping turned up recently on the internet. Perhaps this attack could be linked to that."

"I need to reach out to Farbod. He must know people in government still who can simmer down the heat until we work this out?"

Cross gets up and walks over to a quiet corner of the room. He searches the database in his phone and presses a button.

"Good morning, Daniel. I never thought I would hear from you so soon."

"Farbod, so you remember me?"

"Of course."

Now Cross is comfortable again. He's in familiar territory. "I'm sorry this isn't a social call, my friend. You must be aware of some suspect circumstances in the world?"

"Yes, unfortunately. The more things change, the more things stay the same."

"I am sorry your position in the government was untenable. I haven't watched the news in months. I made the mistake of watching it once recently and now I am here."

"Surely. This has your name all over it," and Farbod laughs ironically.

"Yeah, well, I didn't put it there. It was put there for me," and laughs with him.

"You pissed off the wrong people and they appear to be very influential, my friend. With that come serious consequences."

"Yes, understood," says Cross. "Sorry I have to be abrupt but an incident requiring immediate attention is evolving. Is there anyone left in the Iranian government you can trust?"

"There are still a lot of good people over here. This is radical behaviour that not even the populace wants. It is pure madness. Radicalisation is all about a select few idiots, as you know, and extreme fundamentalism is volatile, dangerous and unpredictable."

"Yes, the madness never stops since sheer power and control are aphrodisiacs." Cross takes a short breather to emphasise his next point. "The West isn't culpable in the sinking of the Iranian oil tanker, Farbod. This is false information and dangerous rhetoric. We need to inform someone within your government."

"I'm ahead of you already. We know this. However, convincing those who make the decisions will be difficult without palpable, credible and verifiable evidence. They also remember the US trying to justify a war with Iraq. Trust will be an issue with this new regime."

"Give me a few days please," says Cross. "We need time to get this information since my group has just received the news."

"I'll work on it. Do you have any idea who is involved?"

"Yes. Remember Wu in Taiwan? He escaped and is now embarking toward their main goal, which is still to take over the White House. His organisation, whoever they are, is using Artificial Intelligence. This likely was their end-game with the virus."

"Ok, Daniel, leave it to me. I'll get back to you."

"Thank you, my friend."

Cross walks back to the table and joins the group in conversation.

"Farbod is already on it. He still knows people in the government and they don't believe we're responsible."

"Let me work on extracting evidence and I'll get back to you." Winwood rises and leaves the room.

"Great. We need to know who is controlling the ships, and how. Two more Chinese vessels went missing the past few days," adds Granfield. "They're beginning to cause massive disruption to trade which may be a key strategy regarding how they will launch control of the White House."

"If what we believe is happening, they will need to switch to the clones."

Granfield nods. "That will be easy with massive disruption to world trade. The leaders will need to convene an emergency summit and will be distracted. We really need to stop the ships from disappearing."

"I've got to infiltrate ISC in China to find out what is going on. Thinking out loud, I also wonder if we can get Graeme Moore Jr. to cooperate. If he believes his parents are still alive, he may wish to help locate them."

Jennings adds his two cents. "I agree, there was something odd there."

"We still have time. The impact on trade due to lost containers will require several weeks to take effect. We need to build your new identity for China,"

"Wait, what new identity?"

"This has to be convincing, Dr. Cross," Granfield adds with a big grin.

"Oh shit."

21

Mr. Wei, Shanghai

Wei walks up to the Immigration booth at Shanghai Airport and presents his passport and documents. The humourless stiff Asian Officer scans in his passport whilst reviewing the visa. He asks some general questions and Wei responds. The officer scans the computer screen with his eyes and then transfers his gaze directly at Wei. After a few minutes he waves him through. The first massive hurdle is over with and he starts to breathe a little easier.

"I'm definitely getting too old for this shit," he mumbles to himself.

Wei mingles with the other people as he threads through Customs with only a carry-on and out into the huge international terminal's foyer. He scans the crowd and sees a gentleman in a black suit and white shirt holding a sign. He walks toward him.

"先生，下午好。我是来自伦敦的英国亚洲控股公司的 Christian Wei." Good afternoon sir. I am Christian Wei from The British Asian Holding Company, he says in perfect Mandarin.

"Hello Mr. Wei. I speak a little English," he says as they shake hands. "Welcome to Shanghai, sir. I am Mr. Lang and will be your driver while you abide here," he adds in broken English.

Lang takes his bag and starts walking out of the terminal with

Wei following at a bit of a distance. It is still light outside but the dense industrial smog attenuates it. Illegally parked across the street is a black Hongqi L5. He'd read about these but has never seen one. Lang opens the rear door for Wei who obliges. Once seated, he hands his travel bag to him.

"Thank you."

Lang walks around and climbs into the driver's seat. "I will drop you off at the Ritz-Carlton Shanghai, Mr. Wei. That is a great location, across from Shanghai Tower."

"This is a Hongqi L5 isn't it?" he states, ignoring Lang's comments since something more interesting now suddenly pre-occupies his attention.

"Yes, sir."

"It is regarded as the Chinese Rolls Royce."

Wei swivels his head around and enjoys the unfamiliar, luxurious vehicle as Lang navigates onto the S1 highway. He's impressed with the supple butterscotch leather seating and the array of executive amenities offered to rear passengers. He is momentarily oblivious to the outside world.

"It is very impressive," he says, switching to Mandarin. "I need to import one."

"This has the 6.0 V12."

"Yes, I heard it fire up when you pressed the start button. I knew it wasn't a V8. China is coming a long way," he says, trying to impress his chauffeur.

They add some more small talk as Lang heads toward the chaos of downtown. Traffic, cars, scooters and people wearing masks are everywhere. As they approach the tower, Wei knows they are close.

Lang pulls up outside the entrance and steps out. Wei has already opened the door and exited as he comes around.

"I shall pick you up here at nine a.m. tomorrow, sir," and they shake hands.

Wei checks in and rejects the mobile app for the room key. After all, what if he loses his phone?

"Key card is fine, thank you."

He grabs his bag and heads through the large warmly-tinted modern lobby toward the elevators. He enters one of them and punches the floor number, after inserting the room key.

He walks into the suite and tosses the bag onto the coffee table. Through the large windows he sees the Shanghai Tower. To the right of that, across the Huangpu River, lie the skyscrapers of downtown. It would be spectacular if it wasn't for the toxic fog limiting the scenic landscape.

No wonder someone wants to take over the White House, he thinks to himself. We need U.S. money to improve our failing cities.

He spots the minibar, walks over and breaks the seal. Upon opening the fridge door, a Zhujiang Beer is staring right at him so he takes it.

As he relaxes on the sofa, a call comes in.

"You made it to Shanghai?"

"Yes."

"Any problems with immigration?"

"No. They scrutinised my documents but let me through."

"Of course they let you in." He chuckles. "Enjoy your evening and fill me in tomorrow after your visit to ISC."

"Ok."

Wei downs his first beer and steps into the shower. He suddenly realises how exhausted he really is and settles for some snacks and microwavable food from the room fridge.

The suite's small control panel at the side of the bed displays 7:02 a.m. as Wei's internal clock shocks his body awake. He opens his eyes and hesitates as he glances at it. Anxiety temporarily envelopes him but he soon regains his composure once he remembers where he is. He knows it is normal for people who excessively travel, and it has happened to him before.

He hears the room doorbell ring so he puts on a robe and walks over. Breakfast has arrived and he desperately needs the fresh coffee.

After eating, he takes a shower and puts on one of his dark European wool business suits. Now he is sure he doesn't look Asian from a distance. He exits his room and grabs an elevator down. Leaving the hotel key with the bellman, once outside the hotel, he immediately sees Lang standing beside the Hongqi. They greet each other and he climbs into the front passenger seat.

"How was your evening, sir?"

"I stayed in the hotel and had breakfast there."

"ISC has its' headquarters downtown. This will be a short ride, or would be without all the crazy people and traffic," Lang adds wincing.

"We have the same issues in the UK."

Twenty minutes later Lang pulls up outside a tall office building. Wei notices the International Shipping Company sign and reaches for his friend strapped to the ankle. He just wants reassurance it is there.

Wei steps out of the limousine and walks through the lobby doors, surveying the surroundings and furnishings. This is another vast structure housing a company making substantial monies. He removes his phone, wallet, passport, watch and belt and walks through the metal detector. Then he retrieves his stuff and meanders over to the main reception desk.

"I am Mr. Christian Wei. I am here to see Mr. Xing and he is expecting me," he says in Mandarin to the young lady behind the desk.

"Let me check, Mr. Wei. Please take a seat," in broken English. It seems they don't like people to speak Chinese here, he thinks.

"谢谢." Thank you, he answers in Mandarin and walks over to one of the leather sofas in the lobby.

A few minutes later the receptionist comes over to the sofa. "Mr.

Xing will be down in five minutes, sir."

Soon an energetic Mr. Xing shows up. "Good morning, Mr. Wei. A pleasure to meet you."

"Mr. Xing, the pleasure is mine," as they exchange pleasantries and business cards.

"I hope you are enjoying Shanghai so far. Please follow me."

"I haven't done anything since my arrival yesterday," says Wei, "but I hope to spend some time afterwards and tour the Great Wall. It has been many years since I was there last."

"Well, it hasn't changed much, I assure you." He laughs. It breaks the ice somewhat and Wei smiles. "I read a little about your family history once I saw your name. Your Chinese father went to England to study and met your mother. I am so sorry about the horrific plane crash."

"Thank you. Their frightfully untimely death impacts me even to this day. But yes, they were a mixed couple which was unusual back in those days."

The sincere empathy portrayed by a new acquaintance halfway around the world strikes Wei very positively.

They step into an express elevator that whisks them to the executive floor, according to the button Xing pressed. Wei follows and is ushered into an expansive office suite that overlooks the city. Wei looks through the window and a mist of depressive heaviness seems to hang in the environment.

"Please take a seat. Would you like coffee or a special Chinese herbal green tea? I will ask for some Chinese pastries too."

"The herbal green tea, please. I drink that at home but am sure it is different here."

Wei likes Xing. He is typically Chinese, which means not too tall, thin black hair with healthy-looking skin and physique. He is wearing an expensive light grey suit which differentiates him somewhat. He has a personality that makes him very affable. Wei estimates his age at mid-fifties. Xing picks up the phone and requests tea and breakfast pastries.

He turns to Wei. "Your desire to meet with me originates from your company's commercial requirements to purchase more advanced container ships."

"Indeed. The new advanced vessels have futuristic electronics and allow for external monitoring and, as an option, external control. We have already discussed our options with some major ship builders but we need to learn more about the electronics. Our companies do a lot of trade together in some parts of the world so you came highly recommended. I will thank you for taking the time to meet with me."

"It is my pleasure, Mr. Wei. Our dock facilities obviously aren't in the middle of Shanghai and we can take a tour there when we have finished up, time permitting of course. However, our control room is in this building. We track every ship in our fleet around the globe from here."

The last comment surprises Wei and he indelibly stores that in his memory bank. He needs to pursue that later.

"In order to do that, you must use commercially available satellite links."

"Yes, of course. We enjoy the height of technology here. This is China and we are given access to military equipment orbiting in space."

Yet another fascinating comment. Wei's eyes light up. He wants to ask so many questions but he's been advised what to do here and cannot divulge what he knows. It's becoming a tad frustrating already but he must remain calm. This is a reconnaissance mission to seek information. Don't do anything stupid was the last piece of advice he was given. I mean as if I would, he protested at the time.

"This is all very interesting."

As Wei says that, a beautiful young Chinese lady walks into the room carrying a tray with a pot of tea, two mugs and a plate of pastries. The women he has seen since arriving all seem to be wearing the same outfit. A red dress just above the knee, a white scarf around the neck and a thick cream belt around the waist seems to be a uniform. Complementing that are white high-heeled shoes. Wei went through a public school system requiring uniforms and he is really impressed so far. People look like they are ready to do some work.

They chat for another few hours or so about what Wei's company is looking for. He opens up documents and charts as he explains his needs. Xing orders a light lunch along with soft drinks and hot tea which someone brings to his office.

After what Wei categorises as a scintillating discussion, Xing stands up and asks that he follow him. "Grab your things too. You might need them where I am taking you."

They exit the office and head toward a seemingly different elevator. They walk in and the doors close. Xing presses the button for the control room but Wei has no idea what floor that is. It could be the basement for all he knows.

The elevator stops and they step out into a room that occupies one whole floor of the building. Wei looks around the area and is relieved to find it isn't the basement and releases his breath. The vast room has windows and he can see structures he recognises from driving in that morning. On one corner of the floor he can see across the river the silhouette of the Shanghai Tower. He makes a mental note that this is a lower floor since it might be useful later.

On one side of the room are what appear to be storage areas. He rapidly calculates on which side of the building they are located.

"Here is our control facility. As you can see, it is vast. Each computer cubicle has access to one container ship." Wei is looking at hundreds of them. "Over in this area," he points as they walk, "We monitor every vessel on this huge screen. The dots and various coloured tracks represent ships and their travel lanes, past and projected. We know exactly what they are doing."

Wei listens to what Xing is saying as he looks at the huge screen. It is a world map laid out flat on glass monitors, set against one wall of the room. The monitors are mounted against each other to form one huge rectangular display. The room is full of operators and technicians. Wei is mesmerised by it all. He looks up at the area around the South China Sea and picks out a few vessels.

He points. "Who is monitoring the ships in this region?"

Xing looks around at another area of the room. "We split this room up globally. Each block of cubicles represents a geographical area. Let me take you over there."

"Do you train or hire already experienced technical people? I cannot imagine many in the world being qualified for this job."

"That is an interesting question, Mr. Wei, because we have been approached by several experienced people over the past twelve months. We did background checks and called their past employers. Everything checked out fine. However, typically, we have to train them."

"How do you receive the data from satellites?"

"We have antennas and dishes on top of the building."

They reach the cubicles comprising the geographical interest Wei has expressed. Xing walks up to a controller who is operating one of the computers. On the screen is a ship she is monitoring. She turns around and Wei sees her name tag.

"This is Chyou. Chyou, this is Mr. Wei from the UK."

She stands up and shakes Wei's hand. He takes a careful look at her without drawing too much attention. She isn't wearing the red dress he has seen other ladies wearing. Perhaps a different dress-code down here. She wears long black pants and a fashionable black shawl-neck sweater with the company logo on the chest.

"Welcome to our facility, Mr. Wei."

She is young, perhaps represents someone in their mid-thirties, but a perfect A.I. specimen. Wei is stunned. He is momentarily at a loss for words but he must restrain his surprise.

"She has been with us for almost one year and is incredibly good at what she does."

Wei finally manages a few words. "Nice to meet you, Chyou."

She nods, turns around and gets back to her work. Wei looks at Xing with a new respect, "Can you introduce me to a few more people?"

"Of course, follow me."

Xing walks over to another cubicle in the same area. "This is Feng. Feng, this is Mr. Wei from England."

Another young adult stands up and turns around to face Wei. "Welcome to our facility, Mr. Wei." The same words Chyou just spoke and they shake hands.

Wei needs to get out of here but he cannot, not yet anyway. Internal emotional conflicts are straining to contain themselves and he is itching madly metaphorically. He takes his time and pretends to review the screen Feng is operating but he wants to go and go fast. He looks at his watch but he needs confirmation from one more robot. He needs to find an excuse to extend this.

"Mr. Xing, it is getting late but I'm so excited at visualising all this. I want to look at another geographical area, perhaps where our two companies collaborate," using his enthusiasm to purposely conceal the desire to get the hell out.

"Of course."

Xing walks over to another area of the room. He selects a specific cubicle. "Qiang, this is Mr. Wei from one of our corporate partners based in the UK," he says in Mandarin.

Qiang stops what he is doing, stands up from the chair and walks around the cramped space in his cubicle. "It is nice to meet you, sir," as he holds out his hand. Wei shakes it.

"Please call me Christian and sorry to disturb you, Qiang. You look busy there and your English is very good."

"Yes, sir. No time to play here," he says laughing. "I studied for a few years in Cambridge. I'm watching one of our ships navigate the Suez Canal which can be very dangerous under certain conditions."

Wei likes this human being and is beginning to calm down. It's obvious this gentleman went through some formal training in a high-end British university environment. "Please, don't let me interrupt you."

As Qiang goes back to his work, Wei surveys the vicinity and catches another person of interest. He walks over but doesn't request an introduction. He just stands behind her and observes proceedings. She is looking at a vessel in the Mediterranean Sea as it heads who knows where. She doesn't exude natural warmth and Wei is getting more familiar with the difference now. Their staggering ability to create life-like robots has human emotional limitations it seems. Wei sighs as things seem to become more complicated.

He turns to face Xing. "Time passed so quickly; we didn't even have a typical Asian beer lunch." He smiles. "I have taken up a lot of your time, Mr. Xing. I really want to sit down here and spend precious hours studying how they operate each vessel. This is the knowledge my company is after. We scheduled two days I believe."

"That's fine, Mr. Wei. We can entertain you tomorrow. I'll make a call and the car will be waiting outside to take you back to the hotel. Take as much time as you deem reasonable and necessary. I'm here to accommodate you."

Xing takes Wei down some stairs via two sets of security doors to the lobby where he signs out. They shake hands and Wei departs the building. He sees the Hongqi parked across from the building entrance which adds to his relief. He jogs over and jumps in the back.

22

A.I. Infiltration

"You have a package that arrived today, Mr. Wei," says the hotel receptionist behind the counter, as she hands him a replacement key card for his room. She steps away and retrieves it.

"Thank you so much." He turns away and heads for the elevators. Walking into the suite he tosses the document cache on the sofa along with the package and grabs the first beer he confronts in the minibar. Standing by the window looking out over the river, he picks up the phone with his unoccupied hand and presses a button.

"Daniel, you are still alive I see, unless you have been infiltrated."

"Why did I sign up for this?" He laughs.

"Well, it's good to see you have your sarcasm intact. It keeps the spirits high and juices flowing. I may remind you it was you who volunteered to go there."

"Yes, I do recall that discussion now, thanks. But I'll need to keep the beer flowing with this assignment, David."

"So, tell me the good word, my friend."

"I don't even know where to start on this one. I'm simply stunned, so let me start at the beginning, wherever that is.

"This is a legitimate company. There is no way I can see Mr. Xing being a part of this conspiracy. He doesn't strike me as being disingenuous and he does seem naïve to the fact that some of the people given responsibility to guide their ships are clones. His body language did not betray him."

"Wait, what? You found what you went looking for already?"

"Oh yes, I know what I'm looking at. My take on this is remarkable, so hear me out. The company hires these technical ship operators and they get taken in to begin their training. Sometime during their training, the real people are switched to their clones." Cross pauses to calm himself a bit. "The company cannot tell these are A.I. because they look incredibly life-like. Being younger they don't have to erroneously age the skin as I saw in Panama and England. This is perfect and no one knows. The employees are gaining some knowledge which surely they must be somehow transferring to their clones before the switch. This would then appear a seamless transfer.

"They wear long trousers and shawl-neck sweaters. This is done to cover up as much as possible to limit exposure."

"That is remarkable."

"Oh, it gets better. The main satellite feed comes from Chinese military installations orbiting the earth. The roof of the building houses the transmitters and receivers. I'm guessing, they either somehow feed into the existing network covertly or they have hidden such a device somewhere in or on the building. I need to discuss this more with Frank because the robots have to be transmitting and receiving data back and forth.

"I met four of their technical operators. Two of them said the exact same thing when being introduced to me which seemed uncanny programming. The third was a real human educated at Cambridge and the fourth was another clone."

"You haven't forgotten that you're really Cross, have you?" he says. "How did your disguise work out?"

Cross takes a gulp of his beer and empties the bottle. He walks over to the bar and extracts another. The procedure now floods his memory banks…

Cross stares in the mirror. He barely recognises himself and the plastic surgeon and her team have done a masterful job. They were assuring him before the minor transformation that reversing it without a complicated procedure leading to scarring is easy. Cross tries to admire his new look just in case they were not being quite honourable, and smiles.

He is standing in the bathroom of a cosmetic clinic in Langley. His eyes and some muscles required pinching in the corners slightly and some skin bleaching worked to make him appear whiter and younger. He no longer has longish grey curly hair. It has been coloured black and cut short.

Cross admires his new identity. To him the transformation looks successful.

"Well, Christian Wei, you look pretty good," he says out loud.

Cross exits the bathroom and leaves the clinical facility. He enters Granfield's office, and Taylor is also there to greet him.

"This is an interesting transformation," he says as he takes a seat.

"Mr. Wei, it is so good to see you."

"Thank you, David. I only hope Parisa likes the new me," he says laughing.

"Don't bank on it. I think she left for Tehran already."

"Very funny."

"If she doesn't, I will," says Taylor and Cross smiles at her.

"Your father was Chinese and your mother English. They both died tragically in a plane crash so no one can try to reach them. Here is your new identity." Granfield passes Cross a package enclosed in a manilla envelope.

"Take a couple of days to expand on your Mandarin and then

we fly you to Shanghai commercially. However, we must send you through London using a different alias for that leg. You appear to have a mixed ethnicity so the new image is fine. MI6 altered an existing shipping company's portfolio based out of the UK and you are the operations director and managing partner. When they research it, it reflects quite a well-established multinational entity, which of course it is.

"The meeting with ISC management has been set up already and they're expecting you. Everything you need to know is in that package. You will, of course, avoid security at Dulles Airport."

"Ok."

"It turns out ISC owns most of the container ships that have been sunk. Something is going on over there so let us find out what."

Cross relaxes for a few days, though he is spending hours refreshing his knowledge of Mandarin…

"Daniel?" Granfield elevates his voice down the secure phone line.

Cross is a little startled and regains his focus. "Sorry, I had to get another alcoholic beverage to help decipher all this."

"Don't become an alcoholic on our behalf."

Cross goes silent again as another thought penetrates his mantle. "When do they do the transfers, I wonder? I saw along one edge of the vast operations room a row of storage facilities. One possibility is they bring them in at night, during nightshifts. There will be less people around. Or they kidnap them from their homes."

"The latter scenario would be even more problematic because it would involve other potential conflicts with family members."

"Wait." Cross hesitates. "What if they are selecting individuals with no family? Or, they only have parents as a single child. It is apparently quite easy to find those in China.

"The other issue I need to solve is how are they not aware that their ships are being lost somewhere? Seriously, they would know, surely. How do they hide this data? If the ships are not arriving at port with their precious cargo, someone is going to call and scream." He goes silent and then suddenly a horrific thought hits him. "How many A.I. lifeforms are out there?"

"A very valid question."

Cross looks at his Rolex and calculates the time in Vancouver. "Let me call Frank. I want him to research two people. I don't have last names so he may find multiple hits. I also have a question about covert transmitter interception and if it can be achieved."

"Good idea."

"Then I want to go visit the building tonight."

"Wait, you want to do what?" protests Granfield, realising the futility of it.

"I will not do anything to jeopardise this mission, but I wish to confirm some things. If they are programming and transferring the clones quickly, their facility has to be close by."

"Be careful and get back to me."

They terminate their call and Cross picks on Wilson next. "Hello Frank, how are you?"

"Jesus, I wasn't expecting to hear from you so soon. Where are you?"

"I am in Shanghai. I need you to research some information for me."

"Ok, go ahead."

Cross fills him in on the information he urgently needs and ends the call.

Cross rips open his package and removes the contents. He slips into a black skin-tight suit, climbs into all-black running shoes and pulls on some black gloves. He carries with him some tools and equipment tethered to a black belt at the waist.

Cross leaves the room and navigates the stairs down to the lobby, escaping the hotel via a side entrance. He walks across the dark road toward Shanghai Tower and finds what he is looking for. Unattended against a railing is a bicycle among hundreds which he commandeers on behalf of the US Government. He climbs on and pedals toward his destination.

People are still milling around in masks, even at midnight, and there is a glow around each light as it reflects against the persistent city smog. Automobiles and scooters still fill the streets and the ever-present constant drone of life in a big city is still banging against the inner senses. Cross lives in a mountain resort for a reason and this is just confirmation of that decision.

As he approaches ISC's building, he slows his forward momentum. He circumnavigates the base of the structure as he surveys the area. Societal life helps here as he is able to camouflage easily between the moving pedestrians and traffic. He now visualises the control area and which side of the building the storage rooms are. His ability to quickly establish bearings enables him to determine which side is correct. As it turns out, they are on the very same side as the loading docks that prohibits traffic. It is also the area that has security people and fencing. "Dammit," he says under his breath.

He cycles to a dark area and leaves the bike against a wall of the adjacent building, but hidden. He may need that later.

Now on foot, he takes out a full balaclava and pulls it over his head. He removes a knife from the belt and walks over to the security booth. The two guards are sitting watching a table tennis championship game. Cross sneaks a peek and wants to watch but has much more important things to do. He looks at the ten-foot security fence and doesn't see anything substantial, except for the barbed wire at the top. He puts the knife back in the belt and retrieves some pliers. He scales the wire fence whilst spinning his head to see if anyone is peering his way. The security lights are not in this area so he is well-protected and difficult to see. As he reaches the top, he snips the barbed wire enough for him to climb over. He drops on the other side.

He takes a gander at the new surroundings. Crouching in between a security vehicle and a small ISC company truck, he heads for the loading dock facilities. Approaching, he sees stairs leading to the floor above the docks. Remembering the number of stairs he took leaving the control room, he concludes that these must lead to the storage areas. This is where he needs to be, he believes.

He releases the device from his belt and turns it on. The symbols start scanning once it powers through the start-up sequence. It finds the building network. He punches another button and it scans again. It takes a few seconds as it seeks to find the password and security codes. Bingo. Now he is able to get into the security portal.

After scanning various locations, he comes across what looks to be a rear security door. He has no idea what that is, so he guesses and turns off the detectors. He scrolls more data and finds the security switch for the loading dock lights. He requests 'off' and within seconds the system turns off the rear lights. He immediately runs toward the stairs and climbs them. At the top he requests the loading dock lights to be re-activated and within seconds they are. Now he crouches again and looks for any possible movement of security personnel. There isn't any as sport is occupying their attention.

The next line underneath 'Loading Dock Lights' Cross sees 'Rear Security Door' and selects 'Off'. Within seconds the door locking mechanism releases with a mechanical thud. In the crouched position he reaches for the door handle. The door falls away from the latching system and starts to open inwards. Cross is methodical and slow as he eases the door wide enough for him to climb inside the building. He carefully latches the door closed behind him but doesn't secure it. He might need that escape later. Now in one of the storage rooms, he scans it to find nothing of any value, except the letter A stenciled on the exit door into the control room.

He finds 'Storage Door A' and turns off the security. He tests the handle and it is unlocked. Slowly he opens the door inwards and peers around the gap. The control room is subdued with nighttime lighting but he can see droves of people at their cubicles monitoring shipping traffic. He removes the balaclava.

Spotting Feng at his desk, he twists his head in various directions looking for the opportunity. He can see no one in the vicinity so releases his gun from the ankle and screws on the silencer slung from the belt. He silently walks up behind the clone and fires two quick shots into the skull. The special bullets penetrate the external cavity and lodge inside the module. The bullets immediately send out electromagnetic pulses and destroy the internal electronics controlling the robot. It slumps onto the computer desk.

"Fantastic," Cross says softly. "I'm getting good at this."

He spins around looking for other personnel in close proximity. There aren't any. Now clear, he drags Feng back to the storage room. Cross removes the robot's clothing and puts them on over his skin-tight suit. He sees a black ISC hat on a storage shelf, puts that on and heads back out to Feng's cubicle.

Sitting in front of the monitor, he sees another vessel beginning to veer off into a storm in the Pacific. He gets up and leaves the cubicle. He stands in front of the huge screen against the wall showing the world map. What he saw on Feng's monitor does not match what he is looking at on the giant screen. That's interesting.

Quickly heading back over to the cubicle, Cross sits down and starts visually processing the data. To the left of the graphical information on the large monitor are the command sequences in Mandarin. In parentheses are the translations in English. He presses a few keys and up comes the ship's vital parameters. His heart starts pounding. One of the details says 'Remote Control Activated' and next to it is a red YES in capitals. He reads the data and hits another series of key-strokes on the keyboard.

"Got it." He smiles.

He types in some more information and the red YES turns to a blue NO. Now he reaches down to his belt and pulls out a memory stick loaded with the software Jeong had given Taylor in South Korea. He plugs it into the computer console and a message appears in a rectangular box on the screen. He hits 'Enter'. Immediately a green slime starts dropping from the top of the graphics pictorially displayed on the monitor.

"Fuck these people. This cubicle is toast."

He looks down at the computer and the typical smell of burning plastics hit his senses. A few seconds later smoke is beginning to emanate from the cracks and fan holes. He smiles sardonically. "Thank you, Mr. Jeong."

Cross stands up and sees some activity off in the distance. Not wishing to hang around, he runs for the storage room and grabs the remains of Feng on the way out.

Somewhere out in the Pacific, on another massive container ship, mayhem has been brewing.

"Captain, we have been released from external control. The vessel's functions are returning to normal and the ship is acquiring data from autopilot again."

"Turn off the antenna and extinguish the ability to transmit-receive data, **now**," he screams the last word. "I don't know what the hell is going on."

"Yes sir," as the first officer heads for the exit. The captain is monitoring the ship's vitals when he sees an icon appear in the top left corner. His heart starts pumping again.

"We are on autopilot," he says to the second officer. "Turn the damn thing off."

Dragging Feng, Cross makes his way across the loading dock area toward the vehicles. He looks over at security and then heads over to an ISC van that appears to be a non-working vehicle. Green mildew on the rear door handle confirms his suspicions. He opens one door which swings outward and tosses the robot into the back. Before he leaves he ensures it is not operational but pumps two more bullets into the A.I.'s head anyway, and closes the van door.

He climbs back over the fence avoiding the severed barbed wire and goes to find the latest CIA-commandeered asset. His heart rate simmers down as he climbs on the bicycle and pedals away into the early-hour pedestrian disorder.

23

The Clone Dilemma

Now in his hotel suite, the endorphins are running rampant and sleep seems a remote likelihood so Cross retrieves his phone. "Hello Frank, what do you have?"

"I researched the names you gave me. You do realise of course that these are popular Chinese names?"

"Yes, that came to mind."

"I narrowed it down to a few thousand." He chuckles. "In any event, it does indeed appear that they focus on employees with no siblings. However, these are people who evidently moved from rural areas of China into the big city to be educated and find good-paying jobs. As a consequence, they have no family close by. Bear in mind, I am limited by the information you provided me."

"Got it. I was limited too because they were introduced to me using their first names only. It could be Wu is implanting these technical people even before their clones take over, is my guess."

"That would be my guess too."

"I admire this project. It is a colossal undertaking which isn't to be underestimated."

"We all agree on that."

"What can you tell me in ten words or less about high-frequency technology?" He laughs.

"Nothing," says Wilson. "Good to see the spirits flowing."

"Yeah, well, I am beginning to lose it."

"If Wu is using A.I. at ISC, they must be able to control them. So, uninterrupted transmit-receive capability is basically essential. They cannot buildout their own system without others knowing so they must tie into an existing infrastructure. They can of course do this covertly, with current technology. They likely have developed their own anyway. Moreover, they have to know what radio frequency and bandwidth the dish, or receptor and transmitter, at ISC's facility uses. Then that signal feeds through a modem which they must be able to communicate with via their WiFi. There it goes off to routers. They tag onto the WiFi so that the clones can move around. It works better than them carrying large spools of cable. Are you following me so far?"

"Yes."

"This all requires security, passwords and codes. The interesting part - a dish is directional, meaning it points at a specific satellite in orbit in order for it to transmit and receive data. If Wu is covertly jumping onto their feed using modulation, they must be connecting to the same satellite."

"From what Mr. Xing told me, it must be a military satellite."

"Exactly. That part has to be correct. They must then have the ability to transfer or bounce that signal to their own network and to their base somewhere in the South China Sea."

"Yes."

"What they could be doing, perhaps something to think about, they could be splicing the signal coming from the dish and sending the modulated information to their own modem inside the building, then on to routers, if they have any and using their own WiFi. Somewhere, they could have split the cabling into a separate box which the clones access. They could be embedding their data packets using a higher frequency, essentially adding it to the transmit and receive signaling that they filter out, which is easily done using their own electronics.

"Based on the electronic board you gave me in Vancouver, these data packets are low power and very difficult to pick up if no one is looking for them."

Cross sighs. He dropped this area of electronics at university for a reason. "I go back into ISC in a few hours. The other thing I noticed: what the clones are seeing on their screens is different from what is displayed on the main system everyone else is observing."

"Once they have breached security, they are at liberty to control anything they want. They must be able to isolate their data on the individual computers from ISC's mainframe. They must have two operating controls. One they use to alter a ship's course and the other to remain intact. This is all technically brilliant."

"Thanks," says Cross, sounding exasperated.

Cross walks over to the minibar. Luckily room service has replenished his supply of alcohol.

"They must have their own IT people," adds Wilson.

"That's a valid point. Of course they must and I hadn't thought of that."

Wilson hears the universally-recognised pop of a beer can opening. "The medicinally-categorised sound of frustration." He chuckles. "How is Leslie?"

"Leslie is good. She likes you and thought you're funny, clever, intelligent and, get this, interesting. She evidently lacks some clarity in her thinking." He laughs.

"Your hilarity is inimitable but thank you, I think. We couldn't find further details in the module from Moore yet. They had a self-erase feature in the software which caused some damage. We're attempting to repair that."

"Thank you, Frank. I owe you. I need sleep, if I can. I get picked up in a few hours."

"Ok." The line goes dead.

The first lieutenant walks into Wu's office.

"We lost communication and control of the ISC Anton in the Pacific."

"Explain."

"Interruption occurred twenty-three minutes ago. We tried to re-establish connection but so far have failed. Feng stopped transmitting data."

"We have another robot failure. Contact people in Shanghai and find out what happened," he says, suddenly screaming.

The first lieutenant turns and hurries out. Wu picks up his coffee mug and throws it against the wall. He is livid. He stands up, storms out of his office and heads to the operations room.

"Someone update me on the Iranian tanker."

Another lieutenant comes over, "The tanker broke in half and sank."

"I witnessed that with my own eyes," he petulantly responds.

"It stirred the Iranian government into calls for retaliation. It seems they are not quite radical enough and it's too soon after the elections. Apparently, the West still has some influence."

Wu reflects on what he is learning. "I have an idea." He's angry but decisions based on emotion are never productive. Animation takes control as he heads for the exit. "I'll get back to you."

Cross calls Granfield. "Clones are everywhere in that facility. I incapacitated one known as Feng and removed him from the building. It stopped their control of ISC Anton and I transferred it back to the ship."

"Excellent work."

"What happened to the Iranian tanker concern?"

"We have that under some control, albeit marginally. The missile strikes came from a drone hovering off Oman. Our allies had no military hardware in that specific zone. We are tracing signals and satellites and Farbod is minimising the political impact, or his people are, as best they can. They have their limitations."

"I suspect Wu is going to be pissed."

"Oh yes, absolutely."

"Frank gave me some detailed information that I'm going to use when I visit ISC this morning. I still believe Xing is a bystander but let me confirm this."

"Be careful. The impact of the disappearing container ships is being felt and we need to step up our game."

"Got it." Cross sighs.

24

Communication Destruction

On the drive to ISC, Cross is thinking about how to approach Xing. Lang pulls the Hongqi up to the entrance and he steps out.

"Thank you, see you later today." He closes the door and walks into the building.

"Good morning, Mr. Wei," says the receptionist. "Mr. Xing wants me to give you a security pass so that you can meet him in his office this morning. Some unexpected business he has to attend to, he said, and apologises." She hands him the card. "The elevator to the executive floor you're familiar with. Insert the card and punch the floor number."

"Thank you."

Cross takes it and walks over to the elevator. He enters Xing's office and already he looks haggard.

"Good morning, Mr. Wei. Please close the door and take a seat."

"Good morning, Mr. Xing."

"I apologise for my poor manners this morning. Something un-expectedly happened last night I had to deal with."

"I am sorry to hear that."

"Feng, one of the gentlemen you met yesterday, is off today. They expect him in later this afternoon but he was in charge of the container ship ISC Anton out in the Pacific. The workstation monitoring it went up in smoke and we lost communication with the vessel."

Cross' eyes are already lit up and his eyebrows lift. "Feng is returning later today?"

"That's what I was told. Replacing the workstation did not restore communication so the ship presumably continues on its path. The security fence was also tampered with."

"A little excitement." Cross smiles. "I want to ask you some questions in private. Is this room secured or can we go somewhere else?"

"Follow me." Xing opens his office door and heads to the elevator. Xing leads him outside and to a café across the street. Cross sees a different café further down a side street.

"I prefer this one." He takes the lead through the crowded pedestrian mess.

They step inside a small café and Xing orders two Green Chai Teas. As they wait, Cross sees an empty table and goes over. Xing carries the teas and sits down in front of him.

"What did you mean when you said the ship is presumably on its course?" Cross asks.

"We have lost contact and the captain no longer responds."

"Is there a direct phone line to the ship that isn't controlled by their electronics?"

"Yes, captains typically carry satellite phones."

"I need this number," demands Cross, politely.

Xing takes out his cell and sends off a couple of messages. He looks at their responses as they come in. "This may take a little time but someone is working on it."

"I noticed yesterday some of the technical people are cold and show little emotion. Qiang on the other hand is upbeat."

"This is normal. Some are focused on what they're doing and do not interact. You need to remember they don't know how to socially behave because some come from one-child families. This we regard as normal, Mr. Wei."

"That's a fair point I hadn't considered." Now for the kicker, "You must be aware some of your ships have disappeared?"

Xing hesitates. The Chinese do not like being embarrassed and come from a strong ancient culture. "This has come to my attention, yes, and we are already looking into their possible sinking."

Cross sips his hot Chai tea. The café is busy and noisy, which helps garble their words. He needs to decipher what Xing knows. "What can you tell me?"

"The ships disappear in heavy storms and are never heard from again. They are designed to encounter extreme weather events so it leaves us perplexed."

He doesn't know if Xing is ready for his next question but Cross needs to know the answer. "What if I tell you I know why they are sinking?"

Xing is clearly agitated. The crowded café means he has no-where to go and needs to confront the question. Cross knew what he was doing when he chose this place. Xing drinks some tea and calms down a little, but not much.

"How would you know? ISC is losing a lot of money and it's tarnishing our reputation. It's also starting to impact trade with the US. These are serious problems, not just for us but for global trade in general. We talked to the ships' architects, designers and builders, thinking their designs must be at fault.

"We have only recently learnt about this, perhaps in the last week or so. We are tracking and monitoring all the ships so it is confusing. We saw they were reaching their destinations but then ports and importers were calling and asking for the changed schedules. We didn't understand what they meant since we hadn't changed their schedules. Our data showed they had reached port."

Xing's reaction is emotional. He clearly didn't know what is happening and is upset. Cross can see beads of sweat above his upper lip. Cross needed to see this. He needed assurance that his instincts are accurate.

Cross places his hand on Xing's arm, "Mr. Xing, the ships are being controlled at ISC in your facility."

Cross could have told him he only had a few months to live. He feels sure the shock would have been the same. Xing turns white and his dilating eyes widen.

Cross continues, "I already know what is going on and why the ships are sinking. I came to Shanghai to find out how, Mr. Xing." He removes his hand.

Xing eyes get watery but suddenly his phone receives a message. He picks it up and looks at it: "We are responsible for the crews and their families." He is clearly distraught and tries to compose himself. "This is the captain's satellite number on the ISC Anton." He shows it to Cross.

Cross dials it in and waits for the signal to filter through. The first time he tries it, it rings and rings. He waits a few seconds and redials but the same thing. Cross punches the redial again, only with more force imagining this would help, and waits.

"Hello," answers the captain in Mandarin.

Cross hands the phone to Xing who exchanges a brief conversation before handing the phone back in a way that suggests the captain wishes to communicate. Cross involves himself in a conversation in Mandarin before asking the captain to keep the satellite phone-feed active. They say their goodbyes.

"Mr. Xing, I am Daniel Cross. I am English and not of mixed race. I live in California and I have been contracted by the CIA to help solve this case." He holds out his hand.

Xing stares at him, not really knowing what to do or say. He removes a handkerchief from his pocket and dabs his eyes. Cross likes him even more than he did before. One cannot show emotions as sincere as has Xing if it isn't truly affecting him personally. Cross understands now there is no way he's aware of what's going on. Xing extends his hand too.

"This is very delicate, Mr. Xing. ISC has been infiltrated by Artificial Intelligence," Cross didn't think Xing could look more shocked than he did a few minutes earlier. "I want to show you what's going on but first I need to fill you in a little info. You cannot react the way you've been doing with me this morning when I reveal things."

"Ok."

"Do you have an IT group?"

"Yes, I will show you the department."

"Department?" Cross's turn for eyes to open wide.

"The technology we use is advanced, Mr. Wei. Sorry, I mean Mr. Cross."

"No, you don't. Mr. Wei is correct." He smiles. "Don't blunder like that again or I may end up dead. I assure you the infiltrator's technology is even more advanced."

"What?"

"Do you have people you trust at ISC?"

"Of course."

"Be careful of those. I mean people who would stand in front of a bullet to protect you?"

"Yes."

Cross fills him in a little on what's going on. He needs to give him some background before they head back. Going dead pale again would not be good.

"Ok, let's head back over before people become aware and concerned with our notable absence. However, before we do, no shocked looks, no surprises, no gasps of air," he says chuckling. "I want to see every IT person you employ when I ask."

They hurry back to the building and walk up the stairs to the control room.

"Observe the screens very carefully," he whispers in Xing's ear.

Cross immediately bee-lines for Chyou's cubicle. She is sitting where Cross was hoping she would be. "Good morning, Chyou, but please remain seated. I don't wish to disturb you. I see you are busy again today."

"Hello Mr. Wei. Nice to see you again."

"I am here to learn something." He stares at the monitor. "I see the ship on your monitor is close to an approaching storm."

"They are designed to withstand storms, Mr. Wei."

"International shipping protocols advise the industry to stay clear."

"Their designs can withstand storms."

"Have a good day, Chyou."

Cross motions to Xing to follow as he walks away. "Chyou is A.I.," he whispers and doesn't bother looking to gauge his expression.

Standing in front of the huge screen on the wall, he looks for the ship Chyou was following, and finds it. "Look at the ship we are monitoring on Chyou's workstation and look at the path it is taking here." He points to the map. "Look very carefully."

He waits for Xing to locate and compare the images.

"Wait, they look different." He hesitates. "On the wall here the path of the ship avoids the storm. On Chyou's workstation, it looks like it is nearer."

"Exactly, but keep your voice down. I noticed this yesterday. The big screen, the one we are looking at, is showing the expected track of the ships. Your people will be monitoring this screen and the data coming off it. What is being projected on Chyou's screen is the affect of her taking control of the vessel."

Xing went silent for a while, which Cross thought was wise. The less he said the better.

"The captain of the ISC Anton told me an external source took control of his ship via the company's satellite feed, which comes from this building. After I destroyed Feng's workstation and restored control, he turned off their antennas and communication devices."

"You did what?"

"I want to visit the IT Department, Mr. Xing, then discretely point out the new employees, if any."

Xing takes Cross up to the twelfth floor. The IT Department occupies half of it. Cross is introduced to the head technical person who has been there some time. She looks like she has, Cross chuckles and says to Xing, "She doesn't look A.I., but might need some help."

They could turn the whole network system off; the antennas, satellites, dishes. That wouldn't solve anything. The shipping industry would be on its own, out in the vast oceans and seas.

"I want to speak with the IT Manager. Can we arrange it somewhere that's not in here?"

"Let me go talk to her."

Xing walks over and Cross sees an energetic conversation between the two and then he heads back. "There is a secure conference room on floor eight and we will meet her down there. She will use a different elevator."

Sitting in the conference room, Cross analyses her. "Hello Yu Yan, I am Mr. Wei," he says in Mandarin. She doesn't speak English.

"Nice to meet you Mr. Wei," but is confused by his mix.

"My father was Chinese and my mother English," he says, trying to make her trust him.

"Oh, thank you for the explanation."

"I own a company in England and want to install a similar communication system for our ships. Where does it come into the building from the systems on the roof?"

"There are a series of built-in vertical and horizontal tunnels which give access to the electrical and mechanical areas within the high-rise structure. The communications cable comes through a series of conduits and onto floor twelve. That is where we have our modems and routers. We also monitor the data traffic that is being sent and received. From floor twelve it gets split and sent around the entire building. It is a very secure network, sir."

"Who monitors the wiring?"

"We have a young man who started last year. He is a wiring technician."

Cross turns to Xing and reverts back to English. "I want to meet this man. Can he show me the wiring?"

Let me see and he turns and talks softly to Yu Yan.

"He comes in later this afternoon and works the evening shift."

"We need to locate where the communication cable to the dishes has been spliced. We believe they are modulating the signals so they can control the robots and add their own data packets."

They revert back to Mandarin and talk some more before Yu Yan exits.

It is dark when Cross returns to the ISC Building. He has his 'equipment' belt although still in a suit. He uses the security card Xing gave him earlier and lets himself into the building. He isn't required to be covert yet and a prior arrangement means he avoids the metal detector whilst acknowledging the security folk. He heads to the elevators and punches in the floor number.

The elevator doors slide open and he gently exits whilst scanning the area and swiveling his head. The IT Department isn't bustling as it was earlier but a select few are still working. He walks over to the location to which Yu Yan pointed where the communication cabling is located. No one sees him as he types in the access code and hears the click of the mechanism de-activating. He opens the door and closes it behind him before turning on the lighting. Over in the corner he sees another door which, according to his reliable information source, should lead to the conduit of cables and ladders that will eventually lead to roof-access and all that goes with it. The 'Authorised Personnel Only' sign in two languages gives it away.

"I guess people who speak other languages are allowed in." He chuckles to calm his nerves.

He quietly walks over and opens it. Peering his head through, he looks straight up and tries to forget the metal ladder he needs to ascend. How many floors, ten, twelve. He doesn't know and doesn't need to. His bad knee might give up before then. The passageway is well lit and he can see channels leading off on various floors. To his right there is a ladder going down to where the conduit and chases extend. He doesn't need to look down there, not being a lover of heights.

His expectation is well founded so he reaches for his gun and starts climbing. A few floors up he sees a hinged access panel on the main conduit that must be five feet wide and opens it. Multi-coloured low-voltage wires neatly secured in bundles are evident. Higher voltage wires are in their own separate aluminium, circular conduits but he doesn't need to worry about those. Then he sees the shielded communications bundle.

"Great." He feels his shoulders relax.

He climbs two more floors before a bullet whistles past his head. He swivels on the ladder and holds on with one arm. The bullet clatters against the metal chase below him. He looks up. A couple of floors up he sees the head of a young Asian partly obscured by wires, piping, metal, wood. Cross looks for an exit and finds one a few ladder-runs above him. Just as he moves his position, another bullet strikes, grazing the flesh in his right thigh. He doesn't scream but he sees blood.

He climbs and jumps into the chase feeding the cabling and

power to that floor, wherever that was. Gathering his strength, he flexes his head so that he can peer upward. He sees the man and fires his weapon. A sound he is familiar with transmits through the cavities of the access area as his bullet pierces the synthetic skin and ricochets off the robot's titanium frame.

"Well, what a fucking surprise."

Another bullet raining down strikes Cross on his right shoulder. This time he lets out a gasp and yells,

"Not my right shoulder, you asshole."

Now he is angry as hell. He hears movement and looks to see the robot climbing down the metal ladder. He fires another bullet but knows it is futile. He needs a head-shot but not from this angle. All seems lost until he finds a high voltage power cable feeding into a Siemens three-phase safety isolation switch box that isn't being used. No wires coming out the other end and it is in the off position.

"What are the chances?" he asks himself.

He yanks at the conduit going into the box. Now he's pissed enough to be oblivious to the pain. The cabling moves. He yanks again and searches for something to aid in this exercise. He finds a crowbar and grabs it. He levers the crowbar and forces the conduit away from the box. Four thick cables are showing with the insulation stripped away from the ends of the fat, stranded copper wires. The robot is only a few ladder runs away now so Cross peels back the green ground cable and thrusts the other naked ends of the cables against the ladder. Arcs and sparks start flashing everywhere as the heavy currents travel through it. The robot stops as its hands and feet are now fused to the metal. The head moves and looks down. Cross sees arcing behind the piercing eyes so drops the cable and jumps into the chase. A few seconds later it is all over as the robot explodes.

He stops to take in what just happened. He looks around but needs to find something as a tourniquet. Some wire is laying around so he uses that on his thigh. His shoulder still works but continues bleeding so he intends to carry on climbing.

A few floors later he finds something suspicious. The large conduit housing the cables has been tampered with. He opens another access panel and looks inside. He sees the communications cable going into a splitter box. One end carries on down presumably to the twelfth floor, he guesses, but the other end feeds out of the conduit, through aluminium piping and into that floor's chase. He steps off the ladder, crawls into the metallic boxed chase and follows it. He sees the communications' conduit exit and right next to that is a hatch leading to a room. Slowly he releases the latch mechanism and the hinged-door slides down. He slowly drops his head through the opening and finds another metal ladder providing convenient access. He quietly climbs down into another small, enclosed electrical area. It has a door but he can hear someone behind it. He looks for the communications conduit to ensure this is the correct area and it is.

Whoever is in the room leaves. He hears the door close so takes this opportunity. He opens the door and peeks through the gap. The lighting is subdued but the electronics are vast.

"How the hell did they get all this in here?" he murmurs.

He immediately goes looking for the end of the communications cable and finds it. Sure enough, they have their own modems and racks of routers, modulators, ultra-high frequency generators, servers, workstations and monitors. It looks like they built redundancy into the system too. He doesn't understand how they have hidden this for possibly a year or more. He sees more cables and wires in conduits exiting the room and at some stage those must end up in the control area on the lower levels.

Time to end this charade. He unplugs the communications cable from their modem and pushes it back down the conduit. He then takes his gun and shoots holes into the modems. Next to receive that treatment are the routers and ultra-high RF Generators. He sees the room has a sprinkler system and smiles.

Complex digital electronics and high power units always work well in water. He searches in his belt and finds what he is looking for. He pulls out a pen, unscrews the cap and sets it under the main electronic console. He leaves the room and walks down the hallway. Behind him there is a large explosion that blows the door open and immediately the fire-alarm sirens bellow and the sprinklers come on.

Down the hallway is a robot that simultaneously loses communications. It is just standing there not moving. Cross looks into its eyes and they are black as the high-frequency umbilical life support ceases functioning. He walks right past it.

Cross searches for the stairwell and finds it. From the nineteenth floor he opens the fire door and starts his long descent.

25

Feng, the Robot

Cross makes it to the bottom of the stairwell, along with fifty or so more ISC employees, but he is feeling the pain. They all file through the fire door onto the street. He quickly tries to assess which side of the building he is on. Fortunately, the loading docks sitting off to his left make the task easier to decipher. The other people are assembling to the right through an open security gate and that is the direction they take. He doesn't.

Quickly Cross moves himself into the loading area and hides. In the small parking area is a little van he has never seen before. Accompanying the vehicle are two powerful Asian men supporting what looks like a body between them. He recognises the face. The two big men are trying to look composed but they aren't as they are stricken with panic and fear.

Cross looks over at the door by the stairs that he used the previous night to get into the building. It remains open. He concludes the two men are not trying to enter but are trying to get the hell out of there.

He removes his gun from the jacket and fires two shots. The big men don't have time to react because they don't see him. The two bullets pierce the side of their heads, one in each subject. They fall to the ground along with the body they are carrying.

Now he sees in the corner of his eye the two security guards approaching the downed subjects. He fires two more shots and they drop.

"Fuck them too."

He moves away from his hiding spot and silently walks over to the body he didn't hit. He stares at it in disbelief. It is Feng's replacement. Cross believes they must have been delivering Feng when he destroyed their communication abilities and it shut down as they were preparing it.

He bends down, scoops up the robot with a grunt and tosses it into the back of the van. The damn thing is heavy and he struggles with his gun-peppered limbs. Finally he closes the rear door, jumps into the driver's seat and cranks the engine. He shifts it into first and drives through the security gates, observing the mayhem outside ISC's building as he drives away.

Cross's phone goes off. "Mr. Cross, where are you?" Xing enquires. He sounds frightened too.

"I have just left the building and heading to no idea where yet. I need help, Mr. Xing, but I need to get out of this area." Sirens are suddenly heard in the background.

"Sounds like you're driving."

"Yes, I shot the occupants and commandeered a black panel van. I have something you need to see but I have been shot twice and losing blood. I'm beginning to fade."

Xing gives him some instructions and Cross implants them into his head. Ten minutes later he drives into an open warehouse building as instructed. He pulls to a stop just as the rollup door closes behind him.

Xing had already called a doctor he knows and she is there when Cross arrives. She pulls open the driver's door and he falls out. Just as he sees her, he fades and his eyes shut.

26

Cross is Lost

Wu is back in the operations room looking at the world image similarly displayed at ISC's building in Shanghai. The only difference being his display on their vast screen also shows the real-time course-change of ships they are controlling. Red lines represent the changes in course of controlling ships and they superimpose those on top of the black path each ship is expecting to take. He was aware of the ISC Anton's loss of communication yesterday after Feng stopped functioning and his workstation went dead. He carelessly viewed this as an anomaly and immediately summoned a replacement clone.

Wu marvels at the technology they designed and covertly installed in Shanghai. The planning to initiate that installation was astonishing. He doesn't suffer fools easily but narcissism overrides some basic human functions.

As he stares at the huge screen, all the red superimposed imagery of each controlled ship's path changes to black. He blinks and turns to the first lieutenant standing next to him.

"What is going on? Do we have a technical problem we need to address?"

"Let me find out, sir."

The first lieutenant runs over to a workstation occupied by someone else and they get into a discussion. The operator is frantically typing on her keyboard, bringing up pertinent data on her large monitors.

Wu walks over. "What is going on?" He's rapidly losing patience.

"Sir, we have lost our modulated signals coming from ISC's building. We are still receiving data from their network but our system has gone down."

"That is impossible. We built in redundancy."

"We have stopped receiving transmissions from the workstations and the clones, sir. Everything we installed is dead."

Wu is pissed. He doesn't understand what's going on. "Get me information on who flew into Shanghai over the past week. If you have pictures as they came through Immigration, this will help. I need that info now."

Wu heads back to his office and just as he sits down, a call comes in.

"We lost all communications in ISC's building after an apparent explosion caused an evacuation. They were replacing Feng at the time but that didn't happen. Two of our men were shot in the head and our security guards killed also. We could not get back into the building because it was closed by their security and local police."

Wu is steaming but must maintain composure and keep his plans moving. They are almost there. So what if fewer ships are lost. He can deal with that.

"I want to put another plan into action." He gives instructions to the person on the other end of the phone.

"Ok."

Granfield is worried. He has received news of the building explosion but hasn't heard a word from Cross.

Taylor is in his office. "We have a corporate plane ready for you. Within the next hour I will decide whether to send you to find Cross. I fear something has happened because he isn't responding."

"Of course. I'll be ready." She rises and leaves the room.

Forty minutes later Granfield's phone goes off. It is Doctor Winwood. "Harris, any news?"

"I called Mr. Xing. Daniel is undergoing surgery to remove a bullet in his already-damaged right shoulder. He is in good hands but lost some blood."

"Thank goodness." Granfield is so relieved.

"The explosion may have halted the loss of their ships, Xing added, but they have no idea what caused it yet."

"That guy Cross is crazy. Must be the English in him." He laughs, more as a release of stress.

"He does seem to be acquiring that reputation, David," and chuckles along with Granfield.

"I will send Taylor to Shanghai and call Parisa," Granfield adds. "I think we should energize Jennings at MI6 and have him go back to Moore Industries."

"I'll stop by your office later today. Sending Taylor is mandatory now since it looks like Cross needs help."

"I agree."

Granfield messages Taylor and Jennings.

27

Mr. Xing's Rescue

Cross opens his eyes but has no idea where he is. He vaguely remembers a lady in a nurse's uniform opening the van door but then it was lights out.

He detests waking up from anesthesia but he can feel someone has done something to parts of his body. He tries to open his eyes but the drowsy chemical effect of the drugs he has been administered makes this procedure very difficult. His head is pounding. He feels pressure on his right thigh and the right shoulder has bandages on it.

"Good morning, Mr. Cross, I am Dr. Li. How do you feel?"

"I feel like someone had a baseball bat and thought I was the ball. I probably deserved it too. Where am I?"

"Mr. Xing saved your life last night. He called me urgently requesting help. I secured your medical stability including an infusion of blood before we transported you to a very private and safe location in Shanghai."

"I feel incisions."

"Of course, yes. The bullet to your thigh was superficial but required ten stitches. We had to surgically remove the bullet in your shoulder but you were lucky with only tissue damage. We also cleaned up other non-serious abrasions and lacerations. You really need to avoid a repeat, Mr. Cross."

"I'll make a mental note and take it under advisement in the future. What happened?"

"I am not at liberty to disclose details. I am only a doctor. I saw you stirring so messaged Mr. Xing. He will be here shortly. In the meantime I suggest you rest while the anesthesia and drugs wear off. Doctor's orders, sir."

She hands Cross a remote. "There is a button you can press if you need me. Your belongings are in the drawer at the side of the bed and hanging in the closet. I'm sure you will need this though," as she reaches for his phone and hands it to him. "By the way, you have an incredible body for a man your age." She hesitates for effect, "This saved your life. However, I see many other scars so my suggestion is you find a new line of work, perhaps something clerical." Cross looks at her with a smile.

"You may not be so lucky next time." She turns around and heads for the door. Before she leaves she points to a button on the side of the bed. "Press that if you need more morphine but there is a timer on it."

Cross smells her perfume as she leaves so he knows he is stimulating his essential senses again. He isn't in a hospital room as he surveys his surroundings. He looks at the remote and sees a button with a graphic for curtains, so presses it. Natural light, albeit suppressed by the shielded sun, floods the room as the cloth materials roll away from the window. The smog at least confirms he is still in the city. The bed isn't a hospital bed per se. There are some medical devices on a trolley close by and those are tethered to sensor pads on his body to monitor heart rate and blood pressure. The morphine drip hangs from a stand fixed to the bed with a feed to the needle in his arm.

He rests his head on the pillow and closes his eyes as the medicinal forces overpower his desire to get up and run. After a while he stirs again to absorb more of the surroundings. Pictures of container ships hang on the walls and there are a few expensive furnishings such as sofa, coffee table, lamps and paintings. A small TV sits on an entertainment centre with surround sound capability. He looks out of the window beyond the environmental issues and sees other tall buildings. He closes his eyes.

Cross is disturbed from sleep by voices on the other side of the door and then he hears a familiar voice. God he needs that and Xing bounces into the room.

"Mr. Cross, sorry, I mean Mr. Wei." He smiles.

"You are hilarious. Please call me Daniel. You saved my life, Mr. Xing."

"We all go through life with some regrets, Daniel. You can call me Liang but I usually go by the English name Liam."

"Thank you, Liang."

"You saved our company. I thought it only right I should save you in return, despite it going against my better judgment and you blowing up part of the building."

"Yeah, well, I obviously didn't take enough into consideration," and bursts out laughing. "My head and body ache. I was running on adrenalin last night fueled by sheer anger. What did I do?"

"Well, in short, you terminated the ability of an outside source to take control of our shipping. You destroyed their electronics and removed the feed that was tying into our transmissions. Also, you had the wherewithal to remove the communications cable from their modem before blowing up the room. This action prevented our network from going down too."

He grins. "I did all that?"

"We found four bodies in the loading dock area. Two were not our employees and had half their heads obliterated. Two were security guards whose morals and integrity had obviously been compromised. This caused a few temporary issues with the local police that money took care of.

"We found Feng in the back of the van you drove up in. Presumably you acquired permission to use the vehicle." He winks. "When you are ready, we will show you. But you need to rest."

"Where am I?"

"This is a private suite used by upper executives and board members. There's a medical facility in this building and you are being well cared for. I spoke with a Dr. Winwood so someone in the US knows. Now rest. I will return in a few hours."

Cross has no choice and rests his head on the pillow, closing his eyes.

Cross is slowly coming out of his medical stupor but he knows this will take time. There is a knock on the door but before he can answer a lady walks in carrying food and a pot of tea. She places it on the swivel table at the side of the bed and leaves without saying a word.

"Thank you," he says in Mandarin as the door closes.

He is hungry so sits up and takes the chop sticks. He pours some green tea into a cup and starts diving into the lotus leaf rice. As he's eating, he picks up his phone and sees about a hundred or so messages. He doesn't even know what time of day it is, or even what day for that matter. He breaks protocol and dials Sadeghi.

"Honey, are you ok? David called me obviously distraught and upset."

"Yes, darling. I miss you but I am ok. I'll talk about what happened when I get home. I want to explain now but you know I can't. I needed to hear your voice and let you know I'm safe," He tries hard to hold back emotion.

"I miss you, Daniel." He hears her crying on the other end.

"Everything will be alright. I promise. I'll be home soon. Are you safe?"

Soon the call ends but he feels better now that he understands her level of safety. He calls Granfield next.

"Daniel, you crazy motherfucker, are you ok?"

"Yes. I had shoulder surgery and stiches in the thigh, but I stopped most of the shipping losses. You did tell me we needed this halted but you didn't put any restrictions on how."

"But not at your expense. Come back alive, will you?" As usual Granfield sounds concerned but clearly grateful Cross made contact.

"I've made a bit of progress over here. It is insanity, David, all of it. Wu must have a facility close by. The van I stole isn't for long distance traveling." He hesitates. "What else is going on?"

"Leslie is on her way to Shanghai so message her. Nick is heading back to Moore Industries but call him when you don't have anesthesia in your system. The Iranian tanker is under control, sort of, but we worry about what Wu will do next. He will be operating on emotion now but a narcissist's brain operates under different rules and will err. That is a certainty.

"The lost ships are beginning to affect trade and it is turning messy. Governments are becoming aroused and they are discussing an emergency UN Security Council meeting. With Xing saving your life, we feel with some confidence the Chinese government has nothing to do with this."

"I saved a robot before I capitulated last night. Xing has it and is perhaps waiting for me to wake up. But this might be better going to Frank. His team has been working on their coding so are more advanced in the development of this technology. That might be quicker than having someone in China decode it."

"A valid point. What else?"

"I also wonder about why they picked ISC's involvement. Were they just after sinking ships to affect world trade or was there more to this? Were they trying to destroy one of the largest import-export shipping companies in the world? That was an impressive electronic setup I destroyed."

"Good question. Get some rest and let your brain recover. Leslie will be there shortly. Fill me in later."

Click.

Cross messages Jennings and waits.

Some hours later he is feeling better but that's speaking relatively. He sees a message from Taylor and pings her back. She will arrive in a few hours. Jennings has also responded and Cross replies with a 'message you soon as I can'. He then calls Xing as he looks at his Rolex. The drugs are keeping his pain at bay but he has had enough. He pulls the needle from his arm and climbs slowly out of bed. He yanks the sensor pads and monitoring cables off his body and turns off the devices. Walking over to the closet Cross expects to see his blood-soaked suit but the clothing is all new. He puts on wide-fit jeans which slide over the bandages and pulls on a Marino wool sweater that stretches over his shoulder. He cannot help but be impressed.

Just then Xing walks into the room. "What are you doing?" he exclaims. "What is wrong with you? Wait, let me rephrase that, have you gone totally daft?"

"I need to get out of here. We've got too much work to do."

"Nevertheless, you had surgery less than twenty-four hours ago. You need the drugs out of your system first and must regain some strength. Are you sure a bullet didn't arc through your cranium?"

"I think I've already proved the latter question. If you have a nurse, get me the following food groups, I will be fine." He proceeds to provide Xing a short verbal list.

Xing passes on the information to whoever picked up at the other end. "Give them ten minutes. How are you feeling anyway?"

"About as well as I look," muses Cross.

"I hope you feel better than that?" He chuckles. "Get your socks and shoes on and let's get going. I want to show you what you found."

They take the elevator downstairs and retrieve Cross' bag of nutrition before walking outside. Standing there is Lang with the Hongqi.

"Hello Mr. Wei. I see your trip turned eventful. I hope you will be ok, sir."

"Thank you, Mr. Lang. My trip was getting boring so I decided to hype up the interest factor." His smile was strained.

Lang opens the rear door and Cross climbs in. Xing steps into the front passenger seat as Lang throttles up the V12. He rotates the transmission selector knob and steps on the gas pedal. Cross takes out a high-protein energy bar from his bag and rips the wrapper off. He also consumes a banana.

Fifteen minutes later they arrive at a small grimy warehouse building and the rollup door is already open. Lang pulls to a stop as Cross and Xing exit.

"I will message when we're ready, Mr. Lang," says Xing, speeding off down the alley.

"Is this the warehouse you directed me to yesterday?"

"Yes, come inside."

Cross follows as they enter the premises and the door rolls down behind them. There are some offices suspended from the ceiling using wooden joist with what looks like fairly recent construction. There are wooden stairs leading to them and Xing walks over. Cross stops as he views the warehouse area. There he sees the van he escaped in last night so walks over and looks inside. The driver's seat and floor remain soaked in his dried blood.

"Come on," says Xing. "The thing I want to show you is up here."

Cross walks up the stairs but the pressure shoots pain down his sutured thigh. He flinches.

"Are you ok?"

"I will be, eventually," he says trying to conceal his discomfort.

Xing walks down a small walkway and steps into a room. On a metal table is Feng. Cross looks at it.

"You have to admire the technology here, Liang. This is astonishing."

"How did you know? I cannot distinguish this from a human, even now."

"My first encounter was in Panama and the second in England. I only knew the first one was A.I. because the real version of the clone was a high school friend. He helped by leaving out important information when they programmed it. It is their demeanor though and the skin. They are discernible if you know what to look for."

"Astonishing indeed."

"When I destroyed their communications, the robots stopped functioning. How many did you find in the building?"

"There are twelve we have found so far, not including the one you blew up. We went back and looked at the missing ships and ten clones appear to be controlling them. When they sank one, they moved on to the next."

"Do you know anything about their programming?"

"We are a shipping company, Daniel."

"Yes, I understand. I have a friend in Vancouver whose team has been looking at the first clone I terminated. I want to take Feng to his lab."

"Be my guest."

"Oh, by the way, I have a CIA operative arriving in Shanghai shortly. She will message when the plane lands. I, or we, need to pick her up at the airport."

"Sure. Mr. Lang will take us." He takes out his phone and sends a few messages.

Cross moves around the table on which lays the clone. He has to marvel at the quality.

"Liang, how do we find out who owns the van? It has a

commercial registration ID on it."

"Did I tell you I own a shipping company?" He laughs. "This is way beyond me. But in regard to the commercial aspect, it should have a registration ID."

"I believe you're correct, yes, you did tell me." Cross adds.

"Ok, let me ask you something else. We thought initially they wanted to disrupt trade but then you said something in the café. You said your reputation is being tarnished which got me thinking. Remember the news story about Tainan in the Panama Canal?"

"Yes, we read about that and saw it on the news."

"I went to visit the ship. They could have blown up the whole canal but didn't. They wanted to preserve it whilst creating confusion. I'm thinking now that part of all this is to control the shipping industry which would generate vast wealth on top of White House control."

Xing sits down in a chair and sighs, resting his elbows on the table. He looks very tired. "This goes beyond my imagination."

"Some of our people are disturbed also. Have you heard anything about a fleet of container ships being built?"

Xing's perceived weariness suddenly evaporates and he sits up, pushing the chair away from the table using its castors. He stands up and walks around the room as his head processes information.

"There is a shipbuilder here on Changxing Island that expanded their facilities and has been pushing construction of a new container ship down to six weeks. We have no idea their client. Ships have been leaving every three weeks for about two years. They even built a private airport there."

"One every three weeks?" Cross' eyes widen. "Where is the island?"

"Right here across from Shanghai's water front, in the middle of the Yangtze River."

"I wonder if they have a lot of black vans zipping around. More importantly, where do they hide all those ships?"

Cross' turn to occupy a chair. He's still recovering from having anesthesia and morphine pumped into him and Xing can see it.

"You need to rest, my friend. You can't mess around after surgery. There is a sofa in the room next door. I will go make some tea."

28

The Koreans Collide

They are sitting in the Hongqi outside a private terminal at Shanghai Pudong Airport when Cross sees the Gulfstream coming in to land.

"That's Leslie." He points to an aircraft landing behind a China Airlines Boeing 767 which is taxiing towards its gate. He glances at Xing. "How did you arrange this?"

"I made a few calls while you were thinking" and chuckles.

The Gulfstream taxis and pulls up outside the terminal. Cross jumps out and immediately wishes he hadn't. Wincing in pain he walks over to the cabin door as it drops. Taylor steps down and gives him a big hug.

"Are you ok? You look good considering," as she kisses him on the cheek.

He laughs. "I will have to be shot at more often. Yes, I am still alive, not that I have a choice. You look good too after a long flight."

Cross tries to take her bag but she refuses. "Don't be silly. I haven't had shoulder surgery."

Cross opens the rear door and she climbs in. He introduces Xing and Lang and they exchange pleasantries.

"Your compatriot here is a loony," Xing says to Taylor. "He needs serious help." Cross is beginning to like Xing a lot.

"I think psychologists kick him out," Taylor responds. "I've secretly seen his file and he is beyond help." They all laugh.

"Mr. Lang is going to take you to a different hotel. The suites are booked using different identities and your things we took the liberty of transferring already. Mr. Wei has some notoriety here and I'm sure it best you hide too, Leslie, if you are going to hang out with this guy.

"I need to get back to the building and sort out the mess. I'm a shipping executive, not a secret agent." He chuckles. "You need more rest, Daniel, and you can do nothing more tonight. Mr. Lang will drop me off and then will take you to the Sukhothai Shanghai. Here are your new identities." He hands Taylor the packets.

"You did all this today?" Cross enquires, eyebrows raised.

"It is never what you know, but who you know. You of all people are already aware of this."

"Yes."

Lang pulls up outside the ISC Building and drops off Xing. They shake hands.

"Message me if you need anything. We can catch up in the morning over breakfast. I will call you. Good night and welcome to Shanghai, Leslie."

Lang drops them off outside the stunning five-star hotel and leaves. Taylor grabs Cross' right arm as they walk into the hotel lobby.

"Just one suite, please, with two rooms," Taylor adds.

"Yes, ma'am," and hands her the key cards.

Cross doesn't protest. He isn't in the mood to and welcomes the company. They find the elevators and direct one of them to the executive floor.

After showering and taking a brief rest, Cross calls Jennings.

"Shot at again? Hope everything is ok."

"Yes, thank you, Nick. But I did my job."

"That seems to be the case. At least part of your job. Ha, ha."

"Yes. Where are you at with Moore Industries?"

"I've done some research on their second building. I am in Hull already so will spend today looking for it. I suspect it will not have a sign on it saying 'Clones R Us'."

"Yes, you may be right, for once. Keep me posted. I need to rest and then tomorrow I think we head to a shipbuilder across the river here. I have a complete robot too and will send that to Frank. We are close."

"Good luck."

Wu is monitoring the huge screen in the Operations Room. It is focusing on the Korean Strait where two ships are close to each other. One identifies with a red lane which means it's under external control. It has deviated from its assigned course and is now heading in a direction that will bring it closer to the other. There is nothing one of the captains can do but there is no collision foreseen by the other ship's crew.

One is a naval vessel with a re-enforced hull designed to withstand ice-laden waters. The other is a cruise ship carrying holidaymakers returning from Japan. Selecting these particular ships for this exercise was purposeful and direct.

"Ten minutes, Mr. Wu."

He remains silent. Wu doesn't care about the time. He is only interested in the outcome and fatalities. The world's reaction will be devastating, he speculates, and the outcome predicated on the number of casualties and the two countries he has chosen. He keeps staring as the red line and the black dot guiding the naval vessel brings it closer.

"Zoom in," he commands.

The Korean Strait now represents a significant portion of the screen.

"Switch the feed and guide their collision."

As he says that, the graphical representation of reality turns to a live infrared satellite view as the naval ship is now barreling full speed toward the other.

"Two minutes," the third lieutenant shouts.

In the top right corner the clock calculating the collision starts flashing red as it counts down.

The naval vessel tears through the side of the cruise ship and rips it apart. The frightened passengers can only look on as they become pawns on the world stage. Fire begins to engulf the ship and passengers as Wu watches some futilely dive into the water.

"I will be in my office. Please update me." He turns away and departs the room.

A few minutes later there is a knock on his door.

"Come in."

The second lieutenant walks in on command.

"Sir, I have a list with photos of foreigners who entered through Immigration from London," and hands the package to Wu.

"Thank you."

It is in the early hours when Cross and Taylor's phones ping. Both put on robes and walk into the lounge.

"What's going on?" asks Taylor as she turns the TV on.

She goes searching for BBC World News and finds it. On the screen is a damaged naval ship with debris of some sort scattered around it. At the scene are rescue vessels and other military hardware. Cross is on the phone's internet.

"A North Korean naval vessel slammed into a South Korean cruise ship carrying holidaymakers. Hundreds are missing and presumed dead."

"This cannot be a coincidence."

"I suspect not, Leslie. Wu is growing angrier and trying to get the world involved, which is only getting us riled up. We need to step our game up. We need to pay this shipbuilding company a visit. We have to stop this craziness one explosion at a time."

"Correct."

Cross sends a message to Granfield and makes some requests.

29

Leslie Taylor's Entry

Xing called early and wanted breakfast. Cross and Taylor obliged since they were already awake anyway.

Down in the hotel's Urban Café they sit sipping coffee and orange juice, enjoying an Asian culinary breakfast.

"How are you feeling, Daniel?" starts Xing.

"Better than yesterday."

"Good. I watched the news this morning. I made some calls already and I have arranged a meeting at Global Shipping Conglomerate across the river at ten a.m. today. Here are your business cards."

"How did you do that so fast?" Clearly Cross is impressed.

"They messed with the wrong people and we're pretty steamed. You put your life on the line. Consequently, you proved to us your sheer determination."

"Who are we going in as?" asks Taylor.

"You are two executives from British Asian Holding Company in London looking to expand. That part was easy. Mr. Lang will be available to drive but we will use a rented limousine to keep up the pretense. We know they will check." Xing pulls out some drawings and a map of the island and facilities.

"I am hungry," says Taylor as she unabashedly consumes large helpings.

Xing continues going over the facilities as they eat. "They have fuel storage tanks here," and locates them on the layout. "This is where they expanded the dry dock area to build the numbers being produced. And that is the airport that was constructed during the expansion."

Xing finishes up as Cross orders more coffee. They are going to need a high state of alertness for the work ahead. He excuses himself and heads to the bathroom.

"Mr. Lang will meet you outside at nine-thirty. Message me if you need anything."

They stand up and all shake hands.

"Good luck to both of you."

Taylor is in a light two-piece suit and low heel shoes. Cross has on a dark European three piece suit but had to remove some of his bandaging to make it fit. Lang pulls up outside the hotel in a Mercedes S-Class limousine and they climb in. The atmosphere is very quiet as he drives over the Yangtze River.

They both survey the mega complex as Lang approaches security. The armed guard asks for identities and Cross and Taylor oblige, along with Lang. He scrutinises them before walking back to the guard shack and picking up the phone. Cross looks around to see what security they have implemented. A few anxious minutes pass before the guard strolls out and hands them back to Lang. He opens the gate and waves them through as Lang drives to the visitor parking area.

"I'll wait here," he says.

Cross and Taylor walk toward the vast building and Cross sees a similar black van parked outside. He swallows hard. They go through security before they hit the reception desk.

"I am Mr. Wang and this is Ms. Carlson. We have an appointment with Mr. Sun," he says in Mandarin.

The lovely lady behind the desk looks at her computer monitor and sees their names. "Please sign in and take a seat. I will notify Mr. Sun," she instructs in Mandarin.

They walk over and sit down whilst admiring the huge lobby area.

"This is another company sponsored with vast financial backing," Cross says, shaking his head.

"Yes, it is. The flow of money seems endless."

A few minutes later a smartly dressed man in an expensive suit comes out of an elevator and walks toward them. He extends his hand.

"Hello Mr. Wang and Ms. Carlson. Welcome to Shanghai and GSC. Please follow me."

He takes them to a lavish conference room adjacent to the reception area. Behind them follows another young lady.

"What would you like to drink? The lady here will get you whatever you want."

They order chai tea and the lady leaves. Small talk consumes the conversation as Sun gets ready.

"I understand you are looking to replace some of your aging fleet with more advanced technology and larger TEU capacities."

"Yes, sir," says Taylor.

"I researched your company and it is quite impressive."

"Thank you," but Cross doesn't know if that is a compliment or whether it makes his fake company a target.

The lady returns with the tea as Sun rolls down a screen on the wall. On the middle of the conference table is a projector hooked up to a laptop. Cross would rather be anywhere than being forced to watch a sales pitch. He seems to know more about this subject than he ever wanted to. In fact he didn't want to know anything before this all started.

Sun starts his marketing spiel. As he talks Taylor asks some questions based on what she learnt on her trip to South Korea and even Cross' eyes widen. He turns and glances at her. She smiles and winks.

An hour and half later he is done and so is Cross but Taylor looks fascinated.

"I have organised someone to take you around our vast facility. They will be here at one p.m. so we have fifty-five minutes to enjoy lunch at our executive lounge. Please follow me."

It is very difficult not to be impressed with the setup as well as their hospitality. Cross marvels at all this; it is simply staggering. They enjoy a very expensive lunch along with a rare beer.

Sun leads them to another building and waiting outside is a young gentleman sitting in a Geely electric car. Sun opens the rear door for Taylor as Cross heads for the front passenger door.

"Yongrui will bring you back here in about two hours. This is a large facility. If you need more time, tell the driver. We will accommodate your needs, Mr. Wang."

"Thank you, Mr. Sun." Cross closes the door behind him and the driver sets off.

"Thank you, Yongrui, for taking us around."

"Welcome to our facility, sir."

Cross freezes and looks at Yongrui in greater detail. He cannot believe it but he needs to refrain from doing something stupid, despite the overwhelming urge. These things are everywhere and he has had enough of this shit. He has masked his pain very well but the thigh throbs from all the walking.

Taylor sees something is wrong with Cross. She knows him now and has a bad feeling. She sees familiar-looking ship-building structures and looks over at the massive construction sites and the two ships on scaffolding in dry docks. Thousands of people are working on the mega projects. Platforms, fuel pipes, electrical and mechanical hardware are laid out everywhere.

"They don't have OSHA here, I guess," she murmurs as she surveys the vast mess.

Next to the docks are two tall fuel storage towers. She doesn't remember Xing bringing these up. She sees that the main storage area is off in the distance. This gives her an idea. Cross is chatting with the driver as he drives through the shipyard.

"Can you pull over here, Yongrui?" she says as she points to a secluded area between the storage tanks.

"Sure."

He stops and Taylor looks around. She removes her firearm and shoots at the back of the driver's head. It penetrates the outer shell and lodges in the power module. Within seconds arcs and sparks flash and it slumps onto the steering wheel.

"Damn, you could have warned me," says Cross as he nearly jumps out of his skin.

"I saw your disposition change when he spoke to you."

"These fucking things are all over the place."

Taylor jumps out and runs over to one of the fuel towers. She finds some electrical control boxes and punches a button that opens up one of the large drain valves at the bottom. Within a few seconds fuel oil starts to pour out. As she does that Cross steps out, limps around to the driver's side and pulls out the terminated robot. He struggles with the weight but somehow manages.

In the meanwhile Taylor has run to the second tower and opens that release valve. Viscous fuel is pouring everywhere. No one sees anything yet as they continue with their busy work building ships. Taylor pulls out a pen and removes the cap, then tosses it onto the flowing fuel. She jumps into the Geely.

"Get us out of here, fast."

"Where to?" Cross presses the floor pedal.

"To the airport."

As they speed off, there is an explosion behind them. This sets the fuel oil on fire which is beginning to seep into the dock area. At least they thought it was fuel oil. Ten or so seconds later the fire ignites something else and there is a massive explosion in the first tower. No one knows what is going on. The Geely is a company vehicle with GSC logos and blends in with other shipyard traffic. People look confused.

The first tower topples onto the first vessel under construction and sets it on fire. The burning fuel runs down the side of the hull and sets the scaffolding alight.

"Quicker, Daniel."

Security personnel are beginning to arrive carrying Chinese weapons as they jump out of trucks. They don't know what is going on either until Cross puts his foot down. Some jump back in the vehicles and start chasing them. Off in the distance, between two large buildings, Cross notices the airport and sees a Gulfstream coming in to land.

"We are running out of time," Taylor yells.

They hear another explosion which sends earthquake-like shudders through the facility. Cross looks in the mirror and sees a huge mushroom cloud disappearing into the smog.

"What the hell was that?"

"Don't worry about it. Keep going."

Gunshots are beginning to penetrate the skin of their small electric vehicle and the rear window shatters. Cross takes evasive action as Taylor returns fire through the open window.

"Hold on."

"Thanks for telling me," she says as she collapses on the back seat.

He weaves between buildings and behind some storage containers. Anything to find cover that gives them more time. In front the Gulfstream touches down and rapidly slows. As it reaches a suitable speed it turns around.

"Head for the Gulfstream."

"What? It isn't ours. The livery and colours are different."

"Head for it now," screams Taylor.

Cross floors the Geely and now he understands the response of electric compared to gasoline engines.

Taylor looks behind and sees huge fireballs. The two ships under construction are ablaze and they hear more explosions.

Cross drives around behind the corporate jet and stops. The Gulfstream is now protecting them from the assailants and the cabin door is open already. They step out of the car, charge toward the stairs and climb inside. The aircraft engines are already accelerating as the door is pulling up. They don't have time to strap in as the Gulfstream races down the runway.

Cross looks out a window to see the security guards far behind. They are firing their guns but nothing is happening and the exercise seems futile.

The pilot reaches V1 and a few seconds later rotates. The nose lifts up and climbs into the air. Cross looks over at downtown Shanghai as the plane disappears from ground view and into the city smog.

30

Escalation of Conflict

Cross is slowly waking up. The anesthesia and chemicals are still activating and he truly detests their presence. It can take several days for his body to adjust to normal, whatever the hell normal is anymore. Taylor sees him stir.

"Welcome back to planet earth. I brought you a coffee." She hands it over and sits back down in her chair.

Cross knows he is still in a plane because he can hear the drone of the jet engines. His shoulder is aching and he can feel the pressure in the thigh but, fortunately, the pain is manageable. He looks out a window and sees the ocean about 35,000 feet below them. He doesn't recall finding a blanket to cover himself.

"Thank you, Leslie," he murmurs and takes a sip of coffee. "Can you tell me what happened back there? Exactly who are you?" He acts as if he's in suspense.

"David messaged me but I had already taken care of things. After you left the table at the hotel this morning, Mr. Xing said we could use one of their corporate jets and he provided me the pilot's cell phone number. The Gulfstream took off and circled around Shanghai waiting for my signal. As soon as we finished lunch, I sent that."

"You knew what was coming?"

"Of course." She smiles. "I didn't plan on procuring any of their ships today, did you?"

"What time is it anyway?"

"You climbed into the seat and once you strapped in, I saw you fall asleep so put a blanket on. I could see you were struggling a little. You only slept for about an hour but it is five-twenty p.m. China time."

"Thank you. I was trying to hide my physical difficulties." He appreciated her tenderness. "Did you feel those explosions? I wasn't expecting the towers to go up like that."

"That was admittedly a bonus. As for who am I? I am you, only with better legs, a chest, a gorgeous face and dark skin." She laughs.

"Wait! I have nice legs," he says. Then he calms his chest convulsions from laughing and focuses. "Where are we heading?"

"We got permission from Mr. Xing to head to Vancouver."

"What? We need the specimen."

"Daniel, look behind you."

Cross lifts himself and swivels his damaged body in his chair. On the floor behind him is a body covered in a cloth.

"I arranged this at breakfast. Mr. Xing admires you."

"I saw him change and he started to open up. He is a funny man when the cultural requirements of Asian executive protocols are removed."

"You have this ability, Daniel."

"No. We can all have this ability when our heads are removed from our arses."

"Mr. Xing made a call and had his contact get permission for the Gulfstream to circle over Shanghai. As we speak, allegedly they are deploying the Chinese military to move in on GSC. They required some assurances of their culpability in all this. They suspect a few members of CCP of being involved at some level. I sent that confirmation from the back seat of the Geely. Of course the Chinese government will deny all this."

Cross rotates the chair back around and takes another sip of coffee. He is in complete awe of it all.

"You are a remarkable lady. I think you saved my life a second time now."

"Don't worry, I'm keeping tabs."

He notices she is in different clothes, wearing heeled shoes, a nice short black skirt with contrasting yellow blouse. She has cleaned up.

"Where did you get the change of clothing from? You look so radiant and relaxed."

She smiles at him and has this air of self-confidence which complements and amplifies her beauty. He knows she is flirting but Cross isn't taking the bait.

"Our bags were transferred from the hotel suite. I took a shower and there are clothes hanging in the closet back there for you. Go freshen up. It will help in the recovery and make you feel better. How are the incisions by the way?"

"The thigh hurts but Dr. Li called it superficial. It makes me wonder if she said that because she was told to. The shoulder on the other hand doesn't feel too bad, as long as I'm not being chased by maniacal renegade security men shooting at me." He laughs.

The hostess comes down the aisle and brings them two aged whiskies. "I am preparing some dinner before I resign from my position," the Asian hostess says in broken English. All three burst out laughing.

He shrugs his shoulders. "Please don't, and miss all this?" She smiles and walks back. "I nearly forgot," adds Cross, "what are the Koreans doing?"

"North Korea is about to lob missiles at Seoul. This needs to be defused. Iran wants to be involved also so it is becoming a veritable tinderbox. While we're discussing politics, the UN Security Council is convening an urgent meeting. We don't have a date set yet but it has to be imminent, surely, in New York."

"This might be the time when Wu plans on switching his clones. I need to call Nick in England. He was looking for Moore Industries' other warehouse."

"Let's enjoy the delightful dinner before our hostess resigns," said Taylor. "Go take a shower. I will inform David when we leave Chinese airspace."

Cross gets up and stares at the covered Feng as he heads to take a shower.

31

Loss of Shanghai's Resources

The news is filtering through and Wu is livid. He can see the remnants of the explosions on Changxing Island as he stares at the TV monitor on the wall in his office. Visual images filtered through dense smog portray for the whole planet via satellite feeds from other countries. The grainy videos show two vast ships, one almost finished, collapsed in their respective dry docks as the scaffolding supporting them has burnt to a cinder. One of the gates in the second dock appears to have been destroyed and water has filled that area. Infrared telemetry is very telling regarding what is going on.

Chinese military troop transporters appear to be invading the facility but it's difficult to fully see. China is repeatedly denying anything is going on but Wu sees it.

He storms out of his office, but not before tossing his workstation monitor against the TV. He heads to the operations room. He walks in and everybody stops moving whilst the deafening new silence waits in anticipation of what is to come. His mood isn't buoyed any by a huge TV screen hanging from a wall depicting the very same images he has just been watching.

"Can somebody tell me what the fuck just happened?"

The first lieutenant, the man put in charge, runs up sheepishly and attempts some dialogue. Wu pulls a gun and shoots him in the head.

"Next person."

The second lieutenant purposely walks up, trying to portray confidence whilst hiding his true demeanor.

"To the best of our knowledge, GSC had two executive visitors this morning from England. They represented British Asian Holding Company and were looking to expand their container shipping fleet. Their identities and company credentials were all verified by security at GSC before the meeting was even approved. These are their photos taken in the lobby."

On a monitor by Wu, the second lieutenant pops up the images of the two visitors. "This is Mr. Wang and Ms. Carlson, sir."

Wu stares at them in disbelief. "Wait." He runs off to his office and retrieves the file of personnel who have entered Shanghai from London recently. He runs back.

Holding the file he flicks through the immigration pictures of the people entering. Then he stops and pulls out a file. He looks at it and at the image on the monitor.

"This is Mr. Wei who entered from London. The black lady has changed. She looks a little different. She altered her hair colour but it is longer and she lost some weight too. She is very beautiful. I don't see her profile in any of the entrants." He looks closer at the screen. "Could this be Leslie Taylor?" He studies Wei in more detail. "These two are inseparable, it seems, aren't you Mr. Cross? A fitting Asian look, my friend." He cannot help but admire his adversaries and double-takes the images before turning back.

"Just before the explosions, we lost contact with a driver at GSC, sir."

"That is irrelevant. How did these two visitors escape?"

"A Gulfstream landed at Changxing Airport but it wasn't an American-registered jet."

"Where are they heading?"

"Their transponder is off but we tracked them heading northeast over the East China Sea, possibly towards Korea or Japan."

"Our Shanghai resources are now non-recoverable. This was a contingency we had planned for but not this early. We need to keep the plan moving forward. Where are we at with the diversionary Korean and Iranian incursions?"

"North Korea is preparing for war. Iran wishes to join in."

"And?"

"The UN Security Council is negotiating a meeting in New York."

"Good. You are promoted to first lieutenant."

Wu storms out of the room.

After a ribeye dinner, Cross and Taylor are enjoying a sweet wine when Cross' phone vibrates.

"David, how are you?"

"I'm asking you the same question."

"A little tired but feeling good. Leslie was brilliant today. I didn't know she is being groomed to kill me off."

"Yeah well, someone has to." He chuckles. "Exemplary work again today. I am watching the news, well everyone is. Those are stunning but grainy images of fire consuming the ships. I guess that wipes out their Shanghai connections."

"That would seem to be the case, yes."

"As I said, we have issues in Korea and Iran wants to join them."

"Wait, I thought Iran was stable."

They traded barbs. "About as stable as you, Daniel."

"As stable as all that?"

"You are about an hour away if we have you turn back. I will get back to you as soon as I can but I'm worried about a diversion. This is just another deception. We have personnel on the ground in South Korea but the North Korean Supreme Leader is a psychotic moron."

"Yes, I heard this from many people. To be fair, he did list that as a quality on his resume."

"It isn't funny."

"Oh."

"Are you on medication?"

"No. Only what is left after the surgery two days ago." He is perplexed. "Why?"

"You get funnier when taking opioids, which is also on your resume. Let me get back to you quickly."

"I say fuck North Korea." Then he remembers something important. "David, before you disappear, we need to search for about fifty huge container ships out in the South China Sea. They must be hiding somewhere but how does one hide ships of that magnitude."

"Precisely, to both."

Click.

"What is going on?" enquires Taylor.

"Well, apparently he is grooming you to kill me off and we might be heading to Korea, so hold on."

32

Change of Plan

Cross picks up his phone.

"Daniel, I found the building. I was correct since it doesn't have Clones R Us on it." He hears Cross laugh. "It is, however, free-standing and very discrete, located in the middle of a residential area along with a few other commercial properties."

"Have you scouted the area?"

"Yes. This is a quiet neighbourhood."

"What are you thinking? Leslie and I are heading to Canada but we could be going to Korea first. I must admit Korea doesn't sound appealing. We need to get to Frank so he can learn more about the full specimen we're carrying."

"Hang on, you have a clone?"

"Yes."

"Be very careful. Have you disconnected anything? You have to ensure it cannot be accessed and started up."

"No, but that's a good point. I'll work on that after this call."

"Graeme Moore Jr. knows you are friends with his father. My game-plan would be that he waits for you since he will likely be more amenable and comfortable seeing you. If his parents are still alive, and they would have to be to keep him involved, he will trust you more. Can you be here in a few days? Leslie doesn't need you in Canada."

"I have no idea. If we divert to Korea, I can fly direct from there but I will get back to you. Iran is siding with North Korea and a UN meeting is imminent. My guess is that Wu would likely plan something then. We might not have enough time. Do you have other people with you?"

"Yes, why?"

"UK government clones are already in the UK. This means transfer has to happen there so we need a back-up plan. I will get back to you, Nick. Be careful."

"You too."

Cross turns to Taylor. "Nick has found the other building in Hull. We have a finite period to sort this out, I feel."

He stands up and walks back to look at Feng.

"What are you doing?" Taylor asks.

"I want to make sure it cannot be accessed by some obscure satellite we don't know about."

"I removed the transmit-receive circuitry already."

Cross walks back and sits down. Grabbing his whiskey tumbler, he empties the contents down his throat. "This is getting to me. All these friggin robots everywhere. I'm starting to get nightmares."

"Yes, I understand."

Just then Cross receives a text from Granfield and feels the plane banking to the left. "I don't get this. What can we do in Korea?"

Taylor shrugs her shoulders and then her phone buzzes. "There is no 'we'. I am dropping you off and then continuing per schedule."

"Yes, I see that. I have just received my instructions. There is something I can do in Korea after all."

33

HMS Rockland, Korean Strait

The Gulfstream lands at Tsushima Airport. As the plane comes to a halt Cross unbuckles and favours his thigh as he moves with his bag. He kisses Taylor on the cheek and then opens the cabin door. At the bottom he sees US military personnel.

"Tell Frank I say hello and keep me posted. Please be safe, Leslie." He limps down the steps.

Cross looks at the badge on one of the Marines as he steps onto the tarmac.

"Welcome Dr. Cross." He salutes although looking a little perplexed.

"Thank you, Sergeant Delaware," and Cross copies him. "This is my makeup for this mission, Sergeant," and grins.

The man says, "Thank you," but does not wish to extend the conversation, "Follow me, sir. As you can see, the Sikorsky helicopter is just over here."

As best he can, Cross follows. The downforce of the rotating chopper blades make it harder as they approach. The sergeant manoeuvres through the open door into the rear compartment and Cross does the same. The sparse environment of a military helicopter immediately swallows up the leather-bound luxurious comfort of the Gulfstream.

"Take a seat and strap in, sir."

As he does so he sees the corporate jet turn around to be ready as a refueling truck arrives. Then the helicopter abruptly lifts off leaving his stomach on the tarmac.

"Put on your headset." He points to a set hanging from his seat. Cross obliges.

"Thank you. I couldn't hear a damn thing."

"This will be rough for a while. We have strong winds from the northeast. However, the ride is short, about an hour. We will arrive on HMS Rockland which was involved in exercises in the area. A British naval ship will make you feel right at home, sir."

"Actually, no. Holding an aged whiskey sitting on a sofa in the mountains with a beautiful lady in my arms will make me feel more at home, Sergeant."

Delaware laughs. "I was told you can be a comedian. I cannot help you there though."

An hour later Cross feels the slow descent of the Sikorsky. His bones are about to shake loose. "How do soldiers have the strength to jump out of one of these and fight bloody wars?"

"Drugs and alcohol aid that process, sir."

Cross chuckles.

In the dark Cross can see the lights and vague silhouette of a navy destroyer as they approach. Through the glass canopy surrounding the pilots, he sees a large yellow H on one of the helipads as the wheels touch down.

They remove their headsets and unbuckle. Someone outside slides the compartment door open and they both step out onto the steel helipad.

"Follow me," shouts a Naval officer and so they do just that.

They enter the ship's main structure and the officer takes them through narrow hallways and up two sets of steep stairs. Cross is struggling but restrains himself to low groans. They enter a room that seems nicely appointed, for a naval ship. Screwed to the door is a wooden sign that reads 'Rear Admiral's Quarters'. Someone had scribbled in pencil underneath it, 'Enter at your own risk' with a smiley face at the end. Cross enters anyway. As he walks in a tall, extra-large, figure in white naval attire approaches him with his hand out and Cross shakes it.

"Welcome aboard, Dr. Cross," he booms. "Your reputation precedes you, sir. I am Rear Admiral Morgan of Her Majesty's Ship Rockland. This is Captain Smith next to me."

"Thank you, Rear Admiral Morgan. Please call me Daniel. This is Sergeant Delaware from the US Marine Corps." They all exchange their pleasantries.

"Please, come and sit down," states Morgan, as he walks over to the sofas. "I have ordered some fresh coffee. We are not allowed alcohol when discussing military operations but that is a daft rule if you ask me."

Cross and Delaware follow and all four sit down on two sofas opposite each other.

"Well, Daniel, what have you been up to? I guess I should say up to again," and bellows his snort.

Cross suspects he doesn't get to laugh too often out in these hostile regions. "Well, sir, how long do you have?" as he looks at his watch.

"I was well informed by David Granfield of your spirited personality. He also told me to take very good care of you. When someone in his position tells me that, I garnish it with deep admiration.

"We have seen the world news feeds today. Changxing Island looks like your work, especially with your modified appearance. China continues to deny such activity took place on their soil. I also heard you got in the way of some bullets heading in your direction and had surgery two days ago. I hope you are recovering."

"In truth, only partially my work since Leslie Taylor takes responsibility for that, Admiral. And yes, I am still recovering from some trauma, but thank you."

There is a knock on the door.

"Come in," barks the admiral.

In walks a lieutenant commander with fresh coffee and chocolate cake. He places them on the coffee table and quickly departs.

"Please help yourselves," and they promptly do.

"As you know, a naval vessel broadsided a cruise ship in the earlier hours today which has created a slight political problem, as well as killing hundreds of South Koreans. The North Korean Supreme Leader, being the stable man he is, is about ready to toss nuclear-grade missiles at Seoul from his Korean naval ship. The problem is we cannot get in contact with this ship and are mystified. There appears to be some kind of electronic shield. Furthermore, it appears someone is controlling from an external source. The Koreans are blaming each other and the South Korean government is very angry for obvious reasons."

"I am guessing you cannot just toss a missile either."

"Very astute. That would be like tossing petrol on a fire to put it out. We need a little diplomacy and discretion attached to this endeavor, but I like your thinking."

"Huge container ships have been sinking at an alarming rate. Somewhere out here in the South China Sea is a hidden facility that is controlling them. There is an operation to take over the world's shipping industry, amongst some of the things the perpetrators want to do."

"Wait," says Captain Smith, "you're telling people in the Navy that ships are being controlled externally?"

"Yes, captain, that is exactly what I'm saying." He didn't appreciate his condescending tone.

"That is impossible, sir. A civilian cannot determine that."

"Actually, with all due respect, a civilian already has, Captain," trying to sound as patronising as he is. "What we are doing now is trying to stop it. That was the reason for being in Shanghai which is where I have just come from."

The admiral places a hand on the captain's arm to calm him down. "I will fill you in later, Captain," as he looks at him. "But this line of conversation isn't productive." He turns back to face Cross.

"Our plan is to drop you on the stern of the North Korean ship which has a helipad. Infiltrating the ship is required in order to halt the external communications. We have already determined the operation as being paramount. This warship has a state-of-the-art stealth helicopter and it is ready as I speak. You will be supported by a small regiment of twenty Royal Marines Special Boat Service members, or SBS."

"I've read about them. Wow. But I do have a question, Admiral. If it is being externally controlled, how can the supreme leader launch missiles from it?"

"Whoever is controlling their mission is still allowing some functions to operate. They already perceived North Korea's reaction. They know he will want to lob missiles."

"Got it. How many crew?"

"This naval ship was donated by the Iranian government. It is state-of-the-art and fully automated. We estimate around two hundred and fifty. We doubt they are all qualified and some will be asleep. We imagine a large number will want to defect."

"Ok. We might need a bigger chopper, Admiral." He smiles.

"The SBS are prepared already. You will be shown a cabin down the hallway where you will get ready. Time is of the essence, Daniel. You will be ok, right?"

"Yes, I'm good." He wasn't, not for this.

"Right."

The admiral presses a button and the same lieutenant walks in. "Take Dr. Cross to his quarters. Sergeant Delaware will join his chopper crew in their own quarters."

"Good luck, Daniel." He shakes his hand.

Cross puts on a black skin-tight suit and lathers his face in black paint. He pulls on his full-face balaclava but fits it around his forehead. He next pulls on a thin black jacket that is waterproof and he hangs the C8 Carbine SAS-commissioned assault rifle on his left shoulder. Strapped to his ankle is his CIA old-faithful. Now he is ready and both have silencer upgrades attached.

The lieutenant waiting outside his door leads him aft where the stealth chopper is waiting on the second helipad. Cross leaps inside the cramped cabin and it immediately lifts off once a Marine secures the cabin door. He turns to one of the SBS men, "That clerical job looks good right about now."

The Royal Marine has no idea what he is talking about and just smiles. As the helicopter changes direction and gains speed and altitude, one of the men stands up.

"Our ETA is one hour twenty-four minutes. Our mission is not to sink the ship or to kill everyone on board. Our mission is to disconnect its telecommunications with the outside world."

Cross looks around and sees a few female Marines. He tries to see who is talking but they are all in black with no markings or insignia.

"You have all reviewed the ship's layout, except Cross here. This is our special guest and you will look after him. This order comes from high up in the US and UK governments. The mission has no margin for failure.

"Our first priorities are the communications equipment on top of the bridge. Remember, there cannot be any explosions or weapons firing, unless absolutely necessary. We have to remain off any infrared radar or satellite feeds. A burning North Korean warship on an infrared world broadcast wouldn't look too good apparently, for some reason." He chuckles.

After finishing his pre-ops talk, the commander comes over to Cross and sits next to him. "The two personnel seated on your right will escort you to the communications room. Do as they say and keep close." Now he's yelling above the noise of the chopper.

Cross turns to his right and sees male and female SBS Marines staring at him. He sticks up a thumb.

"They will also carry incendiary munitions."

A flight of rapid low-altitude speed across the Korean Strait in silence and darkness is coming to an end. They must be close now. Just as Cross thinks that, the commander stands up.

"Right, ten minutes. The stealth is working because we have been flying low-level and we hear no electronic chatter from any-where. The lights on the Korean naval ship have been extinguished so they too are trying stealth, but we are better at it."

As he announces that, the chopper starts to decrease speed. Cross gulps.

"Ready. Five minutes." He looks at Cross. "Go get 'em, Cross," and sticks up a thumb.

The Marines pull down their balaclavas and put on their black gloves. Then they remove their rifles and get ready.

"Two minutes."

No one sees anything and there is this indescribable level of trust that only comes with years of training. The chopper slows and the side doors open accompanied by a rush of warm salt air. They put on their night goggles but Cross wonders if they work on robots.

"Go."

Everyone starts to filter out of the cabin and jump on the ship.

There are some early tussles as the Marines start taking out the crew. They jab them with a needle rather than terminate them with a high speed bullet, at least for now. Slowly the Royal Marines progress across the ship. They're trained in what might be termed: extreme stealth. It must result in complete surprise.

A Marine taps Cross on the shoulder and motions him to follow them. They peel off and run across the decks toward the towers housing the telecommunications. They know where the electronic rooms are, so they head off in that direction. As they approach, they keep their heads down. Surprise has eclipsed the enemy crew and so few are prepared.

Two SBS Marines, with Cross just behind them, step behind the two electronic officers and put a needle in their necks. Two others stand outside and cover whilst Cross runs in and dismantles the communications. It takes about twenty minutes for full disarmament to take place. A Marine hands Cross some incendiaries and he carefully hides them inside the electronic consoles. Setting the timers to thirty minutes will give them time to escape, Cross hopes.

Just as he finishes and they are about to leave the room Cross senses something off to the right. Some movement behind a slightly-ajar door has captured his attention, but it is too late. He feels something penetrate his right thigh but he cannot scream. The mission doesn't allow it. He tilts the C8 hanging off his shoulder and fires into the doorway. Immediately a North Korean officer falls, forcing the door to open as he slumps to the floor.

A Marine notices and looks at Cross. "Are you ok?" but Cross' own facial expression answers that and the Marine calls for the two outside to assist.

Two more Marines, always in pairs, are in another part of the structure. The North Korean captain approaches their hideout and traps them, so they believe. They have their rifles ready but know stealth and no deaths are the keys to this mission. Suddenly the person walking the hallway drops to the floor. The Marines look around the stairwell they're hiding under and see the object just lying there. Scanning the area, they carefully walk over and roll the body.

"Jesus, this is insane. This means communications have been terminated and we need to get out of here."

"I agree," said the second Marine.

They re-trace their movements back across the top deck and head for the chopper, stepping over Korean crew members as they proceed.

Two Marines help support Cross by the shoulders.

"Take him back to the chopper; his job is done here anyway. We are going to shut down North Korea's ability to fire missiles from this vessel and then we'll head back there also." They run off in search of the missile control room.

The commander sees two Marines helping Cross to the helipad so creates space in the chopper. "Get him in here, quickly."

They carry him up into the cabin and lay him on a small mattress on the floor.

"Are you ok, Cross?" asks the commander.

"Fuck these people. Blow up the whole thing and I'll take the fallout," he mumbles.

"Get some morphine in him, before he crashes."

Just then the two Marines that were hiding under the stairwell climb into the chopper. "Commander, communications are terminated. Cross did his job. We saw the captain of this ship shut down right in front of us."

"Brilliant. Take a seat."

The commander crawls over to Cross who has just taken his first morphine jab. "I want you in my regiment when this is over. You performed a commendable job and well done, sir."

As the team slowly reports, two are still missing.

"We are leaving in two minutes," the commander informs the pilots.

Before Cross totally succumbs to the medication, he scans the Marines who have reported. "Commander, the two disabling the missile controls need a little more time. Trust me, sir."

The commander looks at him and then his watch. He waits as the stopwatch clicks past two minutes. He looks at Cross again who is fading.

"Thank you for waiting, Commander," says one of the two remaining Marines as they run into the cabin. One of them is injured.

"Let's go," he screams to the pilots. "We need to get out of here."

The chopper lifts off and gathers speed as it disappears along the dark hostile waters.

"Excellent work," shouts the commander.

The men and women sit back in silence as they head back to HMS Rockland.

When the stealth vehicle finally lands, a medical team is there to meet them. Removing Cross is their first priority and he is loaded onto a stretcher and carried to the medical facility.

When Cross slowly starts to come out of his medically-induced haze, the admiral enters the cabin and sits in the chair next to his bed.

"What happened?"

"You did your job, Daniel. You also saved the lives of two Marines on this mission. When someone saves military lives, we hang a medal around their necks."

"I am confused. Everyone saved lives here."

"You told the commander to give the men disabling the missile systems more time. They encountered some Koreans and had them to deal with."

Cross closes his eyes and tries to envision a normal life, the one he used to live. He misses Sadeghi and needs her.

"You are one crazy fucker," says the admiral with a little snort. "I apologise for Captain Smith's remarks earlier. He didn't know."

"I didn't take offense, Admiral."

"The doctor will be here shortly but I understand a bullet hit close to the last penetration. I suggest you stick a target on the left leg now so the right one can recover."

Cross laughs.

"I need to brief the prime minister on events but you were correct though. Disabling external communications changed a lot of things. When you feel well enough, one of our choppers will take you back to Tsushima Island where a plane will be waiting for you."

He gets up and shakes Cross' hand before he leaves the room.

Some hours later, while resting in his temporary quarters on the HMS Rockland, Cross calls Granfield.

"Mission successful, Daniel. I hear your thigh has been back in the wars too."

"They sedated me and used local anesthesia to re-open the wound and remove the bullet. I was given antibiotics and pain killers before sleeping for a while. Why do they keep aiming for the same leg? They told me to rest but reality tells me there is a fat chance of that. They also restored my face back to normal."

"We asked them to. A simple procedure but Wu may be looking for the Asian profile so this keeps him guessing. When you are ready, the Brits will helicopter you back to Tsushima Airport. There a Japanese plane will take you straight to London."

"The North Koreans calmed down once they regained control of their ship but not by much. They weren't too happy when the electronics were all burnt up and they could no longer fire missiles." Granfield laughs. "They were shocked at their disabled captain. The South Korean government is still angry as they keep pulling bodies out of the sunken cruise ship."

"Yeah well, can't please everybody but sad about that ship. How is Leslie doing?"

"She's fine. And Feng got delivered to Frank and his team is working on it. I feel we are close."

"What about the UN Council?"

"Next week, six days from now but I will confirm that."

"Are the Chinese releasing any further information?"

"They are a different breed and no. Get some rest. I called Parisa and she cannot wait for you to be home. She is faxing over your resignation letter and forging your signature."

34

Emulating the Technology

A half day of rest and Cross is ready. He says goodbye to the admiral before the lieutenant escorts him to a helipad where a Merlin HM2 awaits. The lieutenant helps Cross climb into the rear and then he buckles in. A few minutes later the pilot is given clearance and it spins up its rotors and lifts off the deck. It banks 180 degrees and heads on a course for the Japanese island, skimming across the sea.

"Approximately two-hour flight time, sir."

"Thank you."

As they approach the island's airport, Cross sees a huge JAL Boeing 777 sitting on the runway. The Merlin approaches and touches down.

"Safe trip back to England, sir."

Thank you." He signals a thumbs up.

Someone on the ground opens the rear door and Cross unbuckles and gingerly climbs out. A US Marine escorts him to the 777's stairs but Cross is aided by a crutch which prohibits speed. Once on board, the front cabin door closes and he hears the engines wind up. He looks around and sees other personnel in the first-class cabin. He straps into a window seat for the near twelve hour flight.

After takeoff he messages Granfield who immediately responds. Rest seems to be a common theme that he has no chance of heeding.

He messages Jennings also, who will meet him in London. Next is Sadeghi but he knows he is breaking silence. He is in essence risking her life too. He is now happy hearing from her and asks if she sent his resignation letter yet.

He calls Wilson. "Frank, how are you?"

"I'm fine, Daniel."

"How is my friend?"

"Oh, she's as beautiful as ever. I wish I looked as good as she did after a long flight."

"That would take some surgical procedures and a sex change, my friend." They both burst out with laughter. "No, silly, I meant Feng, but yes she is."

"I am in awe. Their A.I. is simply stunning. How do you know?"

"How do I know what?"

"They are robots? I can't tell just by looking at them. The technology is astounding."

"I have this sixth sense above and beyond the five basic ones. My skin crawls whenever I come into contact with one."

"Are you under some medication?"

"Granfield asked me that recently."

"We are close to evaluating the clone. It has taken some serious effort and many thousands of man hours. We are reverse-engineering it. In other words, we have an end-product that we are trying to control. We have most of the software sorted out, at least in what language to communicate in. The transmit-receive technology is fairly simple, so we have built that already. We cannot dive into its real programming until we can communicate. It's exciting; we are very close." Wilson sounds energetic and focused.

"It isn't exciting when they keep shooting at you."

"Yes, there is that. I haven't experienced that yet." He pauses and takes a sip of tea. "How are you doing? Leslie told me you've had surgery."

"Yes. Fortuitously their aim seems to be as good as stormtroopers in Star Wars."

Wilson wasn't expecting that and bursts out in laughter, spilling his tea. "You are definitely on medication."

"It's permanently in my system but surgeries went well. Thanks for asking, my friend."

"I saw the fires on the huge container ships in Shanghai. Remarkable." Cross can hear someone entering his shop in the background. "Hold on, Daniel."

Cross can decipher a female voice and ruffling as he holds his breath.

"Sorry, Leslie just walked in. I will put her on since she wants to say hello."

"Daniel, how are you?"

"I have had much better days. My right leg is about to fall off but ok otherwise."

"I was told. Great work from the HMS Rockland. You stalled that sector for a while, at least enough to buy us more time."

"Yes. I don't know how much longer we have. The UN is convening shortly. What are you up to?"

"I delivered your friend." She chuckles. "I…"

"I hate those fucking things," he says, disrupting her conversation, but she understands his anger and exasperation.

"I want to see where Frank's team is at. They have a secret location and they look close technically. You are heading to London so see you in Langley I suspect, if not somewhere else. Good luck over there."

"Luck isn't what I need, Leslie." The call ends.

35

The Clone War, Scotland

The JAL 777 lands at RAF Brize Norton, 75 miles west north-west of London, and taxis to the terminal. Cross looks out the window and sees Jennings as the stairs mounted on the back of a truck pull forward. The cabin door opens and he heads for the exit.

At the bottom they shake hands and Jennings relieves him of his bag. "Are you ok? It looks to me like you're struggling a bit."

"I'm very stiff from being seated for so long, but I am ok, considering. It has been a tad rough lately."

"Well, let me lead you to your favourite mode of transportation according to the navy." He leads Cross over to an Airbus HT1 trainer.

"Everyone is a comedian. What's happening?"

"It helps, my friend, otherwise we might all go insane – not just the people we're chasing."

Jennings assists Cross as they climb into the helicopter and then strap in. He signals to the pilots and they secure clearance for the flight up north. The blade slap of engine motor takes over the cabin noise and Cross feels the chopper leave the ground. They each put on headsets.

"What surveillance do you have on Moore Junior?"

"He has a pattern that he seems to strenuously follow and it isn't an exciting one, not like yours." He looks at Cross, smiles and continues. "He works long hours but mainly seven a.m. through around nine p.m. then goes home."

"He has family, right?"

"Yes, he is married. Their children are in school so she drops them off and then heads home most of the time. We think she does work for Moore remotely. She is always on the internet anyway. They live in the east part of Hull.

"He works six-day weeks and Moore Industries has a private suite at the local KCOM Stadium. He does like his football so watches Hull City home games. This is routine and might be his only vice."

This lights up Cross' eyes and Jennings can see it.

"I don't recommend we knock on Moore Industries' door and ask for a meeting, do you?"

"That hadn't come to mind as a viable plan."

"Ok, good. What else?"

"Their second warehouse is much larger than the one you saw and a lot of people are working there. They get regular deliveries, some from obscure companies but most from specialty metal providers, electronic fabrication facilities, software companies, office supply deliveries. Some of those are based in Asia."

"Have you researched any?"

"We are profiling them now."

"Any deliveries made in large crates?"

"Yes, and these come from a company in Asia."

Cross ponders this new information as he looks outside the window and surveys the lush green rolling English fields about three thousand feet below, zooming past at 145 mph.

"There is another fascinating company based in Livingston, just west of Edinburgh in Scotland. They fly products into Brough

Aerodrome, which allegedly has been closed for ten years, and vans then deliver them to their warehouse."

"This gets even weirder the more we dig into it. What day is it?"

"Friday."

"What year?" He laughs aloud. "I'm just checking to see if I have entered a parallel universe. When is City's next home game?"

"Hull FC play tonight and then City play Millwall tomorrow afternoon."

"Millwall? That seems appropriate." He shows a cheeky grin.

"I don't like that grin."

"Have you ever seen hooligans fight?"

"No, nor have I any desire to."

"I have an idea."

The helicopter lands on a helipad at Humberside Airport.

"Sorry I wanted to divert, Nick. We can refuel here before heading up to Livingston."

"No, this is a good idea. I have arranged for people to meet us up there."

Thirty minutes later they take off and head north. It is dark now as they approach early evening. Suddenly the rotors show a discernable change in pitch as the helicopter slows and descends.

"Where are we landing?" asks Cross.

"I don't know. Some field outside the city."

"That sounds encouraging."

"We get what we can get."

The helicopter lands as Cross and Jennings unbuckle themselves. Jennings pulls open the sliding door and they step out into the cold damp air and onto a wet field.

"Welcome to Scotland," says Cross.

Jennings looks around and sees a road fifty feet away. Parked on the side is a Range Rover with its lights on.

"Come on, let's go," shouts Jennings but Cross can only walk as brusquely as medical conditions allow. He is finding it very difficult to traverse a wet field using a crutch.

The helicopter lifts off and disappears over their heads as they make their way across the field.

"Don't worry, Daniel," he says, reading his mind. "We will hook up at Edinburgh's airport. It has to refuel."

Jennings introduces Cross to his right-hand man in Scotland, Michael Yarwood.

"Nice to meet the infamous Daniel Cross, or did you say famous, Nick?" He shot Nick a grin.

"Pretty confident I said famous, Michael."

"I miss the comedic references," adds Cross laughing.

They all climb into the vehicle as Yarwood floors it. In the Range Rover's GPS is already punched the address where they're going. They head into town and Cross is smitten by the number of new construction projects full of detached homes in nice new developments. They enter a commercially-zoned area that also comprises new warehouse buildings, some only half finished. Yarwood approaches the property address and turns his lights off. He points to another car across the street.

"That is ours also."

Cross surveys the building and sees skylights on the sloping brown metal roof of single-story light-coloured brick construction. On the side is a built-in metal ladder shrouded by a circular steel frame, bolted to the wall. The frame supports contractors and prevents perpetrators and thieves from scaling it, or secret agents, muses Cross. There is a padlock on the gate accessing the ladder. Lights are on in the building emitting light through the skylights and around eight cars sit outside in the car park.

"Who is going to scale the ladder?" asks Cross.

"Darnley will do that," answers Yarwood as he texts him.

Cross looks over at the other car and sees a door opening. Out steps a man, presumably Darnley, wearing all black clothing with a full-face balaclava.

Yarwood and the other driver move their vehicles further away and around the corner, out of building view. Another individual, this time a female also dressed in black, steps out and follows Darnley.

"Follow me, Daniel."

Cross gets out and does as instructed. He has his gun in hand and hides across the street but within view of what Darnley is doing. There is a fence around the building but that is no match. Darnley and the lady scale it quickly. Their motion is slow but methodical. There is security lighting but not on the side where the ladder is. The female runs over and bolt-cuts the padlock. Darnley sees the door open, runs across the unfinished landscape and starts climbing the ladder. It is raining and misty so Cross doesn't see how he's going to climb the roof. That thought stops when he sees Darnley slowly crawl across the roof using small compression suction pads strapped to the knees. He gets to the first skylight, removes the camera and starts snapping photos of the interior.

The lack of security baffles Cross. "Did they select this city and area believing they would be secure?"

"That is quite possible. Would you have predicted a high-tech A.I. facility out here?" replies Jennings.

"Good point."

Cross watches as Darnley crawls over to the second skylight. Just as he does, a shot rings out. Cross looks and sees the female agent shooting at a security guard.

"Shit," says Cross.

Just then the agent drops to the floor as a second guard appears with gun visible. That's it. Cross is done with these assholes. He runs out of hiding, points his firearm and shoots the second guard from the other side of the fence. Darnley looks down and Cross is waving for him to move. He stops the photography session and slides off the roof on his back, dropping about ten feet to the ground. He runs over to the other agent and picks her up. Cross watches as he scales the fence with her on his back. Yarwood brings the Range Rover around and all four climb in as he drives off. The second car follows.

Cross spins his head as he looks for anyone following. He sees a body running from the facility's front door but someone in the car behind them takes care of it. The runner drops to the ground with one single shot.

Yarwood is fast and seems to know the area. Cross is in the back with Darnley who is holding a dead body.

"Dammit," Jennings reacts, clearly distraught. "Slocombe was turning into a fine agent."

A few miles down the road Yarwood pulls over and the other car pulls in behind. Darnley leaves carrying a dead Slocombe and Yarwood takes off.

"It is Edinburgh next. You need to get out of here and back down south."

"I didn't get Darnley's camera."

"It doesn't matter, Daniel. They download automatically to our system. I know a sheltered guest house in East Yorkshire with a good bar, open most of the night, so we can look at them there."

Sitting in the helicopter Cross' phone buzzes. Shouting over the noise of the chopper, he answers, "Farbod, I am a little busy so can you hear me?"

"Barely, but yes."

"How are you?"

"Well done in Korean waters, my friend. Excellent work. It has diffused the situation in Iran a little but they are still angry about their tanker."

"Yes, I understand. The West isn't controlling this but we are making progress."

"It looks like your work in Shanghai."

"I like to leave my trademark," Cross releases a dry laugh. "However, it wasn't all my doing so cannot take the credit."

"The Chinese government is still denying anything happened on the global platform but not to a few Iranian officials. In fact they have asked the supreme leader to keep out of the Korean conflict but the international community is forcing Iran to clean up the expensive oil spill, which could be an environmental disaster. This is very privileged information Daniel, and could get me hanged for treason."

"Thank you, my friend, and I will keep it that way. We are very close to ending this, is my perception. I will update you."

Karimi ends the call and Cross puts his head in his hands.

36

Millwall Hooligans

Sitting at a bar in Elloughton, west of Hull, Jennings connects his laptop to MI6's network whilst they enjoy an East Yorkshire Brewery ale. He signs in and accesses the data bases.

"There they are," and he breathes a sigh of relief. "See, I told you Darnley's entrance into the artistic world of photography is right here."

Jennings brings them up on his laptop and spreads them out in a single file of three rows of six columns. He clicks on one that looks interesting and the photo expands and fills most of the screen. He looks over at Cross who nearly drops his beer but Jennings' excitement turns to fear.

"Is this for real?" asks Cross.

Looking through the skylight are seen several cubicles with people working at tables. Surrounding the tables are various storage cabinets that rotate on a stand. Each cabinet hosts various plastic bins containing specific artificial human items. On one side of each table are monitors with pictures of famous people in various angles and guises. Perched in the middle of each table is a head in various stages of build complete with its neck mounted on a stand. Complex electrical connectors terminate the end of short wires protruding from each neck. The workers, all appearing to be illegal Asians, are transforming the heads to match the people pictured in each monitor. On one of the monitors is the Queen. They are creating clones.

Cross takes the rest of his beer and pours it down his throat, whilst ordering two more.

"My guess is these come after they take control."

"My guess too, Nick. This likely means they have enough clones for their next mission already."

"We kind of knew that anyway but this is confirmation." He brings up another photo. One of the heads is bald and they can see the startling manufacturing process in forming a perfect titanium human skull.

"There is a mesh for the heat to vent from the electronic module." Cross points to the right cheek. "No wonder bullets work in that area."

"This is incredible." He takes a glass and downs half the contents.

Jennings scans through the other photographs just for more reassurances. One of the photos shows a casting of a skin molding about to be installed on a head. In another photo a worker is manipulating and forming the facial features to match the clone's real lifeform.

"Ready to eat now?" asks Jennings.

"Yeah, sushi looks appetizing." They laugh.

"My friend is cooking up steak and kidney pie with chips and gravy. In fact, here she is."

A lady of the house walks up and places two plates on the bar along with condiments and cutlery.

"Let us eat, have another beer and grab some sleep; if indeed we can sleep after these images. Bloody hell. You look dead on your feet. How is the leg? You looked in your element this evening running around in Scotland shooting guns."

"I have started researching a clerical job." He smiles. "I felt ok because the endorphins and adrenaline kicked in and masked the real pain. Now it aches and I feel it. I'll take something to knock me out tonight or I won't catch a wink. Tomorrow is another day."

Soon after 7:00 a.m. Cross is awake already and down in the bar. The chef has made him breakfast and brewed fresh coffee. A half hour later Jennings walks in.

"Good morning, Daniel. How did you sleep?"

"Pretty well actually, after I purged the images from last night. I needed the rest though. How about you?"

"I am ready."

"Yeah, ready for what is the question."

Jennings sits down and his friend brings over his breakfast whilst Cross goes over what he wants to do today.

"What? You are joking, right?"

"No, not really. I am confident we are reading this right."

He ponders this for a moment. "Ok, let me finish and make some calls, but we do this my way."

"I am fine with that."

After finishing his bacon and eggs with black pudding, Jennings moves over to the lounge and starts working the phone. Twenty five minutes later he comes back to the bar. "Got it."

Cross looks at his watch. "We have an hour at least so we can troll around the city centre looking for what we need."

It is noon and they've sourced what they wanted. Cross puts on his Hull City scarf and looks in the Jaguar visor's mirror.

"Fantastic, eh?"

Jennings just looks at him and rolls his eyes. "Time for us to head to the stadium."

Using special passes they picked up in the city, Jennings pulls up and parks just outside the football stadium. Next to them is the club owner's Bentley. Right in front is the access turnstile for VIPs and employees. They walk up and show their Intelligence Service credentials. The gentleman looks and waves them in, pointing to where they need to go. They walk up four flights of concrete stairs and head for the owners' suite. Standing outside are two security men and Jennings shows them his pass. One of them inspects it before the other calls using a hand-held walky-talky. Within a few seconds the door opens and they enter.

Thirty-five minutes later, they step outside wearing hospitality uniforms of black trousers, white shirt and gold waistcoat. Cross is wearing his new scarf.

"You look good, Nick. This should be my next job. I am sick of this shit."

"We needed the owner's help to pull your stunt off. He doesn't need to know why."

"Yes, I got that. Now let's find our private suite."

Carpeting partially covers the concrete floor they walk on as they circle part of the upper stadium. Eventually they find the right suite area. Behind a glass wall is a bar and people are sitting at it already. Jennings opens a private glass door and they walk in together. Behind the bar is a private hallway and off this are the luxury suites. Jennings finds the right suite number and enters. It is empty except for some drinks that someone has started to bring in and place in a small bar area. They visually scan the room which opens out through some sliding glass panels onto a small balcony. From the balcony one sees a meticulously manicured grass playing surface with freshly painted white lines.

"This is pretty impressive for a small club."

"Yes it is, Nick."

"We need to leave and prepare now that we've seen it."

As kickoff time approaches, the stadium is filling up. Twenty thousand people will be screaming their heads off, which makes for perfect cover.

Jennings and Cross move away to another suite they have been told isn't being used where they can control what happens next.

The stadium fills and the noise and atmosphere are building with it. Cross looks out over the grass and sees the away fans bellowing their chants in a corner stand opposite their suite. Police and security are everywhere. He even sees armed police wearing flack-jackets on horseback.

"This is a football game, yes?" asks Jennings.

"For now." He chuckles.

"I hope you got this."

Into the second half Hull scores their second goal and Cross can see the Millwall fans getting feisty. Jennings has already confirmed Moore is in his suite.

"Now," he yells at Jennings.

Jennings picks up his phone and talks to someone at the other end. Within a few minutes a small group of home fans start throwing projectiles at a rowdy bunch of away supporters. Those Millwall supporters are now angry and they start jumping over barricades and seats as they head toward the instigators. The owner's authorised-removal of security people separating the fans in that area leaves a void and there is no one to halt their progress. Cross was correct and Millwall supporters did exactly what he'd predicted. Jennings looks at him, eyes wide.

Police are getting involved now and security personnel are running everywhere. The football game continues, this is normal, but mayhem at one corner of the stadium has ensued.

"Time to go."

They run out of the room and head in the direction of Moore Jr's suite. They open the door and very casually walk inside. Moore Jr. is there with only two other people and Jennings politely asks that they head to the bar down the hallway. He closes the door behind them and turns off the lights.

Moore stares in disbelief.

"Good afternoon, Graeme," says Cross and puts a finger to his own mouth indicating that he does not speak. The sliding glass doors are open and the noise in the background is perfect. Fans in front of the private boxes are standing and yelling which partially blocks anyone looking in.

Moore is speechless and nervous. He looks petrified.

"I am Daniel Cross and we met in your office a few weeks ago. I believe your parents are still alive," he says quietly but above the background noise.

Moore nods in agreement.

"We need your help."

Moore hesitates and nods again.

"Here is a secure phone, Mr. Moore." Jennings hands it to him. "This is encrypted and uses different coding so cannot be tapped. It is also programmed with your fingerprint and voice so only you can use it." He steps back to observe the door and balcony.

"We need to find your parents but require some help." Cross looks at him. "We know what is going on and know what you are doing. A visit to your facility in Livingston last night proved it. You really have no choice if you want to see them again, Graeme. Your father saved my life and provided the support for us to be here. He knew what they are doing."

Moore looks shocked and tears appear in his eyes. Cross knows this is a good emotion under these circumstances.

"How did my dad save your life?"

"I am being contracted by the CIA. Jennings, my partner here, is MI6. Your father missed some programming when they built his clone. He knew I would notice. The clone also knew and killed my partner in Panama City instead of me so I could escape. A.I. is very dangerous in the wrong hands. These robots learn like humans do and your father's clone saw him being tortured as they programmed it. It learnt from that."

"They took my mother too. They had to."

"Yes, I know. They are building and programming these clones in Asia."

"You are mostly correct but I don't know where though. Somewhere in the South China Sea is all I know. We finish them off here and add in our technology and software."

"That is the information we have gathered too. We are actively searching because we believe your parents are there, wherever it is. We have a full robot in our possession. I cannot give any details that can get you killed. I am telling you only what you need to know." His sentences are to the point because of the high background noise.

"Yes, thank you."

"We are programming a device so that it can control the specimen we have. I have an idea once we achieve that goal. Do you know their plans?"

"Not really. The clones we finished already and the software that we have developed for them gives me some idea. My father also did research on making them look more life-like and has a patent on the skin technology. They likely chose him because of his published papers. We believe he is still helping them too."

"We and Our?"

"My siblings know and are being silenced."

"Yes, I know about the patent. I did my research too. We will be in contact, but we have to trust each other before I elaborate further."

Moore nods but Cross identifies him clearly as a disturbed and frightened man.

Cross and Jennings leave the suite and head out through the bar area. The noise is deafening. Jennings looks over at the fighting in the stands.

"We need to stop this."

"Nah. Let them scrap it out. It will dispel their pent-up energy and frustrations. I'm inclined to go over and join them."

37

Graeme Moore, Jr

Sitting at a quiet bar on a narrow street in the old part of the city, Cross and Jennings are enjoying an aged whiskey. Far off in the distance, in another part of town, they can hear Hull supporters celebrating their big victory.

"How did you know?" Jennings enquires.

"How did I know what?"

"How the fans would react."

"I read a book actually written by an American and I have also seen documentaries. Millwall fans are quite notorious and formed part of the introduction of hooliganism in English football. They are nuts, clearly defined this afternoon."

"In their defense, however, any fan being bombarded with projectiles will react that way, made worse by their level of intoxication." Jennings adds.

"Changing the topic: What is Moore's number by the way?"

"We should try it."

Jennings gets out his phone. He reads the number as he messages and Cross programs it into his. Immediately Moore responds.

"This is good. He looked scared when he saw you."

"He is being controlled and manipulated along with his siblings.

They must be watching everything he does. Ask him where we can meet, if there is a place."

"He says he will get back to us later."

Later rolls around, after a few more whiskies, and a message comes in on Jennings' phone. "Tomorrow morning in his Methodist Church on Holderness Road and he includes the address."

"A church isn't a good idea but let's go along with it for now. We don't know yet if we can trust him. Tell him ok."

Cross is sitting in the pew at the back of the church. He is the first there and watches as the congregation gradually enters. Jennings is sitting across the road so he can monitor the scene. He doesn't see anything suspicious. Then he notices a new Audi RS6 Avant and messages Cross. It parks on the street in front of the church and he watches as Moore's family step out. His wife holds the youngest child's hand and Moore escorts their teenager. He looks nervous and is looking around as if searching for someone or something. They all walk into the building. Cross sees them enter and puts on his dark glasses. He should have brought his 'secret agent' cap, he is thinking, to go with the glasses. He rolls his eyes.

Moore recognises Cross but purposely ignores him, except for a slight nod of the head. He sits down with his family and, soon after, the priest comes out with the choir following. Forty-five minutes into hymns and the sermon the proceedings halt temporarily as collection plates head down each aisle.

Cross sees Moore stand up, head over and take a seat next to him. Out of the corner of his eye Cross sees his wife look over briefly. Not a good idea to bring his wife into it.

The priest starts up the sermon again and then Cross opens the conversation in a whisper. "I suggest we go somewhere else. We know you like a restaurant close by here after church."

Moore looks surprised that he knows this.

"I'll meet you over there," he says as he stands up to leave. "You will find me."

Moore walks into the restaurant with his family and it's obvious to Cross the owners know them. Jennings had pointed out which table they always sit at so he found an area where he would be hidden. Toward the end of lunch the cute waitress Cross befriended and gave a few pounds to discretely hands Moore a note along with his favourite cocktail. A few minutes later Moore enters the bathroom and Cross locks the door behind him.

"Sorry, church wasn't a good idea. I had to trust you. Please fill me in quickly."

Moore spends about ten minutes going over what he knows. Cross analyses what he's hearing and fills him in on what he has in mind and what he wants him to do. Moore rightly offers assurances in exchange for promises that he will help track down his parents. He is aware he's risking his family's lives as Cross reminds him.

"I assure you we want to find them too, Graeme."

A message arrives from Jennings.

"I have to go because people outside are taking interest. Be careful and message or call anytime. By the way, in about two minutes, you will have serious stomach problems. Take two of these pills in about an hour and you will be fine." He hands the pills over. "Sorry, these people are evil and we are protecting you. You needed a valid reason to be in the bathroom this long. Don't worry. We already paid for your lunch."

He shakes his hand and puts on a baseball cap before limping out the back door.

38

Successful Coding

Wu's frustrations and anger are increasing. He feels he is still in control, and of course he is. Detecting clones has proven difficult and they are still in place - the important ones. He designed the island for clandestine operations and it is a formidable compound. The Korean ships were just a diversion to take away some attention as he plays the next chess pieces.

Wu sits at his desk reading an email on his replacement monitor, the first monitor having fallen victim to his brutal personality. He was born into a one-child family with life dictated by communism and strict Chinese autocratic laws, made worse in a poorly-governed rural community. His father died penniless from cancer, working in a heavy-labour factory devoid of humane or environmental conditions protecting him. After he passed away early from a chronic disease that was curable with suitable medication purposely withheld, Wu's life deteriorated. His mother then repeatedly beat and raped him. Justifying her premature death, Wu fought authorities, claiming she deserved it. His argument bordered on a psychological disorder, according to state-sponsored therapists, and he would spend his teenage years in a harsh forced-labour camp.

Evidently justifiable homicide doesn't exist in any civilian population but is acceptable within the confines of megalomaniacal dictators. His physical scars are there to see but the mental ones are irreparable.

He never married and doesn't have children, as far as he knows. His lack of empathy and feelings are the direct result of his treatment by others during deprived childhood years cultivated by severe indifference. He intends to make people pay, even if they had nothing to do with what happened to him, and make his globalist investors multi-billionaires.

The email is a report on the Korean ships. As Wu reads it, his heart rate quickens and the anger builds. It must be Cross' involvement again. He feels it and has had enough of him.

"Time to turn the heat up," he says to himself as he gets up and storms out of the office.

"You were right about Moore Junior."

"Yes, it seems that way and Wu's organisation still requires his father which means the poor guy has no choice." Cross looks at Jennings who is driving. "But now he does."

They are on their way back to the airport and going through both old and new developments. Cross explains what Moore Jr. told him. They had pulled into a restaurant on the banks of the Humber and were enjoying a very late breakfast.

"Mind-boggling stuff," Jennings replies.

Granfield calls Cross. "UN has a tentative date for their security meeting. It is next Thursday in New York."

"Have you heard from Leslie or Frank?"

"Yes, you need to call. I told them yesterday you were in the UK and tied up."

"They're on my list."

"There is also some strange decision-making going on with the

US President," says Granfield. "He has started to undermine international agreements and upset long-standing partnerships. It is a weird transition since his election and even his own party is questioning the behaviour. It's a deviation not welcomed. He wants to raise tariffs on shipped goods and talks of a security system no one has heard of to defend the shipping trade. He intends to bring these up at the UN meeting next week."

"This sudden change is fascinating," states Cross. "We found one of Moore Industries' satellite companies based in Scotland. We also located Graeme Moore Junior." Cross discusses their interaction at the church and restaurant. He neglects to mention the football riots they induced which ended up making national news. "We need to stop this."

"Call Leslie," says Granfield and terminates the call.

Cross looks at Jennings, "That man never sleeps. I need to call Frank so let me do that before we head out."

"Hello Daniel."

"Please tell me something I don't know, my friend."

"We have activated Feng but are being very cautious. Leslie helped us program some shipping code since it is supposed to know this stuff. Our communication skills in software language are both primitive and scary but we have a robot drinking tea with us. It isn't recognising our environment yet since it's supposed to be working at ISC."

"That sounds interesting. Any further developments on an island in the South China Sea?"

"We're working on that and don't believe this thing was ever turned on when it was being delivered. It looks like they would have downloaded data once connected to their WiFi at ISC, perhaps to ascertain successful connectivity but also to limit exposure should there have been problems. Not delivering meant their failsafe was still active. Their thought-process is staggering."

"We found more clones in various states of cosmetic recreation to match their donors so we are in desperate need of some information that will help us."

"This robot is searching for a specific signal to connect to. This is our next task: to identify and recreate it but we're very close. Once it finds what it is looking for - a known signature - it will then go looking for its home base which, if you are correct, will be somewhere in the South China Sea."

"A very elaborate system."

"They know what they're doing."

"I need to know the very instant you get that because I will have software for you to install."

"What software?"

"By the way, how is Leslie?"

"She headed back to the US early this morning." He misses her but doesn't say anything.

"When will you know?"

The memories of last night invade Wilson's mind...

They finish up dinner in the hotel restaurant and he is about to leave. Taylor stops him and takes his hand, leading him to the hotel elevator. They walk into the suite and she has his shirt ripped off before they reach the bed. She loves the slow, methodical, relentless pulse of older men who know what they are doing, but this time is an exception. Once he has made her orgasm several times he climbs on top, sliding into a world he has only read about but never experienced.

Wilson fails to answer. "Frank, when will you know?" asking a little louder and with some irritation.

"Sorry, I'm thinking. It is early hours here but we have twenty-four-hour shifts going. No one wants to quit for sleep. This place has turned into Nerdsville." He laughs out loud.

"Wish I was there. We need the info quickly. The UN has

tentatively scheduled a Security Council meeting for this Thursday, Frank."

"Give us another few hours."

Click.

A message from Taylor comes in. "Leslie wants me to stay in London but doesn't say why. She will message later, she says."

"Then let's rendezvous with the helicopter and make our way south."

Cross is on a hotel bed resting. The excursions the past few days have made his thigh ache. The bandages are off as he admires yet another damaged area of his torso.

Jennings had dropped him off at another of his preferred guest houses on the outskirts of London close to Stansted Airport. He just finished devouring fish and chips.

On the side of the bed is a Beluga Gold Line vodka, neat. A private message comes in and he knows who it's from. It reads, 'Developed and transferred, tomorrow is key'. Cross understands the cryptic meaning, confirms its receipt and picks up the vodka glass.

He calls Taylor. "Where are you?"

"I am in New York."

"How is Frank doing?"

"He's almost there. They are able to reproduce the coded signature that Feng's designer will be looking for. They just have to ensure its accuracy; otherwise it will be detected by the recipient, and they will know not to transmit back to it. He is verifying that now but it is complicated. They have artificially created another clone, at least in A.I. terminology, using the module you removed from Moore. This is vast research condensed into a finite amount of time."

"Sounds complicated and splendid. We need to know though

since we only have finite time ourselves." He stops to take another sip. "I got a message from Moore Junior this evening. He delivered."

"Now we need to deliver."

Cross messages Sadeghi that he desperately misses her and wants to get home soon. They send their usual loving messages and say goodbye. He detests having to keep communications short.

Cross continues phone communication. "Hello David, what do you have?"

"We think we have located the container ships but it isn't helpful. They appear to be hidden off Hainan Island which is the southern tip of China."

"That's still the South China Sea, correct?"

"Yes."

"Let me do some digging. Frank is close to verifying their coded transmit-receive signals. We can perhaps put a few more data points onto the map and determine an approximate location. What do you mean by 'we think'? Isn't the CIA's technology more accurate than that?" He giggles, the vodka mixing with some pain meds now affecting him.

"Are you ok, Daniel?"

"No, but we need to keep advancing."

"There is a large cove covered by a massive canopy. The canopy is a technological marvel and refracts satellite imagery. From a distance it looks like water but when zoomed in on and magnified, the images have imperfections and the area of the canopy looks blurry."

"Wait." He ponders for a few moments. "I wonder if their location is the same. Perhaps they use the same technology to hide the island."

"That is possible, but we need some idea. The South China Sea is a vast body of water and we don't have time to lollygag."

"Have someone program software to look for imperfections."

"You read too many Isaac Asimov books."

"Possibly. I will update you when Frank calls."

"I suggest you prepare to head back out to that area, and be ready. US and UK naval ships are already patrolling just south of there and have been for a few weeks. Planned naval exercises with other allies are already going on. I will message you shortly with details. Keep me in the loop."

"Ok, but China may not welcome us with open arms in the South China Sea if we need to get close to their shores."

"That depends."

Cross ends the call and sees a message from Xing so he calls him. "Liang, this is Daniel and perfect timing."

"Good evening, Daniel. You saw my message?"

"Yes."

"I have friends high up in the China Communist Party. They connected a handful of political members of the politburo with Wu. They were arrested yesterday and tossed in Jail."

"Wow, that is quite revealing information."

"This is privileged, my friend."

"I'm already aware of that. I need a huge favour, now that we are on the phone," and he explains his request.

"That is an enormous request."

"We know and the West will look favourably if this can be granted. We need the window."

"Give me a few hours. I should have an answer by the time you wake up."

"Thank you, Liang,"

39

Concurrent Missions Active

Granfield had messaged in the early hours of the morning. He is to head to Stansted for an aircraft waiting for him. A car will pick him up outside at seven-thirty a.m. So, upon waking, Cross gathers his bag and walks downstairs.

He checks his phone. Xing has messaged, approving Cross's request, and he smiles.

On his way to the airport, he calls Jennings. "Heading to the South China Sea from Stansted but I don't know which part yet. They located the container ships GSC has been building, they think anyway. At least that was the precision CIA used last night." He laughs.

"Yeah well, about as precise as any of the other shit." Jennings adds cynically.

"Moore worked on his exclusive domain as promised and delivered last night. Now it is up to you."

"Yes, I'll be there this afternoon. Safe travels and I will update you."

"I've been dying to ask, where did you source the hooligans from?"

Jennings chuckles. "The local jail. We offered them free beer and a pub meal along with revocation of their minor offenses. It wasn't difficult."

It is after midnight in Wilson's territory but Cross calls anyway.

"We got the coding to work. Now we're tracking the satellites to gain mapping coordinates. We should have longitude and latitude angles very soon."

"I want to download a patch of software for you to test. This is very important because it has been installed already out in the field. It will be in use today and I would prefer your verification. I will explain later."

"Sure, send it here." Wilson forwards instructions to a secure server.

Cross messages Moore Jr. with the information and he returns confirmation.

The military driver navigates airport security and drops Cross off at the bottom of the ramp. He heads for the stairs and climbs into a Boeing C-17 military transporter that had been waiting for his arrival. He surveys the SAS soldiers before taking a seat.

Hours into the flight Taylor messages. She confirms her position in New York and Cross acknowledges his destination. Taylor teases. 'Somewhere in the South China Sea is a little nebulous, lol'. He likes her. 'I brought my parachute, snorkel and rubber flippers, lol', messages Cross. The light-hearted banter is welcome.

Halfway into the long flight Jennings calls. "How is the flight?"

"Not very exciting but the choice of alcohol is top-notch, for military."

"I went to Downing Street this afternoon and watched the prime minister and her entourage of ministers. I didn't notice anything unusual in their behaviour, at least nothing beyond the usual ignorance and naivety. She did confirm the UN Security Council's agenda with the Press and will leave for New York tomorrow. She intends to meet up with your president Wednesday."

"Wait, he isn't my president. I didn't vote for him, not now that he seems to be jumping off a political cliff. Did you look closely?" changing subjects quickly.

"Yes. Good luck over there and be safe."

Wilson calls from somewhere in Vancouver. "I got the patch and we installed it. As far as we can tell, it works."

"As far as you can tell?" enquires Cross.

"No. As far as *we* can tell, Daniel. I'm an engineer. I always toss in a disclaimer."

"I'm glad people still retain their humour."

Wu is in a conference room full of lieutenants. On a screen against one of the walls is an image of the UN Building in New York City. Someone has scribbled notes on the slide used by the projector. On another screen is a map of the city. This is what he has been building for. Years of parental abuse and systemic failures are about to write an enormous check.

"We have our people ready, sir," said his first lieutenant. "The UK Prime Minister has already confirmed a meeting with the US President on Wednesday, Washington time."

"Good."

"The Council will meet Thursday morning, US East Coast time. Most Heads of State have stated their intentions to attend. Iran and North Korea are two that have abstained. South Korea is still seething as they keep finding bodies, sir."

"No problem with operations, Lieutenant?"

"No, sir. Everything looks good."

"Nothing from Scotland?"

"Two security personnel and a civilian worker shot and killed.

No break-in, nothing stolen, no authority figures. It all turned silent very quickly."

"There was crowd violence at a soccer game Saturday."

"Yes, sir. Moore Junior reached out and contacted us. He is fine and we have been monitoring his pattern and observe no change."

"Too many coincidences to sound credible and I don't like it. Keep me informed of any new developments." With that Wu stands up and departs the room.

Wilson messages the coordinates they obtained for the satellite feeds so Cross picks up his phone. "Did you receive the latitude and longitude parameters, David?"

"Yes. We have a team working on this. You are four hours away. We are coordinating with Operational Command in the area and will get back to you. It is likely we will use one of the islands close by where you need to transfer to a ship. I'll message you."

"Before you go, we got a conditional forty-eight hour window to operate an armed military mission unimpeded in the South China Sea."

Granfield is stunned. "How did you get that?"

40

USS Montgomery

Cross lands at an airport but has no idea where. The opening of the cabin door draws in moist salt air so he knows it is close to seawater. The emergence of the sun attempting to peak over the eastern horizon as he walks off the C-17 is indicative of early morning, somewhere. Transference to a nearby helicopter with a few other personnel happens with haste and it soon departs.

Sitting next to him is a military officer. "I am an officer of the US Navy, Dr. Cross. You can call me Officer Giles, or just Giles. I have been assigned your escort to take you to the Command Centre on board the USS Montgomery."

"That's an aircraft carrier, one of the largest recently commissioned by the US Navy."

"Yes, sir."

"Oh boy."

"This is an Apache AH-64 attack chopper with extended-range capability. This will be a one hundred and thirty minute flight approximately, sir."

"Where are we?"

"Somewhere over water, sir, and we are armed with missiles for added security."

He turns to face him and stares, "You people are hilarious."

"Sorry, sir. I was given strict orders."

Two hours pass and Cross feels the journey coming to an end as the Apache slows. It doesn't need to descend since it skipped across the sea. Looming larger as they approach, Cross glimpses the monstrous aircraft carrier beginning to fill the chopper's windows as it ploughs through the almost-calm seas.

"Jesus. If that doesn't intimidate the enemy, nothing will. Look at the size of that thing."

"Yes, sir," is all Giles says.

On the aft are Seahawks and one stealth helicopter whilst forward of those are lined F-18 Hornets and F-35 Lightning fighter jets. The chopper banks and slows as it drops onto the deck. Personnel are on hand to tether the aircraft to the rolling ship as the door opens.

Cross follows Giles as he heads off through a doorway in the bulkhead, through some corridors and up steep, narrow staircases. Finally Giles enters a large room with a long table and military people sitting along both sides. On one side wall are maps, charts, pictures and scratched drawings pinned to boards. On the other wall is a maze of monitors displaying war plans with electronics sitting on rows of desks.

Cross' presence immediately halts discussions and the commander walks up to him with his hand out.

"Dr. Cross, welcome aboard, sir. I am Commander Doolittle and it is a pleasure to finally be acquainted. Your accomplishments are becoming legendary." They shake hands.

"The honour is mine, Commander Doolittle. Please call me Daniel," and he smiles. "I don't know about my achievements but if you hear me scream, then I've come across another robot." The room erupts. "I am sick of the damn things."

The commander introduces the group and then gets to the business at hand. "I am not going to stand here and praise this gentleman.

You all have his dossier and briefs of what we are dealing with. We have a small window in which we need to act. Dr. Cross, I mean Daniel, please fill us in."

Cross spends the next hour going over their findings. The room is dead silent as they take in the unprecedented material with some disbelief. Luckily he had created a thumb drive on the flight over and is displaying a few facts pictorially to help support this information. He knows already the military requires evidentiary documentation and it makes his story more credible and compelling, although he is having a hard time believing most of it himself, even as he regurgitates it all. He is thankful Wilson sent him pictures of Feng to demonstrate their capability and enforce the realities of the technology involved.

"That is a clone?" the admiral asks in a stunned tone.

"Yes. Feng was real but we hope these people are still alive. Clones are being recreated from the real people they replace, Admiral."

"This is staggering. The details, the clarity, the perfection. I mean how would you know if you walked by one on the street?"

Some of the participants in the room look shocked and their mouths hang open, possibly without them knowing. Cross sees some shaking of heads as he speaks.

"That is the question." He steps back to take a breather. "This Thursday, East Coast Time, the UN will convene to host a Security Council conference." Cross continues his closure statement. "It is my belief this is where Wu and his organisation will strike, if they haven't already. I feel they program these clones to enter life normally and no one will know until it is too late.

"The coordinates for their perceived location based on satellite calculations have been passed on. This is why we are here. By the way, how are you hiding this mammoth vessel, Commander?"

"Actually, as convenience would have it, we are already involved in naval warfare exercises in this region. It is quite an easy task to camouflage what we're doing."

"Some things are hard to comprehend, even as we learn them."

"Luck has played a part in many a war, Daniel." The commander switches on his serious tone. "I am about to reveal what our intentions are and how we will carry them out. These plans are tentative and fluid. Flexibility will be paramount so backup contingencies are required. We have no idea what to expect so we must be prepared at any moment to adapt and not vacillate. We do not have much time."

Just as Cross walks away from the Command Centre for a break, his phone rings. "Frank, what do you have?"

"Good news. We've tested the software you asked Moore Junior to develop. It does what it is supposed to do and we can confirm this now. It is quite brilliant actually."

"This's fantastic. It has already been installed in the field so this is reassuring to learn."

"Good luck, Daniel. Let me know what else you need."

Cross messages Taylor.

'Where are you?' she texts back.

'No idea. On an aircraft carrier somewhere. How is NYC?'

'Heads of State are arriving already. UK Prime Minister arrives tomorrow.'

'We don't have much time left, must go. Will message with update. Got your pass for UN Building?'

'Yes. Be careful.'

'You too.'

He messages Sedaghi. He just wants to hear her message, metaphorically speaking, but really desperate to hold her.

41

Operation Countdown

"**Yes, I know** there is a flaw with the clones. You are telling me what I already know because they keep fucking terminating." Wu can hardly tolerate listening to the person on the other end. He is angry. "Well, fix the fucking thing. You had the time to deal with this and stop telling me what is obvious to even the most stupid person," he screams, before slamming the phone down in exasperation.

He stomps out of his office communicating silently to anyone when he is at his most dangerous. He had received a request to head over to the communications room so that's where he goes next. He steps into another vast room full of manned workstations. Behind one massive glass wall are banks of computer servers with lights flashing, tapes spinning and drives whining, all interconnected with miles of cabling. Underneath are rows of large cooling fans. The hot air draws away with the aid of huge, fanned ceiling vents attached to aluminium conduits that exit the room, where it is then analysed, processed, filtered, cooled and recirculated.

The communications manager sees Wu enter and walks over to greet him. "Sir, we just received a brief communication from Feng."

Wu knows every facet of the operation. "Wait, Feng was designed as a replacement at ISC in Shanghai. It was never activated."

"Yes, sir."

"Then explain."

"We have no explanation." This was the wrong answer. "When Feng was re-activated, it went searching for its server. The software has been designed to detect if a search-signal is tampered with or isn't coded right, but that wasn't the case here."

Already at a boiling point, he asks her to elaborate.

"Wherever the signal was derived, it was coded correctly. Embedded in their transmit signal was an accurate identification code which our computers filtered out as being Feng."

"And?" Wu asks.

"Once our system verified and confirmed it, it transmitted back a coded acknowledgment signal to the clone, sir."

"No one bothered to tell our massive operating system costing several hundred million dollars that this subject needs to be terminated in its' database?"

"We never received an order dictating those terms, sir."

Wu is visibly livid as the blood veins in his head seem about to lose their natural ability to withstand the pressure. "So what more can you tell me?"

"We have not been able to trace where the originating transmission came from, sir. We are working on it but it is a very weak signal." The manager is becoming more nervous and shaken.

"You mean they have developed the same technology we spent years secretly designing and implementing?"

"I cannot precisely answer that question, sir."

"Can they determine where the receive signal originated?"

"They will be experiencing the same problems we have detecting very weak signals."

"You better be right since your life depends on it." He marches out the room looking for heads to roll.

The second lieutenant arrives in one of the empty office spaces off a conference room. Wu looks at him. "You are promoted to operations manager. Please have the man you are replacing moved out of here." He kicks at the first lieutenant's still-warm body lying on the floor in blood and walks away.

The operational aspects of the mission are drilled into Cross and repeatedly verified and questioned over and over to the point of tedium. The recent exploits and demanding travel have taken a toll. One more mission to go, he reminds himself, but this is the biggest of them all. There's a knock on his cabin door.

"Come in."

The commander walks in the room and Cross immediately climbs off the bed and stands up.

"At ease, Daniel. I'm happy to see you resting, sir."

"This is all mind-numbing stuff, Commander, but we are close."

"Yes, we are, thanks to you."

"A lot of people involved in this. I don't deserve all the credit."

"Of course you won't admit that, because that is what makes you special. Rear Admiral Morgan called me before your arrival on this carrier and filled me in a little. He sends his regards and hopes you are recovering. He wishes you a successful mission to end all this."

"Thank you, Commander. Recovery is an optimistic word," and laughs painfully. "I am not sure I ever will but please pass on my regards to the rear admiral. He was a good man to me."

"I came in to wish you luck. They have given us the green light and our mission commences operations in the early hours.

"We have already started naval manoeuvres to get equipment and people into positions but these will take hours. You have two hours before you need to leave, sir, so do what you need to do. As you're aware, you have a long journey ahead.

"I also came in to see if you have questions about anything."

"Yes, Commander. When did I actually sign up for this?" He has to laugh.

"Humour tells me you are nervous and that is a good emotion. I would be more worried if you weren't. There are some serious unknowns and we will have to transition as we encounter them." He lifts up his hands and shrugs the shoulders. "This is a little different from your past operations but not by much. You handled those exceptionally well so you can handle this one." He smiles, shakes his hand and then gives him a bear hug. "This is not normal protocol in the military, Daniel. I will deny it ever happened. Since you are a contracted civilian, I will have leniency and only lose half my pension."

The commander walks out the door and closes it behind him. Fuck, thinks Cross. He sits back on the bed, puts his head in his hands and finds himself in a cold sweat. He really needs an emotional release.

After some minutes of self-pity, he calls Granfield. "We have the green light. I leave with my assigned crew in a little over ninety minutes."

"Yes, we are in our command centre also and a select few at the Pentagon have us tapped in. We'll know everything that is going on as it transmits to us. The White House knows nothing about anything. The secrecy within the confines of government has been remarkable. Even the UK government knows nothing. It is astonishing really when you think about it but we leave them to focus on missing ships, disruption to world trade and the UN conference. In any event, we cannot trust them until this is over."

"I don't care. I just want to get the bugger."

"That reminds me, we have someone scheduled to be at the White House when the UK Prime Minister arrives. They will update us when the press conference starts."

"Great. I want their reaction as soon as you get it."

"Yes, of course. Good luck, Daniel. Don't do anything stupid. Wait, let me rescind that. Of course you will," and laughs his head off.

They end the call. Cross needed the laughs and Granfield does it every time.

Cross sends a message to Jennings. 'A CIA Agent will be in Washington for the press conference tomorrow.'

'Great. How are you doing?'

'Our operation commences in a few hours. We're ready.'

'Good luck, Daniel,' and ends the connection.

The next person is Taylor.

'How are you, Daniel?' she texted.

'Never felt better, ha-ha. Be ready when I tell you.'

'You must be nervous, I can tell. Hang in there because I know you have got this. Fuck these people, Daniel. They don't deserve our empathy or sympathy.'

'For sure.'

'I am ready for these morons. Good luck and be safe, my friend.'

'Thank you. You too.'

He sends his last message to Moore Jr. before he prepares.

42

The Island Coordinates

"Mr. Wu, we have targets entering the zone again."

"Is this still part of the annual wargame exercises between the allied nations?"

"They are heading toward an island mass three hundred miles south, sir. Computer-mapping their course directs the path around the other side of it, and away from us."

"What are they?"

"A flotilla of twenty ships, mostly American and British with one each from Australia, New Zealand, Philippines, France and Germany. There are a couple of aircraft carriers also."

"These operations have been going on for a month. Do you see anything different, Lieutenant?"

"No, sir. You asked that we update you."

"Yes. We will also use these targets to shelter what we're doing. Keep them locked on and watch carefully."

Wu puts his internal phone down and picks up the satellite mobile. "Are we set for our operations in Washington and New York?"

"Yes, sir. Our soldiers are in place and they are ready for the plan to be implemented."

"The UK Prime Minister arrives in a few hours. Be ready."

"Yes, sir."

"Verify the coordinates. Come on, we must find it," shouts the captain.

Cross and the six Navy Seals left USS Montgomery in a stealth mini-submarine twelve hours earlier. He is tired. They all are. For the past hour they have been traversing a small area of the South China Sea matching the coordinates Wilson had provided. They aren't seeing anything. Their technologically advanced batteries, self-charging from the motion through the water, have enough charge for some time but their bodies don't, not to sustain this level of intensity submerged in such a small craft.

"Give me the coordinates again," Cross asks.

He takes the sheet of paper and analyses the numbers more carefully.

"Captain, the mini-sub has reached its coordinated destination based on the longitude and latitude numbers we were provided but cannot find any island," said an officer in the command centre on USS Montgomery.

"We couldn't either, on our maps. We thought Wu must have built a whole new island hidden from satellite imagery and they would find it. We didn't have the time to work this out before they sailed. Keep working on it. We cannot have them sitting out there untouchable in the middle of a vast sea."

Cross looks at the numbers. Something is odd, he thinks. Then he tries to remember a deficiency in Wilson at University. What the hell was it, dammit? He scratches his head. It has been decades but it was distinctive. Then it hits him but he has to hide emotions in the sub. He grabs a pen and scribbles a change to the latitude coordinate.

"Captain, try this instead," and hands him the piece of paper.

The commander takes it, looks and then turns to Cross.

"Why, sir?"

"Please, I will tell you later."

"This takes us another hour or two north."

"Yes. Please trust me."

The captain turns to the navigator, verifies the new coordinates and instructs him to alter course. Approaching the new designation, some disturbance on the radar appears.

"We found something, Captain," says the navigator. "It is small."

"Can we look at it?" asks Cross, now excited and shot with a burst of energy.

"Yes," replies the captain. "Please slow to five knots. Let's keep our stealth capability and slowly raise the periscope."

As it rises a monitor turns on and immediately images from a camera mounted on top come into view. Then, suddenly a different image appears as the camera extends through the water and breaks the surface. Now there is what looks like a small island off in the distance, perhaps five or so miles away. However, below the sea is an expansive rock that spreads out, as islands normally do. It looks too artificial to Cross.

"Can you zoom in?" he asks.

As a larger image of the island emerges, it is starting to come into focus.

"Look at the platform on the left of the image. It is flat with what looks like perfect vegetation and spreads out and away from the main island rock. It could be a landing strip. It is also difficult to make out but are those camouflaged tree trunks supporting a canopy? This is it, I am sure." He cannot control his energy level and wants to leap out of the sub's hatch and annihilate them all. "Can you turn up the radar intensity, turn our high beams on and we all shout hello?" Cross is ecstatic.

There is light outside but what is left will fade soon as the day moves toward late afternoon.

"Can you find an island close by or at least something we can hide behind?" the captain says to the navigator. "We have to coordinate our next strategic move since timing is of the essence."

"Give me a few minutes, Captain."

"You were right, Cross. A trillion dollar military machine couldn't figure it out."

"Sometimes it takes more than a computer, sir." Cross exudes confidence.

"Commander Doolittle, they have located an island at this latitude." The officer hands him a note.

He looks at the data on the paper. "How the hell did they figure that?"

"Cross changed the coordinates."

"Now we start the countdown, Officer. Do it."

"There is a tiny radar disturbance indicating something a few miles north from here, Captain. There are allegedly some clusters of land masses in this area." He points on the radar screen and grins.

"We don't need anything big, but we need to wait about four hours before we can go in. Timing is important because of the scheduled UN conference."

"Yes, Captain."

"Let's do it."

As they approach a small rock cluster, they guide the sub around the opposite side, carefully navigating through a dangerous terrain. It slowly pumps out ballast and rises to the surface. Now they can visually navigate in order to secure their cover and avoid the seabed.

"We wait for the signal," says the captain.

Cross needs to stretch so opens the hatch and exits the sea-going vessel. He sits on the small conning tower and marvels at the angled surfaces of the software-designed outer skin that prevents detection. The special materials covered in anti-radar paint add to the stealth capability. He sits and ponders whilst looking at the sinking sun spraying a glistening stream of light across the ever-moving water surface.

The commander is waiting for confirmation on USS Montgomery. He receives it, Cross is in place, and authorises Phase 2 to commence.

"Acknowledge our receipt and tell them to stand by, perhaps two hours. We are moving some substantial hardware around without drawing attention, yet."

"Yes, Commander."

Sitting outside the sub, Cross sees messages on his phone, missed whilst being underwater. One from Granfield mentions the UK Prime Minister meeting the US President. Everything went ok except the president is still pushing his strange shipping trade agenda. Otherwise everything looks normal.

The next message is cryptic from Moore Jr. 'All done' were the only words and Cross smiles. He just hopes his plan works.

The last message is from Sadeghi. 'I love you' is all she said and Cross' heart starts pumping. He doesn't need an excuse to risk his life but her words have only empowered him. "I am not going to die honey, again," he whispers to himself.

43

Takedown Begins

Wu is in the operations room staring at the large screen on the wall. Its' pictorial focus is on the UN Building in New York City. The conference is hours away but he sees the city already preparing security-measures for the world's dignitaries.

Just then someone shouts, "Aircraft in the area."

Wu's concentration momentarily disrupts as he spins around and runs over to the radar operator.

"Sir, a formation of aircraft has entered our quadrant. They are on the fringes and not heading this way, yet."

Wu looks at the monitor to decipher the information. "It looks like they're on a path going away from us but alert the necessary forces. Turn off all external lighting."

"The electronic shield is on, sir. They cannot see the island. It doesn't exist."

"Let's hope you are correct,"

Wu goes back to monitoring preparation for the UN Security Council meeting.

"Let's go," shouts the captain to his crew. "Our armed forces are in place."

The mini-sub is readied and the last man in secures the hatch. The surreal emptiness outside is replaced with perceptible warmth from low-level lighting inside. The engine is energised as it makes its way out into deep, open water.

In the cabin there is significant activity as Cross watches the Navy Seals prepare for their part of the mission. Cross put himself together already and sits in his black amphibious gear counting down the minutes. His heart is leaping backwards and forwards across his chest.

The six Seals are ready and sit in two rows against the side of the sub as it powers in dead-silence through the night waters. Cross can see the adrenaline and testosterone levels in their eyes. Their confidence is dripping which adds a comfort level he needs. They are huge men and ready to wreak havoc. One of them looks over at Cross and sticks a thumb up.

Whilst in hiding they had scanned through images of the island and picked out a possible area for their clandestine disembarkation. It is all vague because no one knows for sure.

"Ten minutes," the captain shouts as the true countdown begins.

Cross was nervous before but now his nerves are at top alert. He is ready, for what God only knows.

"Five minutes," comes the next call.

The contingent of selected mercenaries, including Cross, starts getting ready. Cross feels the sub slow and the camera rise. He pulls out a needle and stabs it in his right thigh. He winces but not for long.

"Slow and to port five degrees," the captain tells the navigator. "Someone get on top."

One of the Seals stands and opens the hatch slowly. He scans their proposed landing area and drops back down.

"Looks good enough. Twenty yards, captain."

"Slower, two knots."

The sub slows and then there is a small thud as it hits shallow water.

"Go," yells the captain.

All six men stand in unison and then expeditiously exit in an orderly fashion. Everything impresses Cross as he is the last to leave, but not before the captain pats him on the back.

"Good luck, sir. You know the orders and we will be waiting."

"Thank you, Captain," and he exits.

They step off the sub onto landfill rock and a fake shoreline. As they do so the sub reverses thrust, disappearing under the water. In front is a long flat area hosting trees and vegetation seemingly artificially arranged. It is the area Cross first pointed out. The soldiers quickly scope the area, hiding behind large bushes.

A huge canopy prevents light from the half-moon and clear skies revealing the island. A few stray rays of moonlight are able to provide a small glimpse of what they are looking at. The team puts on special night goggles. What looked small before doesn't when up close and personal, thinks Cross. In fact, it is quite large. Cross swallows hard.

"The main island is to our right. This area looks to have been added for aircraft and over there looks like a main entrance," murmurs the commander.

It isn't precise because they can only guess based on what they see. Through their goggles they observe men patrolling the shorelines.

"We need to neutralise this threat first, men. I have counted around twenty so let's spread out and remove them. We will rendezvous back here. Cross, remain behind. We have been ordered to protect you."

"Yes, Commander."

As he says that, the six soldiers dart out from the bushes and spread out on the platform. Cross watches a Seal slice the throat of the closest patrolling soldier as surprise has given this mission hope. Then he drags the dead body to the side of the runway and shoves it into the sea.

Cross takes his time to look at his surroundings and gather some thoughts. He processes the information because he might need it. He knows they have to enter the complex and looks at security off in the distance. He doesn't see that much of it because surely they are not expecting anyone to sabotage this facility. They would have to find it first, a seemingly fruitless task made more difficult by the fact that no one knows of its existence, until now.

Within ten minutes the first soldier arrives back. Cross doesn't hear him until he's right next to him. Damn Navy Seals. He is carrying some things.

"Put this on, sir. I removed it from one of their guards," and hands it to him. "But stay down; otherwise one of our own might kill you." He grins. "Here is his weapon and munition packs."

Cross doesn't question him and slips it on over his skin-tight suit and hunkers down. The remaining soldiers appear one after the other.

"Surprise is always a key element in clandestine warfare." The commander sounds happy so far. "Well done, men."

"Two aircraft are peeling off, sir. They are heading in this direction."

Wu runs over and confirms their observations. Two dots on the radar monitor have indeed separated from their formation and are now heading toward his island.

"They don't know we exist so let's be cautious and inform the soldiers. Get the missiles armed and ready but you cannot fire until

I tell you. Their launch would announce this island."

"Yes, sir."

To his right Cross sees one of the main entrance doors start to open. He points as the men see what he is seeing.

As the door opens, they can see an expansive entranceway into a long, arched tunnel. Running out of it are armed soldiers who, following Wu's orders, are going to prepare the missile launchers.

"Holy shit," says Cross.

"Something like that," adds another soldier.

"This is our cue. Cross, your turn now. This is it. We will be with you, per instructions."

"Yes, Commander."

Cross steps away from their hiding place, wraps the munitions belt across his shoulder and hurries down the runway holding the Chinese-made assault rifle. Behind him are the Navy Seals but having to hide as they progress. Cross' dark grey uniform helps him to blend with the others crowding the tunnel entrance wearing the exact same thing. He moves in between armed soldiers and no one even questions him as he enters the complex. He is startled but most seem to be robots.

Farther down the tunnel he sees it opening up into a chamber but to the left is a sign pointing to a door. The sign reads 'Research & Development'. Built into the rock next to the door are windows. He peers between slats in the blinds and sees interrogation tables. Behind those is a large window looking down a hallway of some sort lined with more doors. Next to the window is a door leading to the hallway.

Cross opens the first door and enters the interrogation room. He looks around before opening the second. It opens to a narrow corridor full of what appear to be cell rooms on either side. He doesn't understand where the guards disappeared to. He can see all chairs are empty. Cautiously he walks down with gun in hand and glares through the small window in the first cell's door. When he sees the person on the other side blankly staring at him, he nearly has a heart attack.

44

Missing Dignitaries

Cross fleetingly freezes in time and cannot move. The person lying on a small bed set against the back wall on the other side of the door suddenly changes the whole dynamics of this mission.

Cross blinks and snaps out of the trance. He has to think and think fast. He walks down the narrow hallway and looks in other cells. Then he finds the reason he is here. Dr. Moore is lying on his make-shift bed but it is obvious he is in trouble. Torture marks are visible on parts of the body Cross can see and he is frail. Thick-rimmed glasses rest on a table next to him.

He moves down to the next cell and views a sight he doesn't want to see. Her back is against the far wall and one of Wu's guards is attacking. Clothes are partially torn and she is trying to push him away whilst screaming but there is no sound. Terror can do that.

Cross sees the door didn't close properly so quietly enters. The victim sees him but he is fast and overwhelming. His Taekwondo training relies on mental strength to paralyse a victim before he is disabled. But Cross is done with that silent shit. A blow using his left arm to the attacker's neck snaps it and kills him instantly as he drops to the floor.

"I am Daniel Cross, Mrs. Moore. I'm working on getting you

out of here."

She runs up and hugs him. "We knew you would come."

"We don't have much time."

He looks around for something to cover her with. Not finding anything, he pulls off the uniform on the dead man and hands it to her. "Sorry, all I can find." He searches for the device that opens the rooms and finds it, yanking it from around the guard's neck.

"This will help. Is there a back way?"

"Yes, down the hallway, there is a room that will take you to a loading dock facility. From there it leads to the outside."

"I need a signal on my phone so let's move. We will come back for the rest when I've contacted my people."

She leads the way whilst Cross has his gun ready. The door seems locked leading to the dock so he uses the security card. It doesn't work and his patience is zero, so he shoots the damn lock. He quickly pushes the door open and sees others running to intercept them. Their movement dictates who they are so he aims for their right cheeks and down they go.

"I can tell you I am done with these fucking robots. Next time become a horticulturalist." Cross shouts at Mrs. Moore.

He searches for a camera system, finds it and shoots that next.

He looks for a power button to open the rollup and presses it. Once there is enough space to crawl under, he stops it and heads outside with Mrs. Moore. He has signal on the phone again.

"Commander, plans have changed. Get the mini-sub back here fast and have it come to the northwest side of the island rock," as he talks a mile a minute. "There they will find a loading dock."

"Yes, sir." Sensing Cross' state of mind he asks no question.

"We need to remove people off this fucked-up island before we can fulfill our intended mission," as he tells him who he has found.

"Jesus Christ," he replies in some disheveled English dialect.

"This changes everything here and we need to delay temporarily the UN conference somehow. Let me work on that. Doolittle needs to delay the operation. We need more time here. Did you toss all the dead guards into the sea?"

"No."

"I suggest getting their uniforms. It worked for me as I walked straight into the tunnel. I doubt we will have the same luck but worth trying. Most I encountered are robots," and spends the next few minutes going over what he wants from the commander.

"Ok, I am on it."

"I have no signal in the building unless I can tap into their network. Even our satellite phones don't go through solid rock. Let me work on this too."

"Keep me posted."

Cross disconnects and messages Moore Jr.

'I found your parents. Need your help.'

'What do you require?'

Cross sends a cryptic message going over what he needs.

'We can do that.'

'I know you can. You will know the plan when it happens.'

'Ok.'

Cross texts Granfield next and goes over what he has discovered and the consequential change in plans.

'Shit,' is his answer. Cross realises nothing else is required. Shock will be evident everywhere.

45

Final Phase

Cross is back in the loading area and finds a gun. "Do you know how to use one of these?"

"No," replies Mrs. Moore.

"Good. You'll learn. Stay here."

He removes a knife and runs off to the cell where the dead guard is. He chops his right hand off, runs back to a guard quarters and uses the hand and security card to enter. Inside he finds a workstation whose password is already working.

Cross goes searching for a network name and finds it. He removes his phone and checks for available networks and is relieved when it finds it. He types in one of the passwords Moore Jr. had given him. It doesn't work.

"Shit."

He types in the second on the list and the same thing.

"Damn."

The seventh on the list works and Cross is into the island's system. He now has telephonic access and he starts to breathe again, at least for now.

He messages the commander. 'Connection live.'

'Sub on way. 20 mins,' comes the response.

'Going to get others.'

'We are coming. Doolittle knows.'

Cross leaves the guard room and runs down the hallway. He tries the security card and it doesn't work.

Pre-occupation known as tunnel-vision grips the people in the operations room. Wu is seeing his plan coming to fruition as the UN Security Council meeting commences. His people are providing a live feed of proceedings as the secretary general is giving the opening remarks.

"Sir, the two allied planes are still in the quadrant and edging closer as they circle in and out of our zone," says the first lieutenant. "Security is active and the missiles armed."

"Good."

"We lost the cameras in the docking area and are working on them." He was purposely ignoring what may have really happened.

"Update me," but Wu's mind is clearly on the live feed out of New York. Everything else seems superfluous.

"Yes, sir," as he turns around and walks away, relieved he doesn't have a bullet in his forehead.

He hears another guard approaching so hides behind the door in the empty cell. As the man walks past, Cross sneaks up behind him and sticks a handgun in his temple, shoving the free hand across the mouth.

"Open all the cell doors."

The guard offers no resistance and does as he is ordered. The electronic locks de-activate with thuds one by one and as they do the drugged, fatigued and tortured occupants start exiting their respective rooms. Cross just stands there not quite believing what he is seeing. To him it portrays the scene from a horror movie. He removes his hand from the guard's mouth and places it on the side of the head. Using the gun for support, he twists the head and breaks his neck. The deceased guard drops to the floor.

He looks at the gathered group but doesn't see who he came for. He goes to the room and Moore is still on the bench. Cross picks him up, puts on his glasses and carries him into the hallway.

"Cross?" The sound of a frightened, distressed man spits the word out behind him. Cross turns around.

"Yes, and I know who you are, sir. We need to get out of here because there isn't time. Someone please help me."

As he says that, the man Cross knows and another of the captors relieve him and take over.

"Follow me, quickly."

They head to the docking area and he helps them crawl under the rollup. Out onto the loading platform Cross sees a conning tower coming into view. He would kneel down and kiss it if he could. The sub motors to the dock and Cross watches as the hatch opens.

"Good evening," says the captain.

"Dammit. I would kiss you but we have witnesses." He laughs.

The captain looks at the group of people they are rescuing and it leaves him speechless.

"There really isn't anything to say except get these people out of here quickly."

The more physically able are first and Cross helps Moore be loaded on last.

"Get going, Captain," he orders as the hatch is locked.

As the sub disappears into the depths, Cross hears commotion behind the rollup and then the motor turns on as the door starts to rise.

"Here we go. Fuck these people."

Hiding just to the side of the door, he prepares the rifle. He suddenly leaps into view and starts indiscriminately firing at anyone and anything in its path as his anger brews. They drop like flies.

He steps back and pulls out the phone. "Commander, go," is all he says.

He messages Moore Jr, 'Now.'

The final message is to Taylor, 'Watch and get ready.'

It's time to move. Cross puts his phone away and heads for the hallway. Before he exits, he sets the clock and leaves behind one of the smart nuclear bombs the commander strapped on him. He hopes forty-five minutes will give them sufficient time and coordinates his watch timer. He runs through the hallway back toward the tunnel. Entering the tunnel area, there are still security and personnel running all over. Cross suddenly remembers what Doolittle had told him.

"The art of deception."

Almost immediately he sees the Seals. Cross waves them over and points deeper into the rock.

"There is the main facility. Somewhere in that direction must be the operations area. It seems our uniforms are working. I don't think they programmed the robots to look for mercenaries in matching clothes," and chuckles. "Dumb shits. Watch out though, some are human."

"We will spread out and rendezvous where we came on shore," adds the commander.

"We have less than forty minutes."

As they spread out, Cross heads for the large chamber carved into the rock.

Wu is looking at the huge screen. He seems to be fixated on UN events and not really aware of what is going on around him. The first lieutenant is afraid; Wu made them all fear him, but he shouts again.

"Sir, there has been shooting in the loading dock area. All the security locks on the cell blocks have been opened."

Wu is watching the UK Prime Minister give her speech. He looks at his watch. "Her speech is too long. What is she doing? Contact the people in New York. I need answers now," he screams.

The lieutenant shrugs his shoulders and runs to get that information.

A Seal enters the huge computer area and fixes a smart bomb under a desk, then walks out. Other events are distracting people and they are not seeing what is going on. Another Seal installs one in a conference room.

As Cross climbs the metal stairs toward the walkway, a human passes him running down. Something tells him to turn around. As he does, he sees the subject stop running and turn. The shocked expression on his face alarms him.

"Cross?" is the last word he says.

He holds up his gun and pulls the trigger. The first lieutenant drops and tumbles down the remaining stairs. "Yes, it is."

This activity is alerting others around him and he needs to finish. He starts running up the stairs as he surveys the vast space. "Where the hell is the heartbeat of this place," he asks himself.

He looks at his watch. Twenty-nine minutes don't seem long enough. He looks around and notices a few Seals walking fast. It's a bizarre setting.

Wu isn't happy. "She is talking too long and where is the first lieutenant?" he shouts.

He takes out his mobile and tries to call his contact in New York. There is no answer as the line rings and rings. He is getting irritated and frustrated and tosses the phone across the room.

The operations officer walks up to him, "We found subjects terminated on the loading dock, sir. Moore is gone."

"What do you mean he is gone?"

"His cell is empty, along with the others, sir."

"Go find them. They cannot have escaped, not from this island."

The scared officer runs off.

On one radar screen is a very faint blip heading for the island. Fortunately, the radar's operator is too fixated watching another screen with two blips circling in and out of the zone. He doesn't warn anyone.

Cross' phone vibrates so he steps into a doorway and checks it. It is the commander.

'C-130 arrives in fifteen minutes.'

'Ok.'

Cross climbs more stairs and finally reaches an area that looks promising, but it is too late. Their activity and clandestine operation appear no longer secret. Somewhere below he hears gun shots and a small explosion.

"Shit."

He runs into a huge room stacked with electronics, workstations and robots. This is it, he thinks to himself. Off on one wall is the massive screen Wu has been watching and Cross sees the UK Prime Minister giving her elongated speech.

"Brilliant, Graeme," he mutters to himself.

Cross quickly assesses his odds. A man in uniform comes running toward him so he shoots. This startles everyone in the area. He looks for Wu but doesn't see him anywhere. He doesn't have time to dwell on it.

He quickly removes another smart bomb from his belt and sets the timer to twenty minutes. As he runs out the door he lobs it into a side room no one seems to be occupying.

Surrounding him is mass confusion, fear and panic as he bolts for the stairs. It is chaos with humans and robots going in all directions. Alarms are flashing everywhere but interestingly no alarm sirens. He hears a few more gun shots in the tunnel but runs in that direction anyway. It is the only way out he knows.

No it isn't, he reminds himself.

46

Evacuation Route

The C-130 gunship approaches using the coordinates entered into the autopilot and a small island comes into view. They send a message to the Seals down below and the commander confirms.

"Here we go," says the pilot to co-pilot, "And switching to manual mode. I have control."

"You have control."

The machine guns mounted in the wings blow through the fake vegetation on the runway and provide clearing for the plane to land.

"Five hundred yards." The co-pilot is calling out the important landing parameters.

They see a few trails of bullets directed at them coming from the side of the strip so they spray that area with return fire.

"Fifty feet, forty, thirty, twenty," as the Hercules touches down.

The four engines reverse-thrust to rapidly burn off speed as Marines leap out of the opening rear cargo door and spread along the runway before it comes to a complete stop. The pilot turns 180 degrees and pulls the aircraft to a halt. The engines remain with above-idle power in preparation for a rapid departure.

Seen beyond the end of the runway are six Navy Seals exiting the tunnel and coming towards them. However, one is injured and being supported by two others. The Marines see this and their commander orders deployment. Gunfire erupts as they provide artillery support to protect the escapees.

The Seals make it out but the Marine Commander is confused. "There are only six of you."

"Cross isn't with us. He went into the main chamber and we don't know where he is."

"We cannot wait around, Commander."

"This is a mission and he is aware we have a schedule to maintain." He looks at his watch. "The island blows up in eight minutes. Cross will get out. I know he will."

"We will wait only two more minutes. Climb on board, Commander."

"Where is the mini-sub?"

"It is safe."

Everyone climbs on board and straps themselves in along the sides of the fuselage, with one exception. The Seal Commander is the last as he scans the tunnel. Above the noise of the engines, he hears something.

"Come on, Commander," says the Marine Commander.

"Wait, I heard something."

He runs over to the edge of the runway and sees someone swimming toward him.

"Wait for me," Cross is yelling as he tries to swim at the same time.

He reaches the shore and the commander pulls him out. His uniform is torn and there is blood.

"Quickly," as he yanks his arm and runs for the Hercules.

Shots ring out as Wu's men are running across the landing zone. One Marine steps out of the aircraft and a bullet strikes him as he is providing cover. Cross and the commander climb aboard and drag the injured Marine with them, whilst he is still shooting at the people chasing them.

"Go," the Marine Commander yells to the pilots.

The engines rapidly ramp up and the short take-off capabilities of the C-130 are on full display as it departs the hostile island and banks to the right on a steep climb.

Behind them the first huge explosion goes off and obliterates one piece of the island. Within a few seconds another goes off. The sky lights up as the passengers in the plane just stare.

On one side of the structure Cross sees a large communications facility. The next explosion forces it to topple into the sea.

47

UN Security Council

Taylor is in the UN Assembly Hall just as the UK Prime Minister finishes her speech to a huge round of applause. Next up is the US President.

He walks to the podium and thanks the Prime Minister for her support. He briefly discusses their meeting yesterday before he gets going with his written speech. Four minutes into his monologue he stops and keels over. Taylor knows this is her cue as a collective gasp envelopes the hall.

She signals her team and runs onto the stage. She moves up to the podium as three medics behind her are attending to the president. To the heads of state in the building and the rest of the world, it looks like they are administering life-support efforts.

"We are so sorry for this interruption, but it looks like a medical emergency and the president isn't fit to give his speech today."

As Taylor says this, her team rushes a gurney onto the stage and the president wheels away with a drip supposedly feeding into his arm. The people in the room stand up and show their support as they all clap.

"Thank you, ladies and gentlemen, for your support," and Taylor exits the stage.

Aboard the Hercules, Cross is congratulating the service members on a job well done whilst a medic is trying to address his injuries which appear minor at this stage. He requests another shot in the thigh and the doctor obliges. He particularly thanks the commander for waiting for him.

"I heard you did the same thing on a recent mission," the commander responds as he shakes Cross' hand.

Granfield calls. "A job very well executed, Daniel. That was incredible. Call me when you are back on land. I never told you, your house was saved from the fire."

"Thank you, David."

"Are you ok?"

"Physically yes, kind of, but mentally is a story over a beer."

Granfield got the answer he wanted and puts the phone down.

Cross messages Sedaghi and she replies back. He cannot wait to be in her arms.

He calls Moore Jr. "Brilliant job I heard."

"Thank you. We developed the software you asked for and downloaded it to the prime minister and her political entourage. When you destroyed the communications on the island, we were already in control. Fantastic deception so the world would remain calm. I understood the why when you told me."

"Your parents are safe but they will require help, Graeme."

"Yes, I already understand that. Thank you."

Half an hour later Taylor calls. "Fantastic job. Congratulations, my friend."

"It took a group of people, including you. You can take over because I'm resigning." He laughs as best he can through the pain. He is very tired and Taylor knows this.

"The beer is on me when you get back, Daniel. Nick flew over to be part of the UK government's protection command. The illusion Moore Junior downloaded worked. Now the clones are being shut down and the real people returned to power."

"See you in Langley," and he ends the call.

Cross is alone in his quarters on the USS Montgomery when everything catches up with him. All the battle scars, devastation, pressure, anger, deaths and surgical pain boil over and the emotional caldron that had been bubbling under the surface finally erupts like a volcano. He puts his head in his hands and sobs like a baby.

Sometime later whilst attempting to adapt to the surgeon's prescribed rest, his phone goes off. He looks at a number he doesn't recognise but answers it anyway. "Hello."

"Thank you for saving mine and the other captives' lives on the island, Daniel," says the President of the United States.

www.ingramcontent.com/pod-product-compliance
Lightning Source LLC
Chambersburg PA
CBHW071827020726
47502CB00004B/1272